I0730977

## PRAISE FOR EDEN VALLEY

### Selection of Five Star Reviews from Goodreads

I loved it! The characters were funny and likable. I found that it was an easy reading story and I hope to see more of these characters.

This is my first book by Amy Cissell and I really enjoyed it...in fact it was hard for me to put down. I loved the references to the shows Supernatural and Lucifer...both favourites of mine.

I loved this book, it is entertaining and the characters are pretty awesome. Evie is a single mom, who is sent into a crazy "revelation week" from hell (pun intended) and we discover that there is a lot more that meets the eye in sleepy Eden Valley. I'm curious about the other characters and what will happen next in the series. I just found a new series to look forward to and I think if you like fantasy, urban fantasy and hotness everywhere, this book is just for you.

I thoroughly enjoyed Evie's story. A fresh new take on a midlife crisis! All of the characters are so well developed and a joy to read. I loved Evie's friends and family and Lily especially is a precocious little girl. Even Luc's brother and sister were fun to read. I am definitely looking forward to the next book in the series!

# VALLEY OF ANGELS

AMY CISSELL

VALLEY OF ANGELS
Amy Cissell

A Broken World Publication
PO Box 11643
Portland, OR 97211
Valley of Angels
Copyright © 2021 by Amy Cissell
ISBN 978-1-949410-34-1 (ebook)
ISBN 978-1-949410-35-8 (paperback)

Cover Design: Cissell Ink
Edited by Suzanne Lahna, The Quick Fox
Edited & Proofread by Christopher Barnes, Cissell Ink

All rights reserved. No part of this publication may be reproduced, distributed, or transmitted in any form or by any means, including photocopying, recording, or other electronic or mechanical methods, without the prior written permission of the publisher, except in the case of brief quotations embodied in critical reviews and certain other noncommercial uses permitted by copyright law. For permission requests, write to the author at editors@brokenworldpublishing.com.

This is a work of fiction. Names, characters, businesses, places, events, and incidents are either the products of the author's imagination or used in a fictitious manner. Any resemblance to actual persons, living or dead, or actual events is purely coincidental.

**Eden Valley**

Raising a Demon
Devil and the Deep, Blue Lake
Valley of Angels
Guardian of Eden

**Eden Valley World Novellas**

Match Made in Hell
Hell's Bells
Fall From Grace
Devil May Care

*This one's for 'the moms'*
*TH, KS, SC*

*Y'all kept me sane with our rain or shine pandemic playdates 'n' wine*
*Fridays. So glad our demon kids are friends.*

# ACKNOWLEDGMENTS

So many thanks to my advance readers! Y'all are beyond fantastic.

I'm grateful to my editors Suzanne Lahna of The Quick Fox and Christopher Barnes of Cissell Ink for their feedback, plot hole discoveries, comma rehabilitation, and insistence that I add some descriptions and character emotions (ew).

# CHAPTER ONE

"Hello, this is Beverly Hill. How can I help you?" Bev winced as she did every time she said her whole name. She'd had it for forty-four years and still wasn't used to it.

"Miss Hill? This is Principal Ives. I'm afraid I'm going to need you to come pick up your niece. She's been suspended for the rest of the week, but will be welcome to return on Monday. Since this is her first offense of the year—and the first as a middle-schooler—her suspension is only three days long. As you know, she gets two more before expulsion."

Bev massaged her left temple with her free hand, trying to get rid of the sudden-onset tension headache. "It's Ms. Hill. I'll be there in a half hour. Can you tell me what happened this time?"

"She was fighting in the lunchroom and sent another student to the nurse's office. She'll be in the office when you get here. I look forward to meeting you. I understand you knew the elementary school principal well."

The principal's cheery tone made Bev want to reach through the phone and punch him in the face. Maybe calling parents with suspension notices was a daily part of his job, but he didn't need to sound quite so happy about it.

"See you soon," Bev said through gritted teeth. She hung up and went back to the email she'd been composing when the phone had rung. She finished, hit send, grabbed her purse, and stepped out of her glass cubicle. As soon as she stepped foot into her boss's office, he sighed audibly.

"Shelby?" he asked.

"I'll be back after I pick her up. I'm just taking my lunch early today." Bev hated the way she sounded, but she couldn't cover up the placating tone she adopted every time she talked to Jackson Allen. Her new boss was beige—white, medium height, lightly tanned, sandy hair, light brown eyes, forgettable face, and a body that was neither hard nor soft. He'd started a couple months ago after Bev had been passed over for the promotion. Again. The fact that they'd worked together for less than eight weeks and he already assumed, correctly, but still, that she was leaving to get Shelby meant his predecessor had warned him and that made losing the job to him even worse.

"If you're gone more than thirty minutes, you'll have to use PTO." His smile was borderline smug and for the second time in ten minutes, Bev felt like punching someone in the face.

"I'll keep that in mind." She pasted a smile on her face.

"Beverly!" he called when she was ten steps out of his office.

She turned around, but before she could walk back into his office, he raised his voice and said loud enough for everyone in the branch to hear, "You'll need to work on your absenteeism if you ever want to advance your career. You've been the assistant manager for how long?" He shuffled through some papers on his desk as if he was looking for the date while heat suffused Bev's cheeks and a wave of humiliation failed to provide a complementary hole in the floor to sink into. "Fifteen years?" He whistled low in surprise. "That's longer than I've been old enough to drive. Maybe you're a middle management lifer…"

Bev walked out of the bank before she fulfilled the fantasy that had been building for weeks. Every time he was awful to her, she added another layer to her elaborate revenge scheme. Currently she was contemplating paying Lily, her niece's best friend and genuine demon child, to magic permanent boils in between his butt cheeks.

When the fresh air hit her, Bev stopped and took a deep breath. "In with the positive, out with the horror that is a mediocre white man."

"Do all humans talk to themselves, or is that an affectation only necromancers have? Oooh, maybe you're not talking to yourself! Is there a ghost around?" The tall white man wearing dark jeans, a graphic tee depicting a unicorn running after an ark, and a leather jacket turned around, eyes alight as he looked for the non-existent ghost Bev might have been talking to.

"What are you doing here, Barachiel?" Bev asked. She side-stepped him and headed to the parking lot without waiting for an answer.

"Elle says I need to have a bank account so I can buy things and get a place to live that is anywhere but her house, so here I am!" He grinned and fell into step beside her. "And you're supposed to call me Barry."

"I am not calling you Barry." Bev unlocked her car and slid into the driver's seat. Barachiel got in on the other side and fiddled with the seatbelt, trying to buckle himself in. "What are you doing?" Bev wasn't even trying to keep the exasperation out of her voice anymore.

"I'm putting on my seatbelt. Evie says it's the law." The latch clicked home. "First try. I'm getting the hang of your weird travel vehicles!"

Bev started the car. She was at the end of the thirty-minute window she'd given Shelby's principal and didn't have time to argue with an angel. "Fine. We're going to the school to pick up Shelby. You are not coming in with me. In fact, as soon as we get there, you're getting out of the car and heading back to the bank to deposit your money and open an account." She turned on the blinker, looked right, left, right before making a cautious left turn onto Main Street, which was currently almost devoid of traffic.

"What money?" Barachiel asked absently, rolling the window up and down.

"The money for your bank account." Bev stopped at a four-way stop sign, waiting to ensure no one was coming too fast to stop, then pulled into the intersection. The two-mile drive was punctuated with several stop signs, two blind curves, and underbrush too close to the road that could be concealing foolhardy animals ready to jump in front of the next vehicle that sped by. Driving safely—two miles under the speed limit, complete stop at each stop sign, and high alert through the curves and forested section of the road—took fifteen minutes. She was going to be late.

"I thought the bank account was supposed to pay for everything I needed?" Barachiel rolled up the window and pulled the lever next to his seat and leaned all the way back.

"You have to put the money in. The bank holds your money for you, keeps it safe, and, depending on the account and how much money you have in it, pays interest. But the original deposit comes from you." Bev slowed down as she approached the next intersection. She had the right of way, but you never knew. Better safe than dead.

"Where do I get money?" Barachiel pulled the lever again and shot upright.

"A lot of people have jobs." She turned on her blinker and turned right.

"Like what kind of jobs? How do I get one? My friend Andras owns a brewery. You work at a bank taking people's money. What else is there?" Barachiel pressed the lock button and tried to open the door.

"What are you doing?" Bev yelled. "That's dangerous. You sit there and leave the door alone until we're parked."

"Sorry. But you don't have to yell. Nothing bad will happen. I'm an immortal angel of the Lord." He flashed another one of his million-watt grins at her and, for a moment, every bit of tension Bev was holding disappeared.

"Please don't do that again, no matter how immortal you feel." She took a deep breath as he dimmed his light and the stress of the last eighteen months—strike that, twelve years—returned. Angel smiles were a dangerous thing…they took away too much sharpness and replaced it with peace.

"Evie owns the Silver Dollar, Viv is a graphic designer, Sam and

Luc work for their dad. Kind of." She thought about it for a minute and grimaced. "Actually, you don't have many good examples of people with jobs. But you know my cousin Russell, right? He manages a bar, doesn't he?"

"Several of my associates work in alcohol management. Have you thought about quitting your job? Taking people's money doesn't seem like the best use of your talents." Barachiel rolled the window down again. "You could be a detective and solve crimes by interviewing dead people. Detectives are very cool."

Bev signaled, then turned into the school parking lot. After creeping forward and into a space as far away from any other cars as possible, she put her Prius in park and turned it off. "Like there are so many crimes to solve in Eden Valley. Besides, I don't want to be a cop."

"Oh no, not a police detective. I meant a detective like Miss Marple or Jessica Fletcher! They're old ladies in small towns who are always surrounded by murders they get to solve, showing up the police! You could be just like them." Barachiel opened the door to get out, but his seatbelt yanked him back. He struggled with the seatbelt, getting more and more tangled, until Bev reached over and unlatched it. Barachiel stumbled out of the car. His wings popped out as he tried to get his balance.

"Wings!" Bev hissed.

Barachiel huffed, and they disappeared back to wherever they went when they weren't visible.

"Please leave now," Bev said. "I need to go pick up my kid and sit with the knowledge that you compared me to two elderly women who were probably serial killers inserting themselves into the investigations. There's no other explanation for the sheer number of murders around them." She walked to the front door of the school, purse clutched closely to her body.

Barachiel caught up with her. "School isn't over yet, is it? There are no other children around."

"It's not. School doesn't let out until three, but today I am picking

Shelby up early. Now go." Bev hit the buzzer to notify the office staff she'd arrived.

"Yes?" a voice crackled through the intercom.

"It's Bev Hill here to get Shelby." She turned her back to the brick wall and scanned the area in front of her, alert to any potential dangers.

"Your name is Beverly Hill," Barachiel said while they waited for the buzz signifying they were being allowed in.

"It is." She hated her name and had ever since she was a student at this school and a couple classmates decided that it was hilarious and deserving of mocking. She'd sworn then that the minute she was eighteen, she'd change it.

But then she'd used it to enroll in college and after that, assumed she'd get married and could change it later. She got busy with work, then being a doting aunt, first to her sister's child, then to her best friend Evie's daughter. When her sister and mother died in a horrible car accident when Shelby was a toddler, her name seemed like the least of her problems. She'd taken Shelby in and raised her and hadn't had time to reflect on the twisted senses of humor her parents—Richard Wood and Chloe Hill—had called on to name their children. She'd gotten her mother's last name, and her sister Holly had been given her father's.

The door buzzed, and Bev yanked it open and fixed Barachiel with her steeliest gaze. "Weren't you leaving? I am going in here, and you cannot."

The angel looked completely unfazed and peered over her shoulder into the school.

"He can come in with you, Bev!" the school secretary called from her office across from the door. "As long as you have ID to pick up Shelby and he doesn't wander off."

"Thank you, Miss…" Barachiel trailed off as he strode across the hallway and walked into the office.

"You can call me Dawn." Dawn Rosner, who had been the middle school secretary since Bev had been a student there thirty years ago, giggled at Barachiel.

Bev walked into the office just in time to see Dawn wink at him, and an expression of mild horror replace Barachiel's friendly grin. His eyes widened and darted around the room, clearly looking for an escape other than the doors he'd just walked through.

"I'll wait for you outside," he said and fled.

"Who's your friend?" Dawn asked with a silly but acquisitive smile.

Bev sighed. Eden Valley was small enough that Dawn already knew the answer—or at least the answer that had been spread around when he'd returned with Elle two weeks ago. "Cousin of Elle's," Bev said. "He's in town to help her through this difficult time."

Dawn's face drooped down and a look of deep compassion overtook her. "I heard. Poor lady. And how Kevin must feel, losing his father so suddenly." She looked at Bev expectantly, waiting for her to fill in the blanks left by Brandon Jones's "death" at the end of July and Elle's three-month departure to mourn, leaving Kevin behind to stay with Evie Addams, her two children, one of whom, Lily, was Kevin's best friend, and her fiancé Luc. Short for Lucifer. Last name Morningstar. Descendent of the original.

"It was very sad," Bev murmured and wondered what Dawn would say if Bev told her that Brandon Jones hadn't been a real person but was instead a flaming sword in a human body, the same sword that had once protected the gates of Eden and had been used to cut the ties Eden Lake had on Kevin, former Eden Lake monster and current sixth-grade student. She bit her tongue to keep from blurting it all out. "Shelby?"

"Of course, you want to collect your niece." Dawn clucked her tongue and handed Bev a form to sign.

Bev scanned it. "It says she's being suspended for fighting in the lunchroom. Do you know what instigated the fight?"

"They don't tell me that kind of information. I just know what's on the form. Shelby punched another student, sending him to the nurse's office with a black eye." She shook her head mournfully.

"He knocked my lunch tray out of my hands and called me a very bad name," Shelby volunteered as she walked into the room. "He's also an eighth grader, about a foot taller than me, and at least fifty pounds heavier. The only reason he got a black eye is because he hadn't finished straightening up after running a hand down my back looking for a bra strap."

"Nice job, sweetie," Bev said, holding out an arm and pulling Shelby in for a side hug. "It's probably good you have a different lunch schedule than Lily and Kevin this semester, or I'd be sitting here with Evie and Elle, wouldn't I? Let's go talk to the principal. I'm excited to hear how he's going to address the bullying and sexual assault perpetrated on a younger, smaller student." She looked at Dawn. "I'm assuming that if Shelby was suspended for three days for defending herself, the other student was expelled?"

Dawn didn't reply, just picked up the phone and said, "Miss Hill here to see you."

Bev channeled every bit of rage she had simmering as she marched towards the principal's office.

"I'm sorry," Shelby whispered. "I know I'm not supposed to lose my temper and hit back, it's just…"

"You are not in trouble," Bev said loud enough for anyone in the vicinity to hear. "If I wasn't an adult, I'd find that kid and…" She bit her tongue. Threatening to assault middle schoolers probably wouldn't look good on her permanent record. "You are not in trouble. If you want, I'll push for them to reverse your suspension, but if you'd rather spend the rest of the week home, I'll just force them to remove it from your record—this is not a first strike."

"Thank you." Shelby squeezed Bev's hand, and together they breached the principal's office.

BEV WALKED BACK into the bank forty-five minutes after she'd left, Shelby in tow. The principal hadn't backed down on Shelby's suspension but had reluctantly agreed to suspend the boy Shelby had punched, even though he was the one with a black eye. Bev had been ready to take it five steps further, but Shelby asked her to stop. Regardless, the school was going to hear from her, and, if she knew her friends, Evie and Elle, too. And if Sam caught wind of it, there was no telling what the principal would have to deal with.

Jackson waved to get her attention, then held up his arm and pointed at his wrist. Bev took a deep breath, held it, then let it go. She was the embodiment of calm. And she would set a good example for her niece.

"Why don't you head into my office and read. I know you have a half-dozen books in your backpack."

Shelby nodded in agreement, but the narrow-eyed look she shot at her aunt suggested she could tell everything wasn't as peaceful as Bev was trying to project.

Bev forced a tight-lipped smile to the surface, both for Shelby and the few customers in the lobby, before walking to her boss's office for the dressing down she was almost positive she was going to get.

"You're late," he said.

"I'll take the fifteen minutes from my PTO bank," Bev replied.

"You're out of PTO." Jackson leaned back in his chair and rested the back of his head in his hands. The expression on his face was lifted directly from a stock photography search for "smug."

"No, I'm not. I check weekly, and when I looked last Friday, I had almost eighty hours." Bev allowed herself a moment of triumph for keeping her voice steady and not snapping.

"Oh, didn't you get the memo? We're redoing the way paid time off accrues. Starting last month, your vacation and sick days no longer go into the same bucket. Gladys recalculated the time you've taken off this year, and you have a deficit in your sick days—you won't have a full day built up again until December."

"And my vacation? Since I had eighty hours left, there must be even more than that." Bev's heart rate was increasing and keeping her tone even was becoming work.

Jackson shrugged. "Sure, there's time left in there, but vacation days have to be requested and approved a minimum of ten days before the requested day off. You can't come and go whenever you please and call it vacation time. From now on, any unscheduled days off that aren't accompanied by a doctor's note will need to be unpaid days off, and if this continues to be a pattern, we will need to talk about a performance improvement plan."

Bev gritted her teeth, wished with all her might that his hair would fall out in a completely random pattern, and held her breath. When nothing happened, she once again cursed the luck that gave Evie the wish fulfillment and Bev constant, overwhelming fear.

When she thought she could speak without angry crying, cursing, or anything but a pleasant tone, she exhaled. "Can you please forward me a copy of the policy and the plan you had to notify staff of this drastic change at the end of Q1 in the fiscal year? I will be taking the rest of the week off, unpaid. I look forward to discussing my performance with you next week."

Bev spun on her heel and walked out of Jackson's office, nearly running into Barachiel. He grabbed her elbow to steady her, and she wrenched it from her grip. She knew she was being rude, but she didn't care.

"Are you okay?" he asked.

"Don't touch me. Not without permission, and not ever." She didn't want to make a scene. She'd grown up the child of parents who loved to make scenes, and she'd spent most of her life fitting in, fading back, and letting her friends take the spotlight. But right now, she was too angry to rein it in.

Barachiel dropped his hand and took a step back.

Bev pretended she couldn't see the flash of hurt on his face. She raised her voice and concentrated on calm; she was Eden Lake on a still day, reflecting everything back and not letting anything ruffle her surface. "Shelby, grab your stuff."

Bev waited near the door while Shelby scrambled to get all her books shoved back into her book bag. She took a deep breath, held it for the count of four, then exhaled. Viv had taught her this calming technique—and it had to work since Viv used it every time she'd visited her mother. Another breath in. Hold. Exhale. She wondered if it would look weird if she closed her eyes.

"I'm ready," Shelby said in a small, quiet voice.

Bev's smile, forced minutes before, melted into genuine warmth when she looked at her niece, who was threatening to overshadow Bev's height any minute. "Let's get out of here. Milkshake at the diner?"

Shelby's face split into a wide grin. "Yes, please." She slipped her hand into Bev's as they walked towards the door.

Barachiel stepped out of their way, his normally too-expressive face a blank slate. Bev straightened her shoulders. She did not care what the annoying angel thought of her. She reached for the door, but before she could shove it open, a sheet of ice pushed through her from front to back, and when it made it all the way to her spine, the sensation of ice crystalizing throughout her body made her blood pressure bottom out. The world swayed in front of her and bright yellow spots danced in front of her eyes.

She was conscious of a hand—an actual, solid hand—keeping her from hitting the ground, but couldn't focus on anything but the chill that permeated every cell of her being.

"Vengeance." The raspy hiss sounded like it was coming from inside her brain. Nausea threatened to rise, and she knew she had to get outside and sit down before she either passed out or threw up. Or both.

"Outside," Bev gasped.

"I've got you," Shelby said. "Three more steps, and we'll be outside. Twenty more to the corner. Twenty more to the bench outside the diner. Concentrate and count. Keep your eyes closed."

Bev focused on Shelby's voice counting out the steps, trusting her niece to get her to safety. It was getting worse, and she didn't know what she was going to do about the voices that she was having more and more trouble convincing herself were in her head.

"You have to believe in them. If you admit they exist, they'll know they don't have to work so hard to get your attention," Barachiel said from her left.

"What are you doing here?" Bev growled.

"Making sure you don't fall over and accidentally raise a zombie," the angel replied.

"That is not a thing," she said through gritted teeth.

"He's right, Aunt Bev," Shelby chimed in. "You know how well denial worked for Aunt Viv. Don't make the same mistakes she did."

"There is no such thing as zombies. There are no ghosts. I can't hear the dead speaking." Even to her own ears, she knew that sounded ridiculous after the events of the last couple years. Between demons and angels and lake monsters turning into adolescent boys, ghosts didn't seem that far-fetched. But stubbornness had gotten her out of a lot of situations she'd thought she was stuck in, and she was going to ride that wave until it dumped her off.

"If there's no such thing, who wants vengeance?" Shelby asked, guiding Bev to the bench and helping her sit. "It wasn't the bank doors."

Bev took a deep breath and opened her eyes again. "I don't know, Shel. But I don't want this."

"You're the one who told me we don't always get the life we want, and not even the life we might deserve. We get this one life and we do our best to make the best of it." Shelby sat next to Bev and slid close, resting her head on Bev's shoulder.

"I hate it when you kids spout back the wisdom we've tried to impart. You always do it at the most inopportune times." Bev sighed. "You're right, though. This is where I am. I just hope that one of these restless dead jerks can lead me to some buried treasure so I can quit my job and commission a huge sculpture to commemorate how very much I hate Jackson. Milkshake?"

"Milkshake," Shelby answered.

"Does being a zombie still count as the one life?" Barachiel asked. "I don't know those rules. It's an afterlife of sorts, but is it an extension?" He turned his clear, wide eyes to Bev, nose wrinkled and mouth pursed.

Bev laughed. "Don't think about it too hard. Come on, angel. I'll buy you a milkshake."

# CHAPTER TWO

Bev stood in front of the mirror in the employee bathroom at the bank. She squared her shoulders and smoothed invisible wrinkles out of her suit. The A-line charcoal skirt perfectly hugged the soft, generous curves of her hips. Her pink and black floral tunic highlighted her pale skin, bringing out the faint pink of her cheeks—created painstakingly along with the rest of her perfectly applied makeup and artfully styled honey brown hair. The soft fabric draped across her breasts, cinched in a bit at her waist, and unlike most plus-sized clothes big enough to accommodate her chest, wasn't too long—the hem landed just above hip level. She shrugged into her coral blazer, checked her matching lipstick one last time, and left the bathroom.

Her clothes, makeup, and hair were her armor, and she needed them to be impenetrable today. It was easier since Shelby'd started designing and sewing all her clothes. That kid might be a handful and a half, but she more than made up for it by refreshing Bev's wardrobe with clothes that fit and looked good at the same time.

Twenty minutes later, she'd made sure she didn't have any weird emails or calendar appointments left in her work account, swept the office and her computer hard drive for anything she'd miss, just in case her eleven a.m. performance evaluation meeting Jackson had scheduled didn't go well. He'd texted her last night around ten-thirty to let her know. Because he was a sneaky little creep who couldn't have a difficult conversation with a person if they were prepared and on equal footing.

She closed her eyes and took a deep breath. On Mondays, they didn't open to regular customers until ten, and she'd come in early to be as prepared as she could be. She'd rolled Shelby out of bed at six, jollied her through breakfast, teeth brushing, and getting dressed before dropping her off at Evie's with thanks, a quick baby-snuggle, and a promise to bring a bottle of wine that night to make up for it.

Bev scanned her email. There was surprisingly little considering she'd been out of the office for five days. She shrugged. At this point, she didn't care. Regardless of how today's meeting turned out, she was no longer going to give this place anything more than good enough. She had money saved up—her MBA wasn't a complete waste of time and money—and they'd be okay for a few months, even without tapping into her emergency funds. But a few months wasn't long enough to make a complete pivot, take care of a kid, and find a new job in Eden Valley.

"In with the good, out with toxic bosses," she chanted to herself. Everything would be fine. It'd been a while since she'd needed to, but Bev Hill always, always landed on her feet. She wasn't as smart as Viv or as fierce as Evie, but she was tough, determined, and confident. There was no way one jerk boss—or a bunch of vengeful spirits who'd, thankfully, left her out of their revenge schemes the last few days—was going to undermine her self-esteem.

She turned her attention back to her computer, fired off a few emails to potential clients, and reminded herself that dramatic exits were seldom warranted and it'd be easier to find a new job if she wasn't stressed and desperate for something new.

By the time eleven rolled around, she'd faked it enough to be on the verge of making it. After a glance in the small mirror she kept in her desk to make sure she still looked good, she stood, grabbed a legal pad, and headed to Jackson's office.

He didn't look up when she walked in and pulled the door closed behind her. She rolled her eyes and sat in the chair across the desk where his eyes were glued to his computer screen. When it became evident he was going to make her wait to start the meeting, Bev crossed her legs at the ankles and started doodling on the notepad.

She'd completed an entire graveyard scene, complete with tombstones, floating sheeted ghosts, and a zombie hand breaking free from the ground before Jackson looked up from his computer.

"Beverly, do you know why you're here?" Jackson asked.

*Because you're a pompous, incompetent asshole who couldn't manage his way out of a paper bag, so you're taking it out on your employees?* Bev smiled tightly. "Because the complaints I've filed with HR about your agism and general harassment have started to pile up and you need to find a way to get rid of me that falls into company policy and doesn't look like retaliation? Or is it that my employer isn't as family friendly as they profess to be, and you changed the rules without telling me to punish me for caring for my niece when she's struggling?"

Jackson sighed and affected a look of deep sorrow. "Beverly, Beverly, Beverly. There's a difference between being family friendly and allowing you to get away with things no one else needs. Julian has three kids and has never missed a day of work."

Bev bit her tongue before she could point out that Julian's partner had stayed home with the kids until they were all in school, then walked out and filed for divorce, due in part—according to town gossip—to the fact that he'd never made it to a single school event or a doctor's appointment and had stood her up on their anniversary to attend a last-minute meeting with a potential client. Instead, she dug deep for her most even tone. "I'm the only one with a school age kid at home and no partner to pick up the slack."

Jackson tsked, something Bev didn't even know people did outside of books. "And why should the bank lose money to your poor life choices and mistakes your family made?"

Heat built in Bev's chest, and her pulse accelerated. She stood up. "I think we're done here. Give me a written warning or whatever you planned. I'll sign it. I'll tell you I'm going to make my troubled almost-teen fend for herself. But don't tell me I have to sit here and listen to you insult me and my dead family."

Jackson stood and walked around the desk, stopping much too close to Bev for her comfort. She took a step back. "This is your last chance, *Beverly*. Get it together or get out. And, since we're on the subject of your niece, have you ever considered her crazy is due to your inability to discipline her? She's never going to be a productive member of society. Might as well cut your losses now and let her speed her way towards the inevitable first juvie experience."

Bev had never believed the term "seeing red" was anything but metaphorical. Until now. She pulled her arm back and unleashed, executing a perfect right cross her boxing instructor would've praised her for. Jackson stumbled back several steps and raised his hand to his jaw.

"I quit," Bev said.

"You can't quit, you're fired," Jackson sputtered. "And probably arrested when the cops get here."

"If I'm not here when they arrive, I'll be at home. They know where to find me." Bev walked out of Jackson's office through the bank lobby, doing her best to ignore the stares of her coworkers and the few customers waiting in line. She grabbed an empty paper box on her way past the printer and filled it with the few personal effects in her office. She typed an out of office message detailing everything Jackson had said, then shut down the computer, grabbed her coat, and walked out.

It wasn't until she got to her car that the adrenaline wore off, and she started shaking. She got behind the wheel and turned the key.

"Hey Siri, call Viv."

WHILE SHE WAITED for the cops to find her, Bev sat on the front porch of the cabin she'd grown up in—most of the time. It'd been her maternal grandparents, and when they'd died—long before Bev was born—her mother had inherited it. They'd lived here whenever her parents had deigned to settle down long enough to unpack. When Bev was older, they'd tried—they really had. They'd moved in semi-permanently and stayed during the school year, but the minute Bev had turned eighteen, they were in the wind again, taking Holly with them. Holly'd never had the same desire for stability Bev had. She'd been the perfect kid for Richard and Chloe.

Bev had kept the cabin—rented it out as a vacation home once she'd bought her own place. And now she was waiting for her newest potential tenant. She didn't usually have people who wanted to stay during the fall and winter months, and she liked it that way. She didn't want to be a landlady, but she'd never been able to let go of it, no matter how much she'd been offered.

"At least I have a place to fall back on if I need it."

"You're talking to yourself again," Barachiel said, startling Bev out of her memories.

"What are you doing here?" she asked waspishly.

"Elle told me to come here. She gave me this—" he waved a giant wad of bound cash "—to put in the bank so I could have the bank give it to you so you'd let me live here. But when I went to the bank, it was really busy, and someone told me you didn't work there anymore because you'd hit your boss. Anyway, I didn't want them to have my money, so I decided to bring it straight to you." Barachiel held out the stack of bills that barely fit in his hand.

Bev took the money and looked at it. Nothing but hundred-dollar bills bound in $10,000 bundles. "This is a lot of cash to carry around." She couldn't stop staring. She'd worked in banks since she was in her early twenties, and this was still the most money she'd held in her hand at one time.

"One hundred and twenty thousand dollars," Barachiel said. "Elle said it would be enough for me to live on, and that when it ran out, I'd know it was time to leave. Is it enough to live here?"

"How long do you want to stay?" Bev asked. She held the money out towards Barachiel.

He put his hands behind his back and took a big step away from her. "I don't want it. I'm supposed to stay for one year to monitor the situation and make sure Eden is secure. Is it enough?"

Bev stared at the money in her hands. A hundred thousand dollars for a ten-month rental would cushion the blow of her unemployment and inevitable fine for the punch, meaning she wouldn't have to dip into her savings. It was way too much, but Barachiel would give it to her if she told him that was the rent. "Don't you need this for food?"

He shrugged. "I don't need to eat, and so far, haven't seen the point of it. Elle eats your human food, and it's changed her, made her more like you." He wrinkled his nose in disgust and stuck his tongue out in a gagging motion.

Bev took a deep breath. She didn't know why this angel's contempt got under her skin the way it did, but everything he said felt like a personal insult. Everything was getting under her skin lately. "A car, then. Transportation?"

"Why would I drive when I can fly?" The look on his face was so ecstatic, Bev felt like a voyeur. She'd flown once—or been carried, anyway. It was terrifying to not be in control, but if she had wings, her feet might not ever touch the ground again.

"I charge tourists a thousand dollars a week, three thousand if they book a month at a time. Ten months would be thirty thousand." She closed her mouth and did some quick calculations. That was too much. You could get an apartment in Spokane for much less than that. "But for a long-term rental like you're proposing, it'd only be half of that." She cringed. That still sounded like too much—especially for a friend. Or angel of a friend.

Barachiel took the money she held out. He squinted at the labels and handed her back four bundles. "This should cover it."

"It's twenty-five thousand dollars too much," Bev said. "And it's cash. You need to put it in a bank and write me a check each month for the rent."

"The bank sucks ass," Barachiel said, shoving the cash into his pocket. It got stuck—the opening to the front pocket of his trendy skinny jeans wasn't wide enough to accommodate almost a hundred thousand dollars. After a couple minutes of trying to make it fit, he gave up, divided the cash into six equal sections, and put one in each of his jeans pockets and the last two in his jacket pockets.

"How is it you use terms like 'sucks ass' and don't know how money works?" Bev asked. The minute the words were out of her mouth, she grimaced. There was no way she actually wanted to know that information.

"Twitter has a lot of knowledge but not that. I know some people should make more, but not people who already have too much money. And that bit coins are good. Although there are things that cost money that I would like to have. Did you know you can buy a device that slices bananas?"

"You don't eat. Why would you need a banana slicer?" Why couldn't she stop asking stupid questions?

"It's good to be prepared for emergencies."

Bev cracked a grin before she could stop herself. "Banana slicing emergencies? Do you get many of those in heaven?"

Barachiel returned her smile. "More than you'd expect."

Bev shook her head and handed Barachiel the remaining four bundles of cash she still held. "You can rent this house. Let's go inside and get the rental agreement formalized. Then, I'll take you to the credit union and help you get an account set up." She unlocked the door and led him inside.

Barachiel pursed his lips. "If you think I should."

She started to nod, then stopped as a thought hit her. "It's been a long time since I've had to think through the barriers to establishing an account, but I am willing to bet you don't have any identification. ID card, tax ID number, proof of existence…"

"Why would I need to prove I exist? Anyone can see I exist," Barachiel protested.

"But the rest of it? Any photo ID or a social security number?"

"What's that for?" He looked genuinely puzzled, and Bev shook her head.

"You can't deposit all this, anyway. You'd have the IRS on you so fast your head would spin." Bev blew a long breath out through pursed lips. "Where did Elle get the money?"

Barachiel shrugged. "Maybe from her job? Isn't that where you get your money? Maybe she can get me all those other things you said I needed, too."

"Elle doesn't have a job. At least not one I've ever heard about." Bev tapped the side of her face with one finger. "I'm not sure how we're going to figure this out and make it work without doing anything illegal. I am going to pretend it's still never occurred to me that Elle's documents aren't legit."

"Why would it be illegal to get identification documents? I am here. I exist."

"What's your name?" Bev asked absently, thinking through every possibility of setting up an identity of a seeming adult who had over a hundred thousand dollars in cash.

"Barachiel, but you can call me Barry," he answered.

"And your last name?"

Barachiel opened his mouth and closed it again. "I don't have a second name. Do I need one? Bee-once doesn't have a last name, and I'll bet she gets to have a bank account."

Bev paused the scenarios running through her mind and looked at Barachiel in confusion before the light clicked on and she understood. "It's Beyoncé, not Bee Once, and you are no Beyoncé. And she has a last name. I think we can figure this out to keep it legal. Mostly. I'll talk to Luc tonight and see if he has any advice."

Barachiel stiffened his shoulders. "I can't accept any help from him or his family. They are evil."

"They're not evil, not really." Bev protested. "Well, Luc and Sam aren't evil, anyway. I'm not committing you to anything; I'm just going to ask for advice. You're not required to talk to any demons you don't want to talk to."

Barachiel crossed his arms. "Fine. Can I still live here?"

"Yes you can. Here are the keys. We'll figure out the logistics later. You're probably trustworthy enough to not ask for first and last month's rent and a security deposit or whatever regular landlords need from their tenants."

Barachiel took the keys, then looked around the large open

kitchen where they were sitting. "Is this big enough to have parties? I would like to have a kegger."

Bev opened her mouth and closed it again. It wasn't worth it. "We'll talk later. Move in whenever." She walked out the door and directly into Sherriff Mills.

"I'm going to need you to come to the station," Joanne said, then she grinned. "I have been waiting to say that my whole life."

BEV STALKED out of the police station. She still felt the heat in her cheeks that had shown up as she was having her mugshot taken and hadn't disappeared during the way-too-long questioning by the creepy, leering deputy. He'd gone round and round with her until the lawyer Bev had requested as soon as she got there showed up and intimidated Joanne Mills—Eden Valley's sheriff and Bev's high school nemesis—into letting her go.

Sam—the sinfully hot demon who was Luc's sister and Viv's…well, they were being cagey about how they wanted to define their relationship—was standing in front of the station tapping on her phone screen with her thumbs. When she saw Bev emerge, she tucked her phone into a pocket in her leather pants.

Bev tilted her head, trying to figure out how on earth there was room in the practically painted-on leathers for anything, much less a phone.

"I'm here to pick you up and take you to Evie's for wine and the mother of all stories," Sam said. "Evie wanted me to tell you Shelby was at her house and doesn't yet know you were arrested, although she can't guarantee how long she can keep that a secret."

Bev closed her eyes and took a deep, cleansing breath. The heat of humiliation wasn't dissipating. Of course everyone knew. There was no way something like this could've been kept a secret, especially not in Eden Valley.

"It's okay, you know." Sam started walking, but when Bev didn't follow, she circled back around until she was standing by Bev's side.

"You're not going to jail, and although I don't know exactly what you did, I can all but guarantee we can get them to drop all charges. Do you have a lawyer yet?"

"Public defender," Bev said, still trying to claw her way out of the pit that was yawning below her. She never lost her temper—at least not like this. "He's fine."

"There's nothing wrong with a public defender," Sam agreed. "But I know some of the best, most ruthless lawyers in the country. Want me to call one to show up and intimidate that power-hungry sheriff with a grudge and her team of incompetents?"

"I'd rather intimidate Jackson into not pressing charges," Bev muttered.

"Oooh, I can do that. We won't even need a lawyer." The grin that spread across Sam's face could only be described as wicked.

"Wait, no! I don't want things to get worse." Bev clamped her mouth shut before she could tempt a demon into taking more revenge.

"I am offended." Sam *looked* offended. "I never make things worse. I make things right. Now come on. Your kid and your friends are waiting for you."

# CHAPTER THREE

Bev sat on Evie's porch and thought about how much time she'd spent in this spot over the last almost-forty years. It'd been a refuge from the realities of school, almost as much for her as Viv. Countless sleepovers, reunions after they headed their separate ways after graduation, and where they gathered every time something—good or bad—happened. The house was often full of people. Something about Evie and her house drew people in. Maybe it was the calm compassion Evie exuded. Maybe it was the view of Eden Lake nestled in between the peaks of the Cascades. Or maybe, Bev thought as she took a bite, it was the brownies.

Sam reappeared and dropped into the chair next to Bev's, then handed over a glass of wine.

"Thank you," Bev said. She held the cool glass against her forehead. "I can't cool off. I don't know if I'm angry or embarrassed or having a hot flash. But I'm about five minutes of this away from jumping into the lake."

Sam opened her beer and took a long drink. "I do like this smoky porter. Smoke and Brimstone is such a great name. I need to make good on my plans to visit the brewery and entice the owner into partnership. It should be easier than I'd originally thought, now that I know he is a fallen angel."

Bev leaned back and took a drink of her wine. "This is so good. Thanks for the wine."

"Thank Viv. This is the first bottling from her friend's new business."

"Charlie is the best ex-girlfriend ever. I'll let Viv know how much I appreciate her good taste." Bev took another drink, holding the wine in her mouth for a moment before swallowing.

"I look forward to your appreciation and hope you can mix in a little adoration." Viv walked out onto the porch, glass in hand. She slid into the space Sam made for her on the wide chair. "Wanna tell me what you're appreciating today? Other than everything, of course."

Bev held up her glass. "Your excellent taste in women, and your ability to end relationships without burning wine bridges. This is fantastic."

"It really is, right? Charlie has her tasting room at Estaca Corazón all set up, and the cabins are about ready to open for the public. She's going to open to the public after Halloween but isn't really planning on things getting busy until spring." Viv took another sip and smiled in pleasure. "You will not believe what she found during construction. An entire underground series of tunnels that looked like they'd been dug out at least a hundred years ago. They're going to be great for aging. She already has plans for a VIP underground tasting room. It's going to be amazing."

Three loud barks from the trees that started a few hundred feet away from the house drew Bev's attention away from the wine and to the children she knew would be appearing momentarily. Sprinkles, Lily's three-headed hellhound who often masqueraded as a Bernese Mountain dog, almost always heralded their arrival. The tension that had begun to unwind clenched again, and sweat beaded on her forehead.

Three kids who were straddling the line between childhood and adulthood burst from the trees, laughing uproariously. A black dog, almost as tall as Lily, who was, by far, the shortest of the three, barreled through them, nearly knocking Kevin over. When they saw the adults on the porch, they skidded to a halt, then walked much more sedately to the porch.

"Is everything okay, Aunt Bev?" Shelby asked. "I thought you were picking me up after school."

Bev worried at her lower lip, trying to figure out how to break the news.

"What's wrong?" Shelby's voice cracked and her body snapped into a tight line that vibrated like a bowstring about to release.

Bev recognized the signs of an impending panic attack. Shelby'd had more than her share since her mother and grandmother had died in a fiery crash where she was the only survivor. She didn't remember her mother, but she regularly had nightmares about fire and death. Not as many now as she used to, but too many for any child to bear.

"Everything's fine." Bev paused and considered. "Well, not fine. But it will be. I have a confession to make, though, and I am really embarrassed to have to tell you."

"Do you want us to leave?" Kevin asked. "We can give you privacy if you want."

"Besides, we can listen just as well from the upstairs bathroom," Lily said with an impish grin.

"No, don't leave. You'll find out, anyway. Evie and Elle are bringing out lemonades for you, and then I'll tell the whole sordid story." Bev sighed and shook her head.

Shelby relaxed minutely and let Lily steer her to one of the many chairs scattered across the porch.

On cue, Evie and Elle pushed through the door. Elle handed out lemonade to the kids, then took a glass of wine from Evie, who set the rest of the bottle on the small table near the door and curled up on the porch swing Luc had put up over the summer.

Seven pairs of eyes focused on Bev. She felt like the one time she'd tried theater in a college class and froze on stage in the final production, spotlight heating her to near boiling and her fellow cast members urging her on until she broke, recited her lines at breakneck speed and fled before the scene ended. She focused on Shelby. She loved every single person on the porch, but the niece she'd raised since she was two was the one who mattered most.

"I was arrested this afternoon."

"Whoa! Aunt Bev! Are you serious?" Lily's eyes were wide, and Bev couldn't tell if it was awe or shock.

"Arrested? Are you going to jail? What did you do? What will happen to me?" Shelby's words tumbled over each other, and her hands clenched on the arms of her chair, whitening her knuckles.

"I'm not going to jail. I'll probably have to pay a fine and have a criminal record, though. And I don't have a job anymore. But there's nothing to worry about. I have plenty of savings. We will be fine." She pasted a bright smile on her face and hoped it looked reassuring.

"Even if you didn't have plenty of savings, you'd be fine," Elle said. "I have money I don't need."

"I have questions about that later," Bev said. "Magic money is probably illegal."

"That's why I didn't tell Barachiel where it came from." Elle shrugged and grinned. "He's a stickler for the rules, once he figures out what they are, anyway."

"What did you do?" Shelby's voice was insistent, drawing Bev's attention back to her.

"This is the embarrassing part." Bev screwed up her face and closed her eyes. "I punched Jackson Allen." She cracked her eyes open. Now all three kids were regarding her with open mouths and wide eyes.

"No wonder you're fired," Kevin said.

"Good," Shelby said fiercely. "He was mean. It's like when I punched Derek last week. Some people have it coming."

"No! Not ever," Bev said more forcefully than she'd meant to. "No one ever deserves to be punched. And I'm an adult, I should handle my anger better."

"He said something mean about Shelby, didn't he?" Lily asked. "Nothing else would make you mad enough to hit someone. You'll let him be mean to you, but if it's Shelby, that's crossing the line."

"You weren't mad at me for hitting Derek because he was inappropriate first and the adults weren't handling it. You shouldn't be in trouble, either." Shelby spoke with the surety and confidence of someone who still believed life should be fair.

"Unfortunately, hitting your boss in full view of every pre-lunch break customer and all your coworkers is considered assault, regardless of whether he had it coming. I got fingerprinted and had my mugshot taken and everything." Bev was trying very hard to keep things lighthearted and pretend she was just as blasé about her now criminal record as the kids seemed to be.

"Aunt Bev, you're a badass," Lily said.

"She is, right?" Sam pursed her lips and regarded Bev. "I didn't think she had it in her, but now that I know..."

"Papa Abe will fix it," Lily said. "You aren't a criminal."

"Before you call the big evil guns, why don't we try someone a little less interested in trading favors and issuing IOUs," Evie suggested. "If any of you kids have more questions, ask them now. Otherwise, scoot inside. Luc has dinner ready for you and a movie queued up until your adults take you home for a good night's sleep. It's a school night."

"Fucking fine," Lily groused even as she stood. "But it'd better be pizza. Pizza is the only acceptable food for getting arrested."

"I don't think pizza is on the prison menu," Viv said dryly.

"Duh." Lily's voice was scathing, and Bev had to hide her grin when Evie rolled her eyes. "We're not in prison. No pizza for Aunt Bev." Lily winked—well, blinked forcefully with one eye and lightly with the other—at Bev and snapped her fingers. "Sprinkles, dinner!" The hellhound dashed into the kitchen, followed closely by Lily and Kevin.

Shelby stood in front of the adults, fidgeting and not quite making eye contact. "Everyone at school's gonna know, aren't they?"

The question hit Bev harder than anything else that had happened in the last twelve hours. This wasn't about her anymore. Sure, it was disruptive and scary and humiliating, but there was embarrassment and then there was the utter soul-sucking humiliation of getting negative attention in middle school. "I am so sorry, sweetie. But yes, almost everyone will have heard by now."

Shelby squared her shoulders, and the grim set of her mouth made Bev's heart ache. Then Shel raised her eyes to meet her aunt's, and a sly smile crept across her face. "Maybe now the bullies will be too afraid to mess with me. After all, my aunt will hit anyone who talks shit about me."

"Language," Bev chided to cover her shock and apprehension about Shelby's reaction. It was good that she wasn't devastated, but this felt like it was straddling a line. "I'd rather your schoolmates not fear me."

"Okay," Shelby said. "I'll let them know they have nothing to fear."

The duplicitous confidence emanating from Shelby made Bev wince. "Shelby…"

"Don't worry, Aunt Bev. I won't rub it in their faces at all. Promise." One hand was behind her back, and Bev was almost positive her fingers were crossed.

"We'll talk about it later. I don't want to prevent you from spinning this to make it easier on you, but I don't want to make things worse."

"I won't make things worse. I'll make things right." Shelby opened the door and joined her friends inside.

Bev glared at Sam. "Been spending quality time with the tweens?"

Sam shrugged unrepentantly. "What can I say? That kid knows what's what. And all time spent with me is quality time."

"Why don't you tell us everything," Evie suggested, topping off Bev's glass.

Bev leaned back in her chair once she'd unloaded the whole story —everything. Not just the last week, but the last few months of snide remarks that started when she didn't get the promotion she'd been promised when the previous branch manager retired. Every time she'd been dressed down with the door open. The snide remarks about her weight every time he saw her eat. The end of summer party Jackson had thrown for the bank employees that he'd "inadvertently" forgot to invite her to, and where annual bonuses had been handed out. And what he'd said that morning.

"Wow," Viv said. "I can't believe you kept it together all this time. I would've hit him the first time he insinuated I was too old to advance in my career."

"No, you wouldn't have," Evie said. "You would have destroyed him verbally and left him sobbing in his office."

Viv nodded. "Yeah, that's more accurate."

Elle held her glass out for a refill and asked, "The problem is that you struck him, correct? I know there's a zero-tolerance policy at school for fighting. Is it like that?"

"A zero-tolerance policy that's unevenly enforced," Evie muttered.

"Yeah, if I'd just quit and flounced, it would've looked bad, but he would've looked worse, and I might have even been able to make a case for a hostile work environment based on his frequent and egregious comments about my age and ability. But I didn't flounce."

"I didn't realize how bad it was when I offered to intimidate him into not pressing charges. Intimidation isn't enough. I'm thinking emasculation is more appropriate." Red sparks flared in Sam's dark brown eyes, and ebony horns curled out of her head above her ears.

"We can't neuter every man who insults us, baby. But if you want to get your wings out, I'd agree to some nighttime intimidation. We could knock on his second-story windows, and you could wave, eyes glowing." Viv reached up and trailed a finger along one of Sam's horns.

"That's not why you want my wings out." Sam leaned into Viv's hand.

"We need to move on before I start making the really obvious joke here. Put your horns away, Sam." Evie turned towards Bev. "What do you want to do? What do you want us to do? You have powerful people on your side, and we can work to make this problem go away."

"If I can't damage him, why do you get to kill him?" Sam sounded outraged enough that Bev cracked a real smile.

"I wasn't going to kill him. I was going to make the problem go away. With the law. Or his corporate headquarters. Maybe sabotage or mental manipulation." At Bev's exclamation of surprise, Evie said defensively, "It's okay if it's for the greater good."

"Since when, goody two-shoes who regularly freaks out when you accidentally wish something into existence." Viv's head jerked around, and she stared at Bev. Her eyes were vacant, and her face was slack. Sam's horns disappeared, but the glow in her eyes stayed. She slipped an arm around Viv, a necessity, since sometimes Viv's visions threw her off balance.

"What?" Bev demanded when Viv looked like she'd returned to the present moment.

"It was nothing much." She shifted in the chair, and Bev narrowed her eyes at Viv.

"Genevieve Kane, we have known each other for thirty-five years, and I know every one of your tells. You're lying." Bev jabbed a finger towards Viv.

"You are lying," Elle said. "People look different when they lie."

"You're a living lie detector? Wow," Evie said.

Elle nodded. "It makes parenting interesting, especially since Kevin knows. Doesn't stop him from trying to get away with stuff, though. The lengths he went through to ensure I didn't see his last report card were almost impressive."

"Fine. It just seemed too trivial for what we're talking about now, and I didn't want to detract from Jackson and his uncertain but unpleasant future."

"Just tell us," Evie prompted.

"It was Charlie. And us—all of us. We were sitting on the large deck at her tasting room, drinking wine and watching the sun set over the mountains."

Bev glanced at Elle, who was watching Viv. "She's not lying," Elle said.

"That sounds wonderful. We've been talking about doing a girls' weekend for a long time and haven't made it happen. Maybe we should just do it." Evie's voice was back to her regular chipper tone, and it was hard to resist Evie's happiness.

"I guess I don't have to worry about work," Bev said. "But I think I'm not supposed to leave town. I don't want them to think I'm a flight risk."

Sam rolled her eyes. "I'll take care of that. *Nonviolently*," she added when the others turned to regard her with suspicion. "I'm not a huge wine fan, but I am a big Viv fan and don't want to miss meeting Charlie."

"What about the kids?" Elle asked. "We can't bring them, can we?"

"Not only can we not, we do not want to do that. The point is to be kid-free for three glorious days," Evie said. "Luc can handle it."

"Four kids at once? One of whom is in diapers?" Bev asked doubtfully. "I don't think I could do that, but if you think Luc is up for the task..."

"Never underestimate me, Bev!" Luc said, walking outside with baby Alex in his arms. "I don't know what we're talking about, but I've got it covered." Alex leaned forward, almost toppling out of Luc's arms, reaching for Evie.

"Ma ma ma ma."

Evie held out her arms and took her daughter. Alex was an almost perfect meld between Evie's fair skin and delicate features and Luc's dark brown skin, velvety brown eyes, and short, curly black hair. "We're taking Bev to Charlie's new winery for a girls' weekend, leaving you in charge of four kids for three nights."

"Provided Charlie agrees," Viv said. "But she will."

Luc grinned. "That sounds like fun. When's the last time you all got out of town, together, without kids?"

Bev, Viv, and Evie exchanged a glance. "Um, high school?" Bev said.

"Wow, I would've guessed twelve years at least, but thirty? You are overdue," Luc said. "I can manage four children. The oldest three just need limits and basic supervision, and Alex can't even walk yet, so I can manage her."

"Has it really been thirty years?" Sam asked.

"No," Evie said. "We went out of town for my bachelorette party, remember? Girls' weekend in Vancouver?"

"Why Canada?" Elle asked. "Don't humans go to places like Las Vegas to celebrate major milestones?"

Evie grinned and flushed. "I got married young. Right out of high school. Canada was a great place to let loose for three women barely out of high school."

"What she means is the drinking age is lower in Canada than in the United States," Bev clarified. "I had to be the responsible one and keep these two wrangled."

"You're always the responsible one," Evie said rather absently as she positioned Alex in her arms and slipped her shirt down.

"Yeah, you are," Viv said. "It's kind of crap that we put that on you."

Evie leaned forward quickly and then yelped. "She has teeth now and doesn't like sudden movements." Evie settled back into the chair and waited for Alex to latch on again. "I never even thought about it that way, but you're right, Viv. It is crap."

"It's not like that," Bev protested. "We're all responsible."

"Except me," Viv interjected. "I'm out here Peter Panning it every day. You two are the ones who had kids and settled down."

"Why don't we agree that we're all very different levels of responsible and not try to outdo each other on proving who's the least responsible?" Evie asked.

Sam leaned forward and grinned. "But, if we're voting, I think it's Alex. Look at her... Makes others carry her around, total parasite when it comes to food, and won't even express her needs in speech anyone else can understand."

Bev laughed. "You might be onto something there, Sam. Alex is kind of a freeloader."

Viv's phone beeped, and she pulled it out of her pocket. "Charlie said she's free this weekend and would love to have us stay under one condition."

"If it's stomping grapes, I am in," Bev said.

"I don't think they actually put feet in the wine anymore," Evie said. "But as long as the condition isn't hard labor or childcare—"

"Same thing," Bev interrupted.

"—I don't care what she wants," Evie finished.

"It'll be the trial run of her tasting room and wine cabins, so we have to try all the wines and amenities to make sure everything works smoothly."

"Oh no!" Evie exclaimed. "We have to try all the wines? And sleep in her luxury vacation cabins?"

"How much is that going to run us?" Bev asked. She tried not to think about money—it'd been a long time since she'd had to, and she had plenty put away, but if she wasn't going to be working for the foreseeable future, she'd need to be frugal.

Viv typed a response. "I'll find out, but regardless, you don't have to worry about it. This weekend is our treat to you."

"I can't accept that. It's too much." Bev cringed at the thought of being in debt to her best friends.

Viv's phone dinged again. "Wow. Just wow. Charlie says no charge for the rooms, and since it's just us and no other guests, she'll go easy on the charges for the wine and food."

"That's amazing," Evie said, pulling her shirt back over her chest and handing a much sleepier Alex to Luc.

"How much money would something like that cost us if Viv didn't know this Charlie?" Elle asked. "I can give her a very large tip if it would be appropriate."

"I have no idea how much it would cost, but it would be a lot," Viv said. "She's giving us all four of the cabins and not making money on the wine. We're getting an amazing deal."

"I cannot wait," Evie said. "It's going to be so fun. Elle, you're in, right?"

The angel shrugged. "I have never gone on a girls' weekend, but I am willing to try it. I do like wine."

"Bev, you're the only one who hasn't jumped in with enthusiasm." Viv fixed Bev with a hard stare. "Why are you hesitating, and should I be making plans to kidnap you?"

"It does sound great, it really does, but Shelby…" Bev didn't want to tell them the whole reason she was hesitating and bringing up her niece who was struggling with school and life and hearing the dead was at least fifty percent of her hesitation.

"Shelby will be fine." Luc stood, rocking a sleeping Alex gently in his arms. "The kids do sleepovers every weekend, anyway, and sometimes in the summer, they spend entire weekends at one of our houses. She won't be alone. In fact, other than you, she'll be surrounded by the people who love her most. And me. I have full confidence that I can manage to keep them out of most trouble they'd try to get into."

"We're not going that far away," Evie pointed out. "If there is an emergency, Luc will call us, and we'll be home in a couple hours."

"If it's a big, scary emergency that requires your immediate presence, either Elle or I can get you home even faster." Sam hooked her thumbs together and flapped her hands like a bird.

Bev was rapidly running out of excuses—at least the ones she was going to say out loud. She did her best to push the fear back, then thought better of it. It hadn't been too long ago that she and Evie were chastising Viv for keeping secrets; she didn't want to make the same mistake. "It's not the distance. It's not even really Shelby, although that's part of it. It's…" She blew out a long breath. "It's the dead. They're everywhere, and they are not quiet."

"What do you mean?" Evie asked, wrinkling her nose. "I know you hear them sometimes, and when they rose on the island, Shelby was able to help them pass to the other side, wherever that is. But is there more?"

"A bit more." She glanced at Viv as she debated how much to reveal. Viv smiled encouragingly at her, and Bev decided to let it all spill out. "I thought I was losing my mind. That Shelby and I both were. We went to see Doctor Allen who diagnosed us both and prescribed several medications. When Viv told me she thought I might be misinterpreting the dead speaking to me as schizophrenia, I took Shelby to a psychiatrist in Spokane—and found a different one for myself." Bev took a sip of her wine while she organized her thoughts. "Other than hearing voices, which I am willing to admit are more likely the talking dead than auditory hallucinations, I was given a pretty clean bill of mental health."

"Pretty clean?" Viv asked.

"I do have anxiety. Like a lot. I can barely stand to go anywhere anymore. Every place I go, all I can think about is the hundreds of ways a person could die at any given moment. When I'm driving, car accidents, every type imaginable, flash through my head. When I'm near the lake, drownings. At home, there are so many accidents waiting to happen. Cancer, strokes, heart attacks, poisoning, shootings, stabbings… I never have a break. And the thought of going somewhere new, hearing new voices, is sending my anxiety through the roof. I don't know if I can do it." Bev felt her pulse accelerate as she thought about the winding roads to get out of Eden Valley. She'd barely managed the last trip to Spokane for Shelby's appointment and had considered it a gift from the gods of mental health when they were able to do most of the appointments via telehealth.

"That sounds so stressful. What can we do to alleviate your stress but also get you out of town long enough to drink some wine in a place that isn't Eden Valley?" Evie asked.

"If the car ride is too much, we can fly and meet the others at the winery," Sam volunteered.

"You're just volunteering because you hate cars," Viv said.

"And because I'm a nice person who cares deeply about my friends."

"But mostly the car thing. I'm onto you." Viv and Sam exchanged a glance hot enough to warm everyone on the porch.

"I don't know," Bev said. "I want to want it, but…"

"Do you hear them now? The dead, I mean?" Elle asked.

Bev concentrated for a moment. "Yes, but they're not too loud. Same with the running litany of death. It's there, but only a little distracting. I'm used to these voices, though."

"Your objections are reasonable and valid," Evie said.

Bev's shoulders that had tightened up while thinking of all the new places she could be tortured with the requests of whatever spirits were hanging around started to relax. They weren't going to make her go. Not that anyone could *make* her do anything, but…

"However," Evie continued, "I think it would be good for you to give it a try, just to see. You can decide if you'd rather fly to the winery or drive. And, once we're there, once you've given it a fair chance—at least through dinner and a couple glasses of wine—if it's still too much, you can go home. Deal?"

Bev thought it over. She couldn't decide if the objections she was still holding onto were because there was something still wrong with Evie's plan or because she was too afraid to try something new. She let out her breath, pulled up her metaphorical big girl pants, and said, "I'm in."

Bev looked around her bedroom as she packed for her weekend trip. The last week had dragged by. Since she was out of a job, and Shelby's suspension ended the day Bev was fired—quit, she reminded herself—Bev found herself with nothing to do and time on her hands.

Her backyard and garden, her favorite hobby and personal retreat, were ready for winter. Her house was cleaner than it'd been in a long, long time, and that was saying something. The freezer was stocked with meals, she'd updated her resume, end-of-life directives, will, and caught up on her favorite authors newest releases. And that had taken her through Wednesday. Thursday was empty. She'd moved the furniture around in the living room, rearranged her pantry, and was now trying to decide how to overhaul her bedroom to make it more relaxing evening retreat and less utilitarian hostel.

"Be-ev!" Shelby's voice echoed up the stairs and into Bev's room. "Where are you?"

Bev walked out of her room, suitcase abandoned. "I'm in my room. A more important question is why are you here?"

Shelby bounded up the stairs two at a time and nearly careened directly into Bev. "I'm playing hooky."

Bev took a step back and put her hands on her hips. "Are you kidding me right now? What are you thinking?"

"I was thinking that there was no way you'd believe I decided to skip school and then stop at home to tell you first." Shelby stuck her tongue out at Bev.

"Or maybe that's just what you want me to think, throw me off the scent," Bev countered.

"Like I'd ever be that clever. That'd be Lily-level planning."

A pang of sadness reverberated through Bev. She knew Shelby was serious, even if she'd laugh it off as a joke. "I think you're brilliant and talented, and that's much better than clever any day." She aimed a smile at her niece, and the one Shelby flashed back was brighter than the sunlight that rarely deigned to show its face this time of year. "You didn't answer my question, though. Why aren't you in school?"

"It's early dismissal today, and no school tomorrow. State-wide teacher in-service, remember?"

Bev wrinkled her nose, trying to call up the school calendar. "Are you sure? I'm usually pretty on top of things like that, making plans for you to hang out elsewhere while I'm at work."

"You are on top of it, and you did make plans. Kevin, Lily, and I are hanging out. That's always the plan, anyway. I just wanted to stop by and tell you goodbye." Shelby darted forward and hugged her aunt.

"Goodbye?" Fear replaced the sadness still echoing in her chest. There were so many ways she could lose Shelby. So many accidents. So many not accidents. All of them flooded her mind, choking off her air supply and making her lightheaded.

"You're leaving in a couple hours, right? Goodbye 'til Sunday. Nothing else. I promise." Shelby's expression was a combination of exasperation, irritation, and a much-too-adult look of compassion.

Air inflated Bev's lungs again. "Pinky swear?" She held out her hand.

"Pinky swear." Shelby hooked her pinky finger around Bev's and they shook on it. "Go have fun. I promise to go easy on Luc, we all do."

"I know you will. You're so respons—" Bev stopped herself before she could fully lay the burden on Shelby she'd carried since she was the same age. "You know what? Don't be ridiculous, but don't worry too much about being the responsible one. Have fun. Tease Luc. He can take it. Just keep it two steps back from him needing reinforcements."

"What would be bad about that?"

"There are three people he might call for help. Evie—"

"Oooh, yeah. We don't want that." Shelby grimaced.

"Mat, although that doesn't seem too likely after what happened this summer."

"He's kinda creepy. I don't think Luc would call him. He'd just stir up trouble, try to get us to fight with each other, pretend he has secrets, and make everyone miserable. Then Luc would have to call Evie, anyway." Shelby leaned against the wall. Bev tried not to notice how close Shel was to the top of the stairs. One wrong step, a stumble, turning around too quickly—any of those could make Shelby fall down the stairs to the hardwoods below.

Shelby took a step forward and angled herself away from the stairs. "Better?"

Bev nodded, hating that her niece read her so well. "Thanks. The third option is Papa Abe. He's not great, but he does at least care very much for Lily's health and well-being, and by extension her friends. I'd rather not come home and find out a King of Hell has been babysitting you."

"Fair enough," Shelby said. "We'll be good, but not too good."

"Do you need to pack anything?"

"Nah, I have a couple outfits at Lily's that are still clean." She gave Bev another hug. Their heads were almost even now. "Go and have fun. Don't be too responsible."

Bev kissed Shelby's forehead. "I hear my words echoing back at me, and I can't ignore that. What else can I get you to embrace and repeat? Hmmm… I love cleaning my room and ensuring the house is tidy."

"Ha! You can't trick me that easily." Shelby darted into her room, dropped her backpack, and came back out with a bike helmet. "See you Sunday!"

She clattered back down the stairs and slammed the door hard enough on her way out to rattle the picture frames in the stairway.

Bev sighed and went back into her room to finish packing.

# CHAPTER FIVE

"Are you coming out for wine on the deck and a great sunset? Or do you need a minute?" Viv's voice permeated the thick, wooden door of the rustic chic cabin Bev had locked herself into.

Bev looked at the door and willed herself to get up and follow Viv to the main building for a glass of pre-dinner wine while the sun set behind the cascades. "I'll be there in ten minutes."

"You want me to come back here and fetch you if you haven't shown up in fifteen?"

"Yeah. That'd be really nice, actually. Thank you." Ten minutes was enough time to change and touch up her hair and makeup, with time left over to breathe through the voices of the dead and encourage them to pipe down. At least these didn't seem to want anything from her. Yet. No hissed demands for vengeance. No insidious whispers about how they'd died. No pleas for someone—anyone—to see them, remember them…

She shook it off. This is how life was now. No job, poor role modeling, and the really noisy dead.

The sun slipped behind the jagged peaks of the Cascade mountains, lighting the sky in brilliant oranges and purples. Silence hung in the air as the six women watched the last rays of light fade.

"That was gorgeous," Bev said. "I haven't been watching nearly enough sunsets lately."

"That view is exactly why I moved here," Charlie said. She poured another round of grenache into their glasses—even Sam was eschewing her usual beer for wine—then settled into the padded lounge chair on the open deck. Charlie had medium-toned brown skin, light brown eyes, and curly black hair. Right now, curled up on her deck sipping a wine she'd created, she looked more peaceful than Bev had ever felt.

"This is magnificent," Bev said. "The rooms, the property, the view, and this wine. How many people will you have working for you?"

Charlie set down her glass and counted on her fingers. "The winemaking staff—about five people who are just coming on staff—my grapes will be coming off their primary fermentation in the next week or so. There were more at harvest—it was exciting to bring in my first crop this year. Stephanie—my chef—is in the process of hiring the kitchen staff. Between the kitchen staff and the servers, I'll have another half dozen this fall. And then a couple people from town will clean the rooms. If all goes well, I'll double my staff in a year to keep up with demand. I'm hoping to be able to justify hiring a business manager by next year so I can let go of those reins and concentrate on winemaking again." Charlie grimaced. "That was a really long answer to a simple question."

"I love learning more about the business of wine now that I've perfected the art of drinking everything you give me. And if everything is as good as what we've seen so far, I can't imagine Estaca Corazón not being a huge hit," Evie said. "What does the name mean, anyway? I've been wondering."

"I wish quality was enough," Charlie said ruefully. "I named it Estaca Corazón because this is where I've planted my heart. Not to mention my money. The first winery I worked for was amazing. The wines were some of the best I've ever tasted, the location was perfect, and every detail was first class. And it went under in less than five years. I'm lucky—I have the reputation I built at Cairdeas, and their blessing to open my own place so close to theirs. I've been sitting on this land for almost a decade, hoping that the grapes that'd been planted but neglected before I bought it would do something. When this property came up for sale, I knew it was time. It's close enough to my vines to make everything convenient and had all the structures already built. I did some renovations—updated the kitchen and the cabins, added solar. The basic ecological upgrades. I didn't even know about the tunnels when I bought it—and I'm positive the previous owners didn't either or he would've bragged about it and added another zero to the asking price." She laughed and took a drink of her wine. "Listen to me go on. You wished me good luck, and I gave you a speech. Why don't we head inside for dinner, then we can sit in the main tasting room and catch up on the gossip."

BEV GROANED and stretched out in one of the large, overstuffed chairs scattered in front of the enormous fireplace. "That was amazing. If that's the quality you'll be serving your paying guests, you're going to have a lot of full, happy people."

"That's the goal," Charlie said.

"My compliments to the chef. I don't usually eat food, but that was great." Elle smiled and held out her glass for a refill.

Charlie shot her a look, but whatever she was thinking, she kept to herself. "You can compliment her yourself. I invited Stephanie to have a glass of wine with us before she heads home to her family."

A tall white woman appeared in the doorway, looked around, and strode across the room. She had iron grey hair plaited into two long braids, a figure that was strong without being spare—a warrior's body—and bare arms covered in scars. She must have noticed Bev trying not to stare at her arms. She grinned and held them out. "Kitchen scars. Burns, mostly. There is nothing glamorous about being a chef."

"Your food was amazing," Bev said. "Where did you learn to do that?"

"I went to culinary school right out of high school, then worked in a couple higher end restaurants in Seattle before I was forced to give it all up and run back to Chelan." She brought her left wrist to her forehead and sighed dramatically.

"Tell the nice people what 'forced' you to return," Charlie prompted.

"Spoil sport." Stephanie stuck her tongue out at Charlie, then turned back to the others. "I met the man of my dreams at a bar. He was a friend of a friend of a friend, and we clicked immediately. Once things got serious—something that took all of three weeks—we had to look to the future. He was over living in a city, and I was over working in kitchens, no matter how prestigious. We came back to Chelan so I could introduce him to my family, he got offered a job, and we moved here a month later. We've been here ever since, twenty years and counting."

"What she's not telling you is that her husband Marc is the most gorgeous man you'll ever meet, and her twins Katherine and Alexander are the best-behaved teens alive." Charlie grinned at her friend. "I've been trying to steal her away from that man for a decade, but she keeps rebuffing all my advances."

"Hey! I'm here now, aren't I?" Stephanie sat in the only empty chair after filling her wine glass. "The twins are fourteen now, old enough to handle themselves after school, and Marc is home by six every night. When Charlie offered me the opportunity to run my own kitchen, I jumped at the chance. It gets pretty boring at home some-times when no one needs you." Her phone beeped, and after she glanced down at it, she drained her glass and stood. "Marc's here to get me. Thanks for the wine, Charlie. It was nice to meet all of you! I hope I'll see you around." She waved and left the room.

"So. Tell me all about Sam." Charlie refilled everyone's glasses, but her eyes were focused on the demon sprawled on the floor next to Viv's chair. "She looks our age, but no way is a woman in her forties sitting on the floor like that when there are other options available."

Sam grinned. "I'm actually older than all of you. Just very well preserved. It runs in my family. My older brother Luc is engaged to Evie, and he doesn't look a day over thirty."

"You're still planning on a winter wedding?" Charlie asked, momentarily distracted from her questions about Sam.

Evie nodded. "My parents think I'm doing it solely to torture them and are trying to convince me to do a destination wedding in Hawaii, but this is home, and I want to get married here."

"I know we're not quite in Eden Valley, but what about here? We have the space, and unless you're planning a huge wedding, we could probably accommodate most of the guests either here or at Cairdeas."

Evie clapped her hands. "Oh my god. That would be so perfect. I mean, I'd obviously have to talk to my fiancé, but…" Her voice trailed off. "That might not actually work. My soon-to-be in-laws are…a little bit weird."

"Oh, honey, I know weird. There is no way your family could out-weird mine. I promise there isn't anything I haven't seen. Please say yes. Or at least a very strong maybe." Charlie clasped her hands under her chin and fluttered her eyelashes.

Bev narrowed her eyes at Charlie, pulled out of her exhaustion to wonder if that was the hyperbole everyone spouted about quirky families, or if there was something more to this story.

Evie laughed. "Very strong maybe. I'll bring Luc by later this month, and we can chat."

Bev stood. "I'm so sorry, everyone. I'm exhausted and can't stop thinking about that king sized bed and super soft sheets. Mind if I head out?" She tried to stop a yawn, but was too late and nearly split her jaw.

"Go. Sleep. You need it." Viv waved her hands at Bev. "Besides, I know you'll be awake by five."

"See you tomorrow. And thank you, Charlie. So much." Bev headed out into the dark. It was a short walk to her cabin, and the path was well lit, but something felt dark. Almost oppressive. It was almost like the feeling she got in cemeteries, but there wasn't a grave-yard anywhere nearby. The darkness pressed in on her, and she picked up the pace until she was practically jogging. The feeling of being watched intensified, and she held her breath, not easy when you're also trying to power walk. When she hit the small front porch of her cabin, she exhaled forcefully, then darted up the stairs and opened the door. She turned in the doorway, looked out into the darkness, and yelled, "Leave me alone!"

Bev slammed the door, locked it, and crawled into bed, pulling the covers over her head.

# CHAPTER SIX

Bev hesitated at the top of the stairs. She could hear the other women talking, and no one sounded scared or upset in any way, but the darkness she'd felt the night before had intensified the minute Charlie'd opened the door to her wine tunnels. No one else had felt anything weird, and Viv said she wasn't seeing anything new.

"Oh my god," Viv gasped. "Is this for real?"

Bev gritted her teeth and headed down the steep staircase and followed the path of light spilling out in the hallway and leading to another door.

When she walked into the room where everyone was waiting, her jaw dropped. The room was perfectly round and made of smooth-carved stone that shone in the lamplight. Alcoves were placed at irregular intervals on the walls, and Charlie had taken advantage of the space and put x-shaped wine racks in each one. She'd decorated the room in a style that could only be called cozy opulence. Warm leather chairs, inviting lighting, thick, patterned rugs on the floor, and what had to be custom framed art on the walls that fit perfectly with the curvature of the room.

"Wow," Bev said. The voices of the dead were loud here, and it was getting difficult to breathe again.

Elle stepped close to her and put a hand on her elbow. "I can help you push them back if you want. Most have no interest in getting close to the light."

The voices dimmed enough that instead of a cacophony, it was a background murmur. Still irritating, but more easily ignored.

"I don't know what this space was, or even how far the tunnels go, but every fifty yards or so, there's another one of these rooms. I'm not sure how to bring it up to code—I have a contractor coming in next week to go over some options—but this space is amazing. As far as I can tell, this room is the center of a huge star shape, and each of the other, smaller rooms connect to each other. Kind of like a spider web? I did have engineers in early to make sure everything above was structurally sound, and it seem like it is… Even if I can't figure out how to make this the code-friendly VIP tasting room experience, at least I'll have some great places to store wine." Charlie's enthusiasm for the web of tunnels was almost contagious. Almost.

"What do you think this space was originally used for?" Evie asked. Her eyes were wide as she slowly turned in a circle, taking everything in.

"It was a mausoleum," Bev said, then winced. She hadn't meant to throw the death talk into the party. Almost no one was excited to find out their rooms had been full of dead people.

"Huh. I guess that makes sense," Charlie said. "These alcoves are pretty deep, and about the right dimensions to hold a coffin. I wonder where all the bodies went?"

"I don't think they ever left," Bev said as the chattering grew louder again, until it was deafening. "Shut up! If you have something to say, stand in line and take turns. I can't understand you if you're all talking over each other. Come here and tell me what you want!" The noise in her head disappeared, and she almost collapsed with the relief of it.

When she started to focus on the room around her again, the first thing she noticed was Charlie staring at her, jaw dropped.

"I'm sorry. I don't…" Bev let her voice trail off. It was hard to explain why you were yelling at the walls without sounding a little crazy. She pasted a smile on her face and hoped Charlie would let it go.

"Are you hollering at dead people?" Charlie asked. "Because that is weird."

BEV STOOD on the deck jutting out in a triangle from the main house watching the sunset. She was alone. After she'd fled the tunnels, she'd gone on a long walk to quiet the voices in her head. By the end of the walk, things began to feel clearer. Having the voices stop for a few moments gave her the clarity she needed and the confidence she hadn't even noticed was missing.

She'd spent the last couple years pretending nothing was wrong, and even when she knew there was more to it than misfiring neuro-transmitters, she refused to take responsibility for what was happen-ing. And it wasn't just her—Shelby was going through the same thing, although with infinitely more grace than Bev.

And now here she was, alone in silence for the first time since she and Viv had gotten Viv's car stuck in a portal to hell and had to be rescued by a demon. It would be temporary. The voices would return, but they wanted something, they all wanted something, and maybe she could help them find out what that was.

Footsteps behind her made her whirl around. It was Stephanie, the winery's chef, and she was holding a bottle of wine. "The other women headed into town to do a little shopping, but they wanted to make sure you didn't feel abandoned. I have a bottle of sparkling wine with your name on it." Stephanie held out the bottle and there was a label, adorned with ghosts and clearly dug out of an old Halloween decoration bag, with Bev's name written in big, block letters.

"That's awesome," Bev said. "I would love a glass."

Stephanie opened it, and the cork flew off with a satisfying pop. "I'd love to stay and have a glass, but I need to get back into the kitchen so everything's ready for dinner at seven. Let me know if you need anything else, otherwise I'll see you at dinner."

"Thank you," Bev said, taking the glass Stephanie handed her.

"Any time. Enjoy the sunset. And the bottle." After she'd deposited the bottle in the ice bucket she'd brought with her, Stephanie disappeared back into the building.

Bev moved one of the chairs to the very point of the deck and settled in to watch the sun go down and make some new year new me resolutions. This was an opportunity for change. It'd been a long time since she'd truly enjoyed her job—and, if she was being honest with herself, she'd only gone for the promotion because it was expected of her. Promotions were the career path. Branch manager, then district manager, then maybe higher if things went well. Maybe something bigger when Shelby was out of high school and off to university. But banking had never been her passion and certainly wasn't why she went to business school. That had been the job she'd fallen back on when she came back to Eden Valley.

Her real dream was something she'd never shared with anyone. It was silly. Totally impractical. But seeing Charlie's set up here and talking to Stephanie was resurrecting that dream at least as effectively as Bev's presence was resurrecting whichever spirits still walked this land.

She wasn't sure if she was ready to say it out loud, even to herself, but for the first time in over twenty years, she didn't have a job that pulled her along with expectations and ambition she didn't want but didn't know how to leave behind.

Voices behind her, live human—mostly—voices, snapped her attention back to the present. She grabbed her wine glass and headed back inside. Charlie was nowhere to be seen in the great room where they'd hung out in front of the fire the night before. She grimaced. "Sorry?"

"For what?" Viv said. "We all have our quirks. You yell at dead people. It's no big deal. Charlie only wears days of the week underpants. That's way weirder if you ask me."

"What happens if Friday goes missing?" Evie asked.

Charlie appeared in the doorway with a cheese tray and a pitcher of water. "First of all, you were supposed to take that bit of information to the grave. But the answer to your question, Evie, is commando. No Friday means no underwear." Charlie grinned at Evie.

"I used to hide all the Saturdays," Viv said in a stage whisper, hand cupped around her mouth with the back of her hand towards Charlie.

Sam leaned over and dropped a kiss on Viv's cheek. "That's the kind of trouble I appreciate."

"I knew it! I couldn't ever catch you in the act, but I knew it was you." Charlie pointed dramatically. "I will have my revenge!"

Bev laughed watching Viv and Charlie argue about the fines Viv owed for unauthorized underpants confiscation. Bev might be a bit of a freak, but they all were a little. And no one was staring at her or laughing behind their hands. She'd known who she was for most of her life and had seldom wavered. She'd been a daughter—the responsible one who made sure bills were paid and food was on the table. She'd been a friend who made sure everyone got home safe, had all the birth control they needed, and always had a shoulder to cry on. She'd been an excellent employee with twenty years of perfect performance reviews. And she'd been a perfectly adequate aunt to Shelby, fighting for her in school, with her doctors, and with anyone who looked at her kid sideways.

She'd never neglected herself. Self-care was the oxygen mask she wore to make sure she could be there for everyone else. She took the time to make herself feel good. Gardening for her soul and makeup for her body. But watching the banter between these women who were all living their best lives made Bev realize there was one thing she hadn't done for herself. She never let herself dream bigger.

There was a lull in the teasing while Charlie refilled their wine glasses, and Bev took the opportunity to assuage her curiosity. "Think back to when you were a kid—ten years old. What made you happiest then? What did you dream of for yourself? And did you do it?"

Charlie sat down and pulled her chair closer to the fireplace. "Oooh, that's a great question. There was nothing I loved more as a kid than messing with my older brother's chemistry set. I'd sit in the library for hours poring over science magazines, writing down experiments to duplicate at home, and then running off with the chemicals, first from his set, then liberated from the school's science lab, to see what kind of stuff I could create. I would get into so much trouble." She laughed, shaking her head. "I guess I still love experimenting. Wine is chemistry—and a little art. But here I am, living my dream. At least now, I won't get into trouble for sneaking my concoctions into someone's glass."

"All I ever wanted was to be a mom. When we were kids, I made you and Viv play house with me all the time. You were both terrible at it, by the way. Worst kids ever. You're both grounded." Evie pursed her mouth and shook her finger at Bev and Viv.

"Someone had to prepare you for your own demon spawn," Viv said. "But you're right, playing house was never my thing. I don't know what my biggest childhood joy was. Things were pretty crappy at home for a long time, and it felt like every time I found something that gave me joy, my mother found out and took it away." She sighed, and for a moment Bev felt like backpedaling the whole conversation. "You know, though? I loved school. I loved learning. And I loved sharing what I'd learned with other people. I'm not sure if graphic design is hitting that same place, but I get to create ideas and show them to other people who pay me money for the privilege. If you'd asked me at ten if I wanted to be a graphic designer when I grew up, I would've said no. I wanted to be a writer. I had dreams of being the female Tolkien for the modern age. Turns out, writing is not my strong suit, so I had to find another way to share my creativity." Viv grinned at the room, and there was not an ounce of regret at lost dreams in that smile.

"Wow. This is a lot deeper than I thought we were going to get." Bev looked at Sam. She wasn't going to push the demon if Sam didn't want to answer. So far, Charlie was mostly in the dark about the weird supernatural happenings in Eden Valley, although with the ease with which she'd taken Bev's outburst earlier, she might have an inkling about the weird in the world.

Sam flashed a grin and crossed her legs. "I'm not going to be deep for you, Bev. I'm a shallow person, and I will keep it light over here. When I was young, I wanted nothing more than to be a princess. I did everything my father told me to do so that I would be good enough to stand beside him. Turns out, I wasn't qualified." She turned and kissed Viv on the cheek. "My daddy issues and your mommy issues fit together so well, don't they?"

"How are you living your dream?" Charlie asked.

"By letting go of what I thought I wanted because I'd always been told that was what I was supposed to want and going for something that means much, much more to me." Sam smiled at Viv whose cheeks were stained red.

"I can call you princess if you want," Viv said. "But only if you wear a tiara."

"Deal."

Already, things were lighter. Her friends' stories were the confirmation she needed, but there was still one person who hadn't answered. Bev considered not asking—who knew what the angel would say—but didn't want her to feel left out. "Elle, what about you? What did you want when you were young?"

"I didn't have a childhood as you know it. I am an idea, or at least we started as an idea. We sprang forth fully formed, much like that myth of Aphrodite. But we had our formative years as we learned our roles and what She wanted from us. Her will never was too burdensome. We wanted only what She wanted, and that was what I aspired to." Elle was glowing, just a little, and Bev was wondering if she'd made a mistake in prompting Elle to relive her childhood. She glanced over at Charlie who was staring in fascination at the glowing woman with the strange goals and stranger upbringing. The winemaker was taking all this better than any of the Eden Valley residents had, which was more than a little suspicious.

"You switched from 'we' to 'I' at the end," Evie pointed out. "You have individuality now. So what do you want now? What dreams do you have?"

"I dream of the tree and of truth. And what I desire most is to be able to discern the truth without faith." The glow abruptly winked out, and Elle once more looked like a beautiful but totally mortal woman.

"Y'all have a lot more weird in you than my days of the week underpants. I don't know what's going on with any of you, but it's kind of fun. My only regret is you haven't come to visit sooner and glow up my winery." Charlie raised her glass. "To weird, and to sisterhood."

"I love a cheesy toast," Viv said, raising her glass and clinking it against Charlie's.

"I know you do, that's why we're doing this."

"Bev didn't share," Elle said, interrupting the toast. "She made us dig deep, and for a reason—she's looking back into herself—but didn't tell us what she'd found."

"Fair enough. Now that I'm unemployed, I have time to figure this out. I feel kinda like Sam—everything I tried to be, the dreams I had, were someone else's, or my reaction to other people, and not my own. But there's one thing I always wanted to do and never told anyone." She looked down at her hands in her lap, then grabbed her wineglass and took a fortifying drink. "I love baking and throwing parties and having people over. And then I like it when they leave. But I always wanted to—please don't laugh—have a bed-and-breakfast. Just a few rooms for people who want a different experience in Eden Valley. I'd make amazing breakfasts, host wine and cheese happy hours on the porch, and have the most amazing garden where people could hang out, smell the flowers, or pick themselves a snack."

"That sounds so cool," Evie said. "Do you have a place in mind?"

"Whoa, whoa, whoa!" Bev held up her hand to stop her friend. "This is my childhood dream that I remembered tonight. I have nothing in mind but the desire to see how I can translate those desires into something realistic that I can do now."

"Don't be realistic, be quixotic," Charlie advised. "Realism will only get you more of what you have right now. You can't achieve big dreams if you don't dream big."

Bev was looking for the right words to deflect the attention without being too self-deprecating. The one thing she'd never lacked before she started hearing the voices of the dead, and before her child transformed into a tween, was confidence. She'd always known what she was good at and focused on those things rather than striving for things that seemed out of reach. Stretch goals had never been her thing. She needed to find that spark again, but maybe glow it up a little. Reaching for the stars didn't seem like such a bad idea now that everything was topsy turvy. She shuddered. That was scary. Maybe her first stretch goal should a metaphorical toe touch and not cartwheels. And failing that, she was going to fake it 'til she made it. Before she could respond, Evie's phone rang.

"I thought we were going phone free this weekend?" Viv said. "No surfing the 'net, no texting, and no phone calls."

Evie dug her phone out of her pocket. "The only person who could get through is Luc."

Viv pursed her lips. "Fine. That's a good idea."

"Hey, what's up? We've only been gone twenty-four hours. Did the kids burn the town down already?" Evie grinned at the phone as she teased Luc.

Bev watched Evie's face morph from light-hearted to concerned to afraid. Evie glanced over at Bev so quickly she would've written it off as a coincidence if she hadn't been watching for it. It was Shelby. She should never have left. Fear chased away every trace of the confidence she'd been willing back into place.

"What is it? What's happened?" Bev asked. She heard the panicked note in her own voice but didn't even think about trying to hide it.

"We'll be back as fast as we can. Elle and Bev will be home first. The rest of us will be a bit longer." Evie paused a moment, then smiled. "Love you too. See you soon." She shoved the phone back in her pocket and turned back to the group.

Evie looked perfectly calm, but Bev knew that mask. Evie was quietly freaking out and trying to keep everyone from doing the same.

Evie smiled at their host. "Charlie, I am so sorry, but we're going to have to cut the weekend super short. Well, Elle, Bev, and I are, anyway. There's no reason for Viv and Sam to go home if they'd rather stay."

"Of course. Is everything okay?" Charlie picked up the abandoned wine glasses. "And are you okay? How much wine have you had?"

Evie looked down at her glass and grimaced. "More than is a good idea if I want to drive two hours home, in the dark, on windy mountain roads. Sam, I don't suppose you'd take me home? You can drop me off and come back for the rest of the weekend with Viv."

Sam looked at Viv, who shook her head. She was also trying to keep her fear off her face. Bev knew her friends well enough to see what they were doing and appreciated it so much. She didn't think she'd be able to think if either of them broke down. The tensing of her jaw, over and over, was the only sign Viv showed of how freaked out she was.

Sam took her eyes off Viv; they were backlit with amber. Not enough to be obvious across a room, but enough to look otherworldly to anyone close. Like Charlie. "Of course I can take you home, Evie. Let's go talk while Bev and Elle get packed, then we can make a decision."

Viv let Sam pull her out of the chair she was ensconced in. "Charlie, I'll be back in ten to let you know if we're ditching your amazing hospitality. But either way, I'll be staying for dinner. If Evie doesn't think I'm needed right away, I can take that much time, anyway."

Bev was already across the room and headed towards her cabin, Viv on her heels. She didn't know how her stuff was getting home, but it didn't matter. She knew the reason Evie'd told Luc Elle and Bev would be home first was because they'd be winging it. She shivered. It was going to be cold. And terrifying. So many ways to die when you're being carried through the air.

Fortunately, she hadn't really unpacked—you never knew when you'd have to make a quick exit. She pulled out the warmest clothes she'd brought, changed, and shoved everything in the bag before anyone else made it to her cabin.

"Don't worry about your stuff," Viv said. "I'll make sure you didn't miss anything and toss it in the car."

Evie walked into the room and put an arm around Bev's shoulders, pulling her into a side hug. "It's going to be okay, Bev." She glanced back at Viv, who shrugged.

"You can do it," Sam said. "I've got you. I promised."

Viv reached out and grabbed Bev's hands, then closed her eyes. Bev watched her face as it cycled through concentration, pain, and relaxation as she tried to pull a vision of the future out of the ether rather than waiting for it to come to her as she usually did. Viv let go of Bev's hands and fell back into Sam's arms. Sam led Viv to a chair, then rubbed her temples.

"Nothing useful. Just Evie's ex-husband riding a cow and Shelby holding the cow's leash," Viv said, grimaced. "I'm still making sense of it. Evie, tell us what's going on."

Evie took a deep breath. "The pet cemetery is missing quite a few occupants, and Shelby's missing."

# CHAPTER SEVEN

Bev looked up from the hands she'd been resting her face in after she'd dropped to the bed. She slowed her breathing using an exercise her therapist had taught her to deal with her frequent anxiety attacks. Once she was sure she wasn't dipping into pure panic, she asked, "What do you mean Shelby's missing? Where is she? When did she disappear? What the hell, Evie?"

"The kids were in the woods, apparently setting up their new, very secret fort in the old, abandoned Masters house. They had flashlights, snacks, and it was afternoon. Luc thought they were in the witch's clearing—that's where Lily said they were going. But they'd gone a bit further afield. To their credit, she and Kevin fessed up immediately. Anyway, they split up in the mansion to find the best room to serve as the official headquarters. Shelby didn't come back." Evie's voice was shaking by the end of the explanation, but the arm she still had around Bev was steady.

"She's still in the house?" Bev wasn't sure if that was good or bad. So many accidents possible in a house that hadn't been occupied in at least half a century. Rotten boards, loose stairs. But if she'd left the house, left Lily and Kevin behind, that was a very different scenario and one that brought a host of other possibilities to mind.

"The kids couldn't find her. They looked before running home to tell Luc. Luc called me right away but was going to send Barachiel to the mansion as soon as we got off the phone. He'll be able to fly her back quickly if she's injured." Evie turned towards Viv. "What did you see?"

Viv hesitated long enough that Bev's panic started to return.

"I'm not sure. All my visions lately have been the undead showing up, usually superimposed over Jer's face." Viv wrinkled her nose in disgust.

"Jer? It wouldn't surprise me to find out he was a ghoul," Evie muttered.

"But Shelby?" Bev took pride in the steadiness of her voice.

"Her aura is obscured by darkness, and I can't see through it," Viv confessed. "I was so sure that what I'd seen was here, that this is where the dead would rise. I'd hoped we could do a combo girls' wine weekend and zombie apocalypse… Or at least send them back to sleep. But now, I don't know. I've never been wrong before."

"You've misinterpreted things, though," Sam reminded her. "Remember when you thought you were going to drown in the lake?"

"And it turned out to be my long-dead aunt opposite-drowning? Yeah… But this was different." Viv shook her head as if to clear it.

"Is there anything you can tell me? Anything that will help?" Bev was ready to get out of there but didn't want to go before she had everything possible to help her find her niece.

Viv looked down at the floor between her feet. "Start with Xena."

"The warrior princess?" Evie asked. "What does that mean?"

"No, not the warrior princess. Xena was Viv's cat, wasn't she?" Bev said.

"I don't remember. When did you have a cat?"

"For three months the summer after sixth grade," Viv said absently. Her brow was wrinkled in concentration.

"Viv, what happened to Xena?" Bev asked. "She was just gone one day, and you said your mother was allergic and had given away your cat."

Viv's eyes flashed open. "Mother wouldn't have taken the time to find a good home for an unwanted pet she probably wasn't allergic to in the first place."

"The pet cemetery," Evie said. "If she didn't throw her in the lake, she would've buried her in the pet cemetery. That'd be the easiest place to avoid notice. It's been overgrown for longer than we've been alive. No one goes there anymore, and even if they did, finding a fresh cat grave your mother had dug wouldn't raise any alarms."

"Okay. The pet cemetery is the starting point. Anything else?" Bev zipped up her jacket and pulled the strings of her hood tight, tying them under her chin.

Viv shook her head. "I'll call you if there's anything else."

"I'm ready to go whenever you are," Elle said. "Viv will pack my stuff."

"Let's go. The sooner I get home, the sooner I can find Shelby."

They walked out into the grassy area separating the cabins from the main building. "How do you want to carry me? I've only traveled by angel once before."

Elle regarded her. "I will scoop you up like a child, but you must put your arms around my neck and do your best to stay still."

"I will not move." She let Elle pick her up, wound her arms around the angel's neck, and braced herself for launch. Takeoff was anticlimactic. Instead of a crouching leap into the sky, Elle's wings appeared, and they rose lightly like a helium balloon. They were mere inches off the ground when the pull Bev associated with the dead grabbed her attention. She looked over Elle's shoulders into the shadows between the cabins. A figure stood there. He was solid, unlike the few ghostly forms she'd seen out of the corners of her eyes. His gaze caught hers, and he raised one impossibly pale arm and saluted her before melting back into the darkness.

THE FLIGHT HAD BEEN UNPLEASANT. There were other, harsher words Bev could've used to describe it, but she tried to save up her profanities for when she really needed them. Her face was frozen five minutes in, and Elle wouldn't talk to her. It felt like hours, but when they'd touched down and Bev had checked her phone, fewer than twenty minutes had passed.

"Thank you." Bev stomped her feet, trying to warm them up enough to walk.

"You are welcome. I will talk to Kevin, then return to see if Evie wants to come home, leaving Viv and Sam to have a romantic interlude without us." Elle spared Bev a look of compassion and a brief, beatific smile that burned away a little of the hopefulness and despair, then walked up the path from the wide clearing between Evie's house and the lake and disappeared into the house while Bev stumbled behind, yelping as feeling returned.

The kitchen was bright and warm. Luc was bouncing Alex on his hip. She was crying hysterically, and from the exhausted look on Luc's face, this had been going on for quite a while. The demands she'd been prepared to make about why he hadn't left Alex with the other kids and gone to look at Shelby himself died on her lips.

"She started screaming about fifteen minutes before the first animal crawled across our lawn and hasn't stopped since." Luc switched positions and cradled her against his shoulder rubbing his hand over her back, a motion that seemed, if anything, to make everything worse. "She's not hungry, doesn't need a change, won't sleep, and refused to be quieted by any of the usual tricks."

"Can I?" Bev held out her arms, and Luc deposited the screaming child in her arms.

"Thank you. She gets heavier by the minute and I've barely been able to set her down tonight. I'm going to check in with Elle, Lily, and Kevin to make sure they're all still there and okay. Do you need anything? Wine? Water? Elle to turn one into the other?"

Bev shook her head and gazed down at the baby in her arms. Her mouth was open wide and her tiny face was red as she screamed her displeasure into the night.

Luc disappeared from the room. Bev expected Alex to redouble her protests when her father left, but instead, the wails quieted as she focused her big, honey-colored eyes on Bev's face and reached a hand up to touch Bev's cheek.

Alex stopped crying and just stared. Bev was used to small children and the way they could fixate on a ball or a light or a face, but Alex's regard ran a shiver down her spine.

Luc reappeared in the kitchen and looked back and forth between Bev and Alex. "Damn. I might have to hand in my dad card if all it takes to soothe her is a woman's touch."

"I don't think it's the fact that I'm a woman. There's something else." Bev shook her head. Alex might be a half-demon, but she was still a baby. "Tell me what happened."

The story he recounted was almost word for word what Evie'd reported. "I tried to call Barachiel, but he didn't answer his phone. That wasn't surprising; he's still not great at using technology and almost never remembers to charge it. So I left Alex with Lily and Kevin—who felt so guilty they didn't even complain about being saddled with a screaming baby—and headed to his place. Your place. You know what I mean."

Bev nodded. "And?"

"He wasn't there. I did the quickest circuit of town I could do without looking inhuman, but he was nowhere to be found. I flew over to the mansion, but other than the signs Lily and Kevin had left behind on their rush to get out and get back here, I didn't see anything else. Shelby isn't in the house, Bev."

Bev took a deep breath. Shelby was missing. Inhale. Exhale. Pause. "Did you call the cops?" Bev wasn't sure that she would've, but it's what you were supposed to do when kids went missing.

"I tried to file a missing person report, but they said she hadn't been gone long enough and that Shelby was a stereotypical runaway." Luc closed his mouth and took a deep breath through his nose. His eyes reflected a ruby sheen, and Bev knew he was angry. "I know that's not true, but what I don't understand is why it's trotted out so often. However, I didn't want to take the time to argue and damn their souls to hell—paperwork can be a real time waster. But they will be hearing from me once we find Shelby, and they will not like what they hear."

It was nothing different than Bev had expected. She refocused her attention. "You told Evie the pet cemetery was missing some occupants. What did you mean?" Bev asked. That, along with what Viv had seen, was what Miss Marple would call a clue. "The old one in the woods? I'd forgotten it was there until Viv's vision earlier."

"I didn't know about it, but when the animals—and I'm using that word loosely—started appearing, I had questions. Lily and Kevin had run through the cemetery instead of going around like they usually did to get home faster and told me it looked like freshly dug dirt and there were a few bones on the surface or in the dirt that looked like they'd been left behind." Luc grimaced. "I know I'm a demon and spent the entirely of my formative years helping my father receive souls in hell, but when I flew over the pet cemetery, it creeped me out."

"Are the kids okay?" The tightness in Bev's chest that had taken hold when Evie got the phone call from Luc clenched harder and spread, pressing on her lungs and making it difficult to take a full breath. She knew the dead rising had something to do with Shelby; a herd of zombie pets and a missing baby necromancer weren't coincidence. Now she just had to figure out how to use the clues to find her kid.

"Lily said it was much less creepy than what happened on the island when Kevin and the lake monster separated. The only thing they were worried about was Shelby." Luc ran his hand through his short hair and, for a moment, his grimace created lines on his smooth, ageless face. "I don't know why I thought a group of tweens could be trusted."

"I think the collective noun is 'an irresponsibility of tweens,'" Bev said, trying to breathe through the anxiety that was teetering on the brink of a full-blown panic attack.

Sprinkle's deep, boom, three-part harmony barks echoed down

the stairs, followed closely by the heavy footfalls of the hellhound. She burst into the kitchen, then through the back door.

Luc sighed, lines of exhaustion once more marring his smooth skin. "She's been doing that all night. Zombie cats are her drug of choice."

Lily clattered in the dog's wake. "Sorry! I thought she was sleeping, and she made a break for it," Lily called as she ran through the door and called for Sprinkles.

Kevin and Elle descended the stairs more sedately.

"He doesn't know anything more than he's already said. The children are completely honest. I will go get Evie now and be back within the hour. Please let her know to be ready." Elle stopped in front of Bev and put both hands on her shoulders. "It will be okay."

"Promise?" Bev asked, trying to smile.

"No. I can't make a promise like that, but I can push hope into you." Elle dropped her hands and walked through the back door. Her wings arched out and up, and she shot up into the air.

"I'm going to the pet cemetery. Whatever happened, that's the key." Bev handed Alex back to Luc, then opened the hall closet and snagged a hat and pair of gloves from the basket of cold-weather gear.

"There's a flashlight on the table. Take Sprinkles. She might be obsessed with finding a kitty snack, but she'll be able to protect you against anything you come up against." Luc grimaced as he bounced Alex gently in his arms. "I should come with you..."

Bev bundled up again, grabbed the flashlight, and flicked it on and off. "You should stay with your baby. I have my cell. Call if she turns up."

"Bev, I am so sorry. I should've..." Luc caught Bev's eyes, infusing his gaze with guilt and remorse.

"How many times have we let those kids run wild in the woods until dark? How many times did Evie, Viv, and I do the same thing? This isn't on you. I just hope I get a chance to ground Shelby until she turns thirty-seven." Bev aimed a watery smile at Luc, then went outside to send the kids back in and borrow the hellhound for her search.

Lily immediately agreed that Sprinkles was the perfect companion for Bev's search but tried to invite herself along as well. "You know she'll listen to me and Kevin better than you!" She bent over and slapped her hands on her knees, then reached out a hand and scratched Sprinkle behind her center head right ear. "Ready girl? We're gonna go find all the dead cats! Won't that be fun!"

Sprinkles barked excitedly and tried to chase her tail, something infinitely more difficult when one has three heads. She straightened out and trotted forward towards the trail that wound around the lake.

"You are eleven and definitely not walking through the dark woods full of dead animals to find Shelby. And if I find out that either of you ignored me and snuck along behind trying to avoid notice, Shelby won't be the only one under house arrest." Bev infused every bit of Commanding Mom Voice into her words, and when Lily's defiant look faded, she knew it had been effective.

Lily's lower lip started to push out in a pout, but she must've thought better of it. "Fine. But if you won't take us, you need Dad. Wait here." She and Kevin ran back to the house, and moments later Luc strode out of the house.

"Alex is asleep and Lily and Kevin are staying with her. You will not do this alone. Sprinkles, go home and guard the kids."

Sprinkles woofed, and for all the world, it sounded like she was arguing.

"Sprinkles, home. Go to Lily." Luc's eyes glowed red, and his black wings unfolded from his body.

The hellhound whined but turned and trotted away.

Bev wanted to argue, but she was grateful for the company. Not to mention, having a demon along to walk through the forces of the undead—even if it was cats and dogs—was comforting.

"It'll be faster if we fly," Luc said.

Bev grimaced. She knew he was right, but flying wasn't her favorite. At least she was more prepared this time. She tucked the flashlight into her coat pocket and held out her arms so Luc could scoop her up.

Bev looked around the pet cemetery, sweeping the beam of her flashlight out, looking for any clue that she might be overlooking. "Every grave is empty," she told Luc. "Whatever happened was thorough."

"What do you think it was?" Bev heard the care he took with his words and knew he was trying to avoid assign blame.

"I'm not sure. Shelby is a lot more comfortable with the dead than I am. She doesn't talk about it much. Looking back, I think it was an effort to not make me uncomfortable rather than hide her own discomfort." She shook her head. "I wouldn't be surprised if she was doing illicit web searches for necromancy training or something like that. Those weren't the words I selected to trigger a notification from her devices."

"Does she have the power to pull all these animals from their graves?" Luc crouched down, then made a noise of visceral disgust, stood, and stumbled back several steps.

"What is it? Did you find something?" Bev jogged over to Luc.

"Stop!" He held his hand up and shone his flashlight back at the ground.

Bev peered where he was spotlighting. "I don't see—" The ground moved and she bit back a shriek.

"What kind of horrible person keeps pet spiders? And then buries them here?" Luc shuddered.

"At least we're not finding fish. I don't know what a zombie fish would look like out here, and I don't want to find out." She strode forward and squatted next to the undead tarantula.

"What are you doing? Get away from it." Revulsion laced through his voice.

"Luc, are you afraid of spiders?" She reached out and touched it, trying to find the spark that was animating it so she could turn it off. She could sense it, almost see it, but couldn't grab onto it. It was like trying to grab a toy from a claw machine.

"No. Of course not." His voice was no longer near her.

Bev opened her eyes and looked up. He was on the other side of the cemetery hovering about five feet above the ground. "No shame in a phobia." She closed her eyes, and the spark flared. There it was… Fear and horror welled up at what she was about to do. Dead or not, this animal was alive, and ending life, no matter how much it was necessary, felt wrong somehow. Dark side stuff. "Ahhh… Found it." She pinched her fingers together just above the spider and it collapsed to the ground. "You can come down now. It's dead. Dead-dead," she amended.

Luc glided over the cemetery and dipped down so his feet were almost on the ground. "Are you sure?"

"Positive. And I can do it again, as long as I'm close. Do you see anything else I can lay to rest?"

Luc flew up a few more feet into the air. "I think a hamster or gerbil a few feet to your right."

Bev threaded her way through the makeshift grave markers. She was sweeping the beam of the flashlight from side to side, trying to catch the movements of the undead rodent, when a flash caught her eye. She swung the light back and forth until she saw it again. Hamster forgotten, she walked to whatever shiny was on the surface of a now-empty pet grave. It was probably a collar that had rotted and fallen off when its wearer went for an unauthorized walk, but she had to be sure.

When she found what she was looking for, a pang of disappointment hit her. It was nothing more than a feather, probably from someone's pet parakeet. She picked it up. It was in remarkably good shape for something that had been buried for who knows how long.

"This is too big, and it's not the right shape." She held it up. The feather was almost two feet long and was so white it glowed even without the light focused on it. "This isn't a bird feather. This belongs to an angel, doesn't it?"

Luc landed next to her and took the feather. "Yes. This is an angel feather. And unless Elle came this way on her way back to get Evie or we have unannounced company, we can assume it belonged to Barachiel."

"Why would he be here? Do you think he knows something about —" Bev gestured wildly around her "—this?"

"I have no idea, but I know how to find out." Luc strode to the middle of the cemetery—the only place that wasn't overhung with branches—and shot straight up into the air. A burst of sparks erupted into the air. The sparks solidified into five streams of light, each streaking in a different direction. One returned to Luc, two disappeared into the eastern sky, one dropped towards where Bev thought Evie's house was, and the fifth sped off to the north so fast Bev couldn't track it before the surrounding branches obscured it from view.

Luc landed next to her and stumbled. His wings drooped, the tips dragging in the grave dirt. His human visage was gone, and in its place was a horror worthy of the engravings that decorated the Malleus Maleficarum. The horns that usually curled gracefully out of his head when he let them, looked like ancient, twisted bone, and his shoes had been replaced by cloven hooves. His skin had shrunk over his skeleton, leaving him gaunt, and the wings were more bat and less sexy dark angel from a television show.

He held out his arms, and she only hesitated for a second before hopping into them. Bev tried not to look at his face. She knew it was Luc—and his eyes were the same—but he was more than a little horrifying.

"Thanks for being quick. The lights won't last long, and it'll wipe me out for at least twenty-four hours once they fade."

The breeze rushed by her face, and she tried not to contemplate what would happen if the lights faded before they landed. She closed her eyes against the biting wind and kept them closed until they slowed. Luc set her down and wiped a hand across his face. "We don't have much time." He staggered to the side and nearly collapsed. Bev got a shoulder under him and held him up. In his human guise, he was slightly above average height for a man, but with the lean physique of a long-distance runner rather than a body builder. As a demon, he was at least a foot taller and much, much bulkier.

"Where are we?" Bev grunted under the weight of the demon.

Luc looked around. "Don't you recognize it? We're still within the bounds of Eden."

Bev shone her flashlight around her, trying to pick landmarks out of the open field they were in. Something looked familiar, but she couldn't quite put her finger on it. "I don't know. Do you see the light? What is it, anyway? How will it help us find Barachiel?"

"Too many questions. The light touched down over there." He waved off to their left.

Beverly held him up as they trudged through the thick clumps of grass that'd mostly died back. Lights appeared in front of them.

"I see it now!" Bev said.

"That's a regular light. Are we back in town? I'm too tired to have a sense of direction."

"No, this isn't town…" They rounded a stand of trees. On the other side, a floodlight illuminated a huge yard anchored on one end by a huge, red barn and on the other by a sprawling farmhouse that aspired to rival Evie's but without the upkeep or style. "It's Jer's house. Dammit. Viv said something about Jer but didn't elaborate."

"Unless Evie's ex-husband is a secret angel, he's not what we're looking for. It's in the barn." Luc tripped and nearly went down. "Jusssss a little further," he slurred.

Bev ducked under his arm and got a better grip around his waist. "It'd be a real weird day if we found out Jeremy Kantek was an angel this whole time. Although maybe that'd be the most normal thing about today."

Luc laughed, but it quickly turned into a gasping cough.

"We're almost there." She tried to hurry him along; the slow pace felt excruciating.

Finally, she pushed open the small door and dragged Luc into Jer's barn. It was filled with shiny farm equipment and shinier four-wheel-drive pickups. In the middle of the space, surrounded by a bubble of light, was Barachiel, wings wide and curved around like a mother hen. Bev ducked out from under Luc's arm, helped him to the ground in a controlled tumble, and ran towards the light.

She skidded to a stop before she got to the angel. The figure he was shielding wasn't Shelby.

"Jer?"

Evie's ex-husband looked up with unfocused eyes and a rictus grin. "Thank god you're finally here. Did Evie send you?"

# CHAPTER EIGHT

"Beer?" Jer asked.

Bev shook her head. She was practically vibrating with impatience, but every time she'd tried to talk, Barachiel had interrupted, making sure Jer was comfortable, that he had a beer, and a soft blanket, and the space heater was on. He was going overboard with the mother hen impression at this point.

Jeremy, still under the literal wing of Barachiel, had led them to his office, leaving Bev to haul Luc to his feet and get him to the leather couch across from Jer's desk. Once she'd covered Luc with a blanket, she sat on the edge of the matching leather recliner.

When it looked like Barachiel had gotten Jeremy as comfortable as he could and wasn't going to fuss too much more, she broke her silence. "Where's Shelby?"

Barachiel's wings drooped. "I was hoping you'd know. She's disappeared."

"I know she disappeared. That's why I'm here and not drinking wine with my friends on my much-anticipated and long-overdue vacation. What I'm interested in is how you know, why you didn't call me or answer Luc's phone calls, and why you're here with your wings around Evie's ex-husband." Bev's voice rose steadily until she was almost shouting.

Barachiel shrunk back. "Don't yell at me. I knew you were gone, so I didn't call you. When I felt the magic surge, I had to find it before something terrible happened. Unfortunately, I was too late." He waved a wing at Jer, who hadn't said anything other than offering cheap beer to everyone.

"What's wrong with him?" Bev asked. "Normally, I wouldn't care, but he's obviously off. He hasn't insulted me yet, and he's didn't even comment on Luc's current appearance."

"That's why I hoped you would've found Shelby. She was here and can tell us what she did and if we can reverse it. I can't fix his mind without knowing what she did to him." Barachiel tucked his wings back. "How did you know to look for me?"

Bev pulled the feather out of her jacket where she'd been holding onto it since she'd picked it up.

"My feather!" He reached out for it, but Bev pulled it out of his reach.

"You can have it back if you start at the beginning and tell me why you think Shelby did this." Bev hid the feather behind her back.

Barachiel pouted for a moment, then sat down in the only open chair—a rickety rolling chair behind an ornate antique roll-top desk. "I was watching the children. They are precious to you and were acting oddly—like a game of spies. I followed them to an old house with peeling paint and many rooms. I was about to leave them to their games when I saw a shadow. It wasn't Luc or any of his family, and none of my family absorb darkness the way this figure did."

"Did you feel it?" Bev asked, handing his feather to him. "Was it oily?"

Barachiel tilted his head to one side. "Yes. Oily is a good word. Not a nice oily, though, like when you're eating bread with dipping sauce. It was the oil that leaks from your vehicles and stains the roads and makes the earth weep."

Bev nodded and got in her next question before Barachiel could go on a tangent about the environment. She didn't disagree with anything she'd heard about it so far, but now wasn't the time. "Did the oily feeling make you want to flee or vomit or curl up in a ball until it went away?"

"No, of course not, but I am not a human subject to such emotions or physiological reactions. I had a mild aversion, but my curiosity and concern were greater. You speak of this shadow as if you've met before?"

Bev shook her head. "Not met, not really. But Gwen—Viv's mother —had a dark shadow with her before Sam destroyed her mirror and focus stone. It was oily and when Gwen was channeling it to try to banish Quinn, I was afraid and unable to move."

"Did you find the source of the dark magic?" Barachiel asked. He spun around in the chair. Bev watched a delighted grin grow on his face, and he pushed off to spin around again.

"We didn't. It'd fled by the time we could look. But what does this have to do with Shelby? Did it take her? Is she in the lake?" Bev stood, ready to steal one of Jer's trucks—a row of hooks with a dozen sets of keys hung next to the door. And maybe a boat. He had to have at least one in his huge garage. The panic that wouldn't dissipate climbed another notch.

"It didn't take her. She ran out of the house to meet it, and they walked away together. I followed as they walked into the place where human dispose of their non-human companions. She stood in the center and called them up. When they broke free from the dirt, she took one of the creatures, tucked it into a pouch on her shirt, and reached out towards the shadow. They disappeared from view, and a stream of dead headed towards the lake." Barachiel spun around a couple more times before continuing. "I tried to follow, but this is as far as I got. This man was laying in the middle of the dirt crying and saying Evie's name over and over. He was surrounded by poorly resurrected and very large creatures making a noise that sounded like this." Barachiel stopped spinning, looked at Bev, and mooed. Then he stood, tripped over his feet, swayed, and hit the ground. "My head feels weird."

"You're dizzy from spinning around too much. And are you saying

Jer was being menaced by a herd of zombie cows?" If the situation wasn't so serious, Bev would be laughing hysterically picturing Jer shaking in the face of undead cows.

"Cows, yes. That is the correct word. I believe your friend has had a great shock to his system, and the cows have been very persistent. I cannot tell if they have affection for him or not, but he was not excited to see them."

"So instead of continuing the search for my daughter, you stayed her to protect a grown man from a herd of cows?"

"They may have meant him harm. Your child appeared to be in no danger and was going willingly with a person who was teaching her how to use her powers over death." Barachiel climbed to his feet and settled back into the chair.

"We have to find her. I don't care if she went willingly. She is a child, and she doesn't get to decide who will teach her how to raise the dead. Will you help me look?" Bev stood and looked at Luc. She pulled her phone out and opened the group text. *Luc is at Jer's in the barn. He's sleeping and said he'd be out for at least a day. He's also in his birthday suit. I'm going to keep looking for Shelby.*

A second later, Evie replied. *I need more explanations. Why is Luc naked in Jer's barn?*

*Zombie cows threatened Jer. Luc and I flew here following Barachiel's light. Shelby ran off with a shadow. More later. But come get Luc before Jer snaps out of his cow fear and sees the demon in all his glory snoozing on the couch.*

*We'll be there in fifteen minutes. Check in soon,* Evie replied.

Bev shoved her phone back in her pocket. "Come on, angel. Help me find my daughter."

Barachiel stood, swayed slightly, and bowed his head. "I am sorry. I thought I was doing the right thing, helping the person who looked like they needed help. I should've prioritized your child over this adult man who has drawn the attention of so many bovines."

"It's okay. Well, it's not okay, but if you help me find her, I'll let it go eventually. At least now, I will always have the mental picture of Jer surrounded by zombie cows." Bev felt the anger welling again, and along with it, whispers of the dead. Her fist twitched, and for a moment she let her mind fill with an image of punching the stupid angel in his stupid face for choosing Jeremy Kantek over Shelby. As soon as she allowed herself to take him out mentally, the fog cleared and the voices receded again. It still wasn't okay, but at least her words no longer felt like a lie.

"It's not just a mental picture. I used the camera on my phone to take some pictures before I saved him, in case he wanted to know what had happened." Barachiel held out his phone.

"I'll look later. This is the kind of anticipation I want to savor." Bev walked out of the barn and into the yard. A small herd of cattle had gathered around the corner of the barn and were lowing quietly. Bev didn't know the rules of zombie creation or large animal disposal, but it didn't feel right that there had been a bunch of dead cows close enough to raise from the dead. Weren't there rules about stuff like that? Bev walked up to them, found their sparks, and pinched the light—when she'd been in the pet cemetery, it'd felt like putting out a candle. This time, though, nothing happened except a wave of dizziness that threatened to knock her off her feet.

"What are you doing? Why are you pretending to pinch the cows?" Barachiel asked from somewhere above her head.

Bev looked up. He was floating and slowly rotating, his hand shielding his eyes from the weak light of a crescent moon obscured by hazy wisps of clouds. "I was trying to put them back in the ground, but apparently necromancy comes with a fuel tank, and mine's on empty. What are you doing?"

"Looking for the darkness."

Bev bit back the comment she really wanted to make about needles and haystacks and darkness at night. "Do you sense anything?"

Barachiel landed beside her. "Yes. It's growing. Soon, everyone with a glimmer of magic in their souls will be able to feel it, whether or not they have the spark of the divine inside. I have made a mistake. This is evil. I thought I knew what evil was before, and this feels akin to what I knew, or who I knew, but this is more than I ever believed possible."

"Where?" Before Barachiel could answer, she felt it. "The lake? I thought the lake was fine now that we broke the tie between Kevin and what he used to be."

Barachiel didn't answer her concerns, just looked at her and shook his head. "I will go find her and bring her back here." He floated up into the air.

"You will not leave me here." Bev grabbed an ankle with both hands and held on.

"Let go of me. This is unseemly, and these are very expensive jeans. Mr. Beyoncé wears this kind." He kicked ineffectively at her.

"I'm not letting go until you give me your word as an angel of your lord that you will pick me up and take me with you as you go investigate the source of the dark magic and find Shelby." Bev ran the words over again in her mind making sure there weren't any loopholes.

"I am not a demon," he replied stiffly. "You don't need to put so many restrictions on my promises."

Bev shrugged. "It's my kid. I'm not leaving anything up to chance. The only reason you're not laid flat on the ground is because I need you to get to her as quickly as possible."

"Fine. But I don't like carrying humans." He stopped trying to get away and landed next to her. "How do I carry you?"

"Elle and Luc put one arm under my upper back and one under my knees." Bev mimed the hold.

"This will be easier." He picked her up and slung her across his shoulder in a firefighter's carry. "Plus, I believe this is undignified, correct?"

Bev didn't answer. She didn't want to antagonize her ride any more than she already had in case he'd decided to set her down in the lake from a great height.

Barachiel shot up into the air and flew rapidly with none of Elle's smoothness or courtesy.

"We're here," the angel said just before leaning forward and dropping her unceremoniously on the ground.

Bev looked around. They were in a nondescript clearing wreathed in fog that glowed faintly in the weak moonlight. She glared at Barachiel. "Where exactly is here?"

"The lake. I fulfilled my promise." Barachiel shook his wings, then folded them against his back. "You were less awful to carry than I anticipated."

"Thank you?" Bev did a slow circle. "What do you mean, the lake? I don't recognize this piece of the shoreline... Oh crap. This is the island. I thought it was gone."

"It is. It sunk back under the surface last summer. This is the island that doesn't exist in your version of Eden anymore. At least not visibly." He flicked his fingers over his jeans and leather jacket, removing whatever traces of dirt he saw marring his look.

Bev took a deep breath, and the air tasted thick. She gagged on the feel of oil coating the fog she'd inhaled. "It's here. But if the island doesn't exist, and we're on the island, how...?"

"I don't have time to explain it, nor would you likely understand if I did, but it would save us both a lot of time and aggravation if you tried to believe me until we find Shelby and retrieve her from this place. This is the island, but it exists outside of your time and space right now. Once we are safe, I will see if I can find the words that will make sense to your human brain." He strode to the edge of the clearing and walked the perimeter.

Bev watched him pace the circumference and opened her senses. She'd felt the dark magic before, and she was sure if she concentrated, she'd be able to find it again. Instead of a generalized darkness, she found a tar pit. It stuck to her, and the more she tried to disengage her mind, the further in she was drawn.

Light blazed, and she stumbled back and into Barachiel's arms.

"Don't do that. We're too close, and your mind is untrained." He resumed his pacing and came to a stop in front of an exceptionally wide shrub. "Here."

"Is that how Shelby got stuck?" Bev asked. The thick vapor was weighing down on her, feeling more oppressive than fog had any right to feel.

"I don't know, but probably not. She went willingly, which might mean she was lured instead of captured like a fly in a web. If she wanted power and knowledge, she would be open to darkness the way you are not." Barachiel reached forward into the shrub. His right hand disappeared until it looked like there was a clean cut halfway up his forearm. "This is it."

"This is what?" Bev eyed the shrub that seemed to be made of void.

"Where Shelby is being held. It is the entrance to the dark sorcerer's lair." Barachiel strode forward and disappeared into the bush. One moment he was there, the next he was gone with no trace.

Bev's heart hammered in her chest as she willed her feet to move forward and follow the angel into the dark.

Barachiel's head reappeared, and Bev shrieked and jumped back.

"Are you coming or not?"

She took a deep breath and walked forward. The darkness sucked at her, making her feel like she was walking through a giant leech. It released her with an audible pop, and she took several steps into a room that was lit with darkness.

"How?" The walls were obsidian and glowed with a purplish light. It was like walking into a black light.

"Sh." Barachiel put his hand on her lips to quiet her, and the lack of repulsion she felt at his skin on hers surprised her almost as much as anything else that had happened tonight.

"Where are we? Is Shelby close?" Bev whispered against his finger. He snatched it away and glared at his finger.

"She's here, but so is the sorcerer. With any luck, we will not only find her before the sorcerer finds us, but she will be willing to come with us quietly." He shook his wings slightly, and a circle of dim light surrounded them and extended about six inches out from Barachiel. "Stay close."

Bev moved as close to him as she could without touching him, and they inched forward.

"Why aren't we hitting the wall? It wasn't this far away." Bev reached out her hand, expecting to hit cold stone, but there was nothing there.

"This place isn't real. It exists in the mind of the sorcerer and now in our minds. It finds what you expect to see and creates it, trying to match it with the non-reality space we're in to give shape and context. It exists only as we perceive it, and only a little. Keep believing that we are in a finite room, though, please. I cannot because I know how reality bends in here and can't make myself believe anything else. Your inability to grasp the complexities of thought required to create a space like this are all that's saving us right now." He increased his glow a bit more.

Bev looked around at what she could see and held on desperately to its existence. She wasn't sure what kind of dire consequences there were if she stopped believing in floors, but she didn't want to find out.

"Good job," Barachiel said. Bev felt like she was being praised by a college professor for spelling her name correctly. Or by Jackson when she turned in her monthly reports on time. Like she had done every month for twenty years.

She pushed back her feelings about Jackson... He was almost out of her life forever. Now she needed to concentrate on Shelby. She pushed her mind out, more cautiously this time to avoid getting stuck in the tar pit of black magic that permeated this not-island.

"I don't know what you're doing, but things are moving. If you are thinking about scissor monsters or men in hard plastic masks, I would invite you to move your thoughts to something more innocuous."

"I wasn't, but I am now," Bev snarked. "Please don't give me any more advice on what not to think about. I'm trying to find my niece, and you suggesting I avoid remembering my food-related nightmares in vivid detail will be for the best."

"I will not ask about your nightmares now, but I am interested in how food can be threatening." Barachiel paused and Bev brushed against him. He glanced down at her but didn't move away.

Bev concentrated again, pushed away all thoughts about being chased by French carrots on bicycles until she got to her wedding with a six-foot-tall lobster who had charmed her parents but left her sister skeptical. Instead, she closed her eyes and recalled the essence of Shelby. It didn't take long. They'd spent almost every day together for the last twelve years. She'd held her when she had nightmares as a child and when she'd tried to walk away from them when she was eleven. She'd grounded her for destroying her garden and given her the tools she needed to expand her creativity and come into herself. They'd listened to the voices of the dead together and gone for milkshakes after. Shelby might not be her daughter, but she was her heart.

"Good," Barachiel whispered, and this time it didn't sound condescending. "Close your eyes and follow the path opening in front of you. I won't let you fall. I promise."

"I trust you," Bev said. She froze for a second, then realized it was true. He might be a clueless jerk who was more invested in being quirky than learning to live in the world, but he was genuinely trying to do his best.

"Thank you. I am going to touch you now. Just your elbow so we don't get separated. Is that okay?"

Bev nodded, then realized he might not be able to see her. "Yes. Thank you for asking."

His hand clasped her elbow and held on tight. "Now pull yourself to the picture you've painted in your mind, and no matter what you hear, don't open your eyes."

Bev called up the essence of Shelby she'd created. She felt herself moving, too quickly, it seemed. She opened her mouth to ask Barachiel about it, but was interrupted by the sound of claws on a chalkboard. Shivers went up her spine and stayed there, splaying out goosebumps over her body. Nausea followed, and she started to let go of the spark that was Shelby.

"Concentrate," Barachiel hissed. "I will take care of everything else, but you're the only one who can find her." His voice changed, and he spoke, although the language wasn't anything she'd ever heard or even imagined could exist. It was almost more horrible than the claws scraping against the cave walls around them.

"Shelby, Shelby, Shelby." The mantra shut out the sounds of Barachiel chanting and the monster chasing them. She didn't stop, couldn't stop, because if she did, the horrors in the dark would over-whelm her. It wasn't the dead—they were terrifying but passing famil-iar. This was something so much worse.

Arms wrapped around her waist. She started to pull back from whatever monster had grabbed her, but then the smell that was so uniquely Shelby reached her. Summer sunlight, autumn leaves tinged with campfire, and the strawberry shampoo she insisted on using no matter how many times Bev tried to get her to switch to something a little better.

Tears fell from her eyes and splashed off Shelby's head.

"Now, think of somewhere safe, both of you. I will shield you from anything that comes at us." Light flared behind Bev's closed eyes and warmth surrounded her. She wrapped her arms around Shelby and filtered through all their happiest memories. Every time, she came back to the same thing.

"You can open your eyes now," Barachiel said.

She looked around. She was on the large swing on Evie's porch, Shelby curled up next to her. The girl's face was filthy; the only places her pale skin shone through were where tears had traced canyons down her cheeks.

Barachiel stood in front of them, still glowing—wings out and ethereally beautiful.

"Thank you. I couldn't have found her without you. Thank you." Bev's voice shook. Now that they were back and Shelby was in her arms, she could feel herself starting to fall apart.

"It was my fault she got so far away. My priorities were incorrect. It was the least I could do. I will notify those inside that you have returned and suggest they find you each new clothes. Will you stay here tonight?" Barachiel's glow faded, and he tucked his wings back. His beauty diminished until he was merely gorgeous and not other-worldly.

"Shel? Do you want to stay here or go home?" Bev asked.

Shelby cried harder, great gulping sobs. "Ho-ho-home," she choked out.

"There's your answer. After I check in with the others and let Lily and Kevin know Shel's back, we'll head home."

"As you wish." He inclined his head to her. "I will collect your friends and wait to escort you home."

"I'm sorry," Shelby said through her tears. "I screwed up."

"You did, and we will definitely be talking about how and why and what we're going to do about it, but for now, you're home, you're safe, and I'm too relieved to be angry." She pulled Shelby even closer. "But don't you ever dare do this to me again, or I swear to all I hold sacred I will lock us in your room and only converse with you in puns."

Shelby giggled. "Anything but that. I'll be good." She drew her legs up and scooched onto Bev's lap, somewhere she hadn't fit for at least three years.

Her maneuverings were interrupted by a very loud *maiow.*

"Xena! I almost forgot!" Shelby reached into the pouch on her hoodie and drew out a tiny black kitten. "Isn't she so cute! Can we keep her?"

# CHAPTER NINE

Bev stared down at Shelby, who'd barely stayed awake long enough to shower and put pajamas on. She was splayed out on her bed, managing to take up more of a queen-sized bed than any five-foot-tall middle schooler had a right to.

Next to Shelby's head, curled up on her pillow and purring like mad, was Xena. Bev hadn't fought it too hard. At least not tonight. Tomorrow was soon enough to have a conversation about adopting zombie cats that'd been buried thirty years ago, regardless of how cute it now appeared.

When she'd satisfied herself that Shelby was safe, Bev took a shower, put on her softest, coziest pajamas, and went downstairs to turn on the fireplace and pour herself the largest glass of wine. It was only midnight, but it felt impossible that six hours ago she'd been drinking wine with her friends and thinking about how to open a B and B in Eden Valley.

Her phone beeped as she was rummaging around in a drawer for her corkscrew. She grabbed it and swiped it on.

*Hey. I'm outside your door. I was going to knock but didn't want to freak you out. Let me in, please. I brought your stuff and a special gift from Charlie.*

*PS - Your angel is out here lurking. He says he's standing guard. Want me to send him away?*

Bev opened the door. Viv walked in, dropped Bev's suitcase, and pulled her in for a hug.

"Are you okay? No, of course you're not okay. Sit. Put your feet up. I am here to take care of you and make sure you get some sleep."

"Hi!" Barachiel followed Viv inside. "She said I should come in or go away. I will stand watch tonight to make sure Shelby is safe."

Bev allowed herself to be guided to the couch where Viv fussed over her, tucking the blanket around her and handing her a glass of cabernet sauvignon.

"It's kind of a big wine for midnight, isn't it?" Bev asked, taking a deep drink of the earthy, tannic wine that reminded her of the forest in autumn with notes of tobacco and blackberries.

"You deserve a big wine," Viv said. She grabbed a bottle of sparkling water from the fridge and curled up in the chair across from Bev.

"Should I sit down or stand vigil in front of Shelby's bedroom?" Barachiel asked. He was shifting from foot to foot and biting his lip. He looked almost...nervous.

"Why don't you sit down and have a glass of wine with me," Bev said. "This is really good."

"I don't drink. Or eat. I've told you that. Human foods do weird things to angels." Barachiel sat on the edge of the loveseat next to the chair Viv was occupying.

"Suit yourself. You're missing out, though. This wine is perfection." Bev took another long drink and winced as her stomach growled. "Oops. I don't think I've eaten...anything."

Viv hopped up. "Don't move. I've been to your kitchen before. I'll be back in a couple minutes with snacks, artfully arranged on a plate so you can feel fancy while you eat."

Barachiel stared at Bev long enough that she started squirming under her nest of blankets, and she took a gulp of her wine to hide her discomfort.

"Did you talk to your child about staying away from black magic?" the angel asked.

"No. We will have that conversation tomorrow, but tonight she was too scared and too tired. I got her cleaned up and tucked into bed. There will be time enough for everything else later."

"Will there? The sorcerer won't let go of her that easily. Your child was in the non-space created by darkness and magic. That means she is tied to the pocket in reality and to the one who created it." Barachiel leaned forward, shifting his weight on the loveseat and fixing her with a stare she couldn't look away from.

"I appreciate the warning, and I will talk to her tomorrow. But unless you can tell me how to break that tie and that it's something that must be done tonight, I'm going to let her sleep as long as I can." Bev took another sip of wine, then set it on the end table to grab the plate covered in bite-sized pieces of cheese and prosciutto, crackers, and olives.

Viv curled up in her chair and pulled a deep burgundy blanket over herself. "There are too many children tied to too many things that go bump in the night. Just once, I'd like to see a nice, normal child who doesn't dabble in monsters and demons and black magic."

"This place attracts those things. Eden is a type of nexus for powers that you would call supernatural."

"Great. Our own personal hell mouth," Bev said, wrinkling her nose.

"Hey, at least it's not the one in Cleveland. If I'm going to have a hell mouth, I'm glad it's in one of the most gorgeous places on earth." Viv held up her sparkling water in a mock toast.

"Small mercies, but cheers to not being in Cleveland."

Barachiel looked back and forth between the women. "It's not just a portal to hell."

"It's a tv show about a vampire slayer," Viv explained.

"Yeah, I'm sure you haven't seen it since the only media you seem intent on participating in is twitter."

"Twitter is a good way to learn about current events and modes of speech without immersing myself too much into humanity and finding myself changed the way Elle and Andras have been changed." Barachiel's voice was stiff and stilted, but Bev couldn't decide if it was out of irritation at her teasing or disapproval of mass media in general.

"So you don't watch tv, you don't eat, you've never had an alcoholic beverage, and you probably aren't out getting laid. Other than indulging in some great designer duds, what kind of pleasure are you getting out of this world? You can't tell me being on twitter is pleasurable." Viv leaned back in her chair and regarded Barachiel with one eyebrow quirked up.

"I didn't say I'd never done any of those things. I have had beer with my friend Andras, but I didn't like it. Or rather, I liked it and pleasures of the flesh are forbidden to those who would not fall from Her grace. You are correct that Twitter is not pleasurable, therefore it is allowed as a way to learn about humanity, most of whom are very angry and justify it in the name of their god who bears no resemblance to mine." Barachiel's gaze didn't waver as he stoically focused on a spot just above Viv's head.

"You seem uncomfortable talking about it, so Viv won't push it any further, will she?" Bev shot her friend a look, hoping she was conveying a strong "leave it alone" vibe.

"At least for now. But I will say I'm so glad I fell in love with a demon and not an angel. Those pleasures of the flesh are out-of-this-world good." Viv smirked at Bev, who rolled her eyes.

"Now that we've talked about Buffy, I'm gonna start it up. I haven't watched all the way through in a while, and that's a comfort show. Barachiel, you can leave if you want to, or ignore it—whatever, but it's my house, and I had a really hard day. Vampires and wine are what I really need tonight."

"I'm in. It's been a while since we've had a sleepover that wasn't one of us dealing with supernatural weirdness, and I hope we get that chance again soon. But in the meantime, I'll take what I can get. Wanna snuggle?" Viv asked, waggling her eyebrows at Bev.

Bev laughed. "I do not, but thank you for asking." She was lying. She did want to snuggle, but not with Bev, and the realization made heat bloom on her face. She hoped the blush would disappear before Viv looked back at her.

"Why is your face red?" Barachiel asked. "I have seen this reaction in many humans and have never been able to understand it."

"Wine on an empty stomach sometimes makes me flush," Bev said, thanking her lucky stars that she wasn't as crappy a liar as her friend Evie. She didn't pull it out often, but when she did, it was totally believable.

BEV SAT at the kitchen bar watching Viv make breakfast. It was a reversal of where they'd been three months ago.

Viv slid the ham and cheese scramble onto Bev's plate along with a side of breakfast potatoes. "Sorry about the omelet. It started out good but fell in with a bad crowd. This is your brain and drugs and all that."

"You are ridiculous, and the scramble is fine. I almost never have omelets unless I'm ordering them from a professional." Bev stood to refill her coffee, then sat down to dig in. "This is really good. Like really good. I'm impressed."

"I can cook. I've always been able to cook. It's just that you and Evie never spend time with me in my own kitchen, so I don't have much of an opportunity to show off my mad stove skills." There was a slight bite to Viv's words that belied the grin she flashed before filling her own coffee cup and dumping in a generous serving of flavored creamer. The toast popping up kept her back to Bev while she slathered butter on all four pieces and then served up her own helping of eggs and potatoes.

"Are the renovations done in your place yet? You should have a housewarming party." Bev took another bite of her eggs and nodded her thanks when Viv put two pieces of the toast on her plate.

"Almost. Ugh. I was so sure I'd be able to do most of the work myself, especially with Elle coming by to clean with her magic angel dust. Wait, isn't that a drug? I wonder if we can bottle Elle's essence and make a killing in the black market or the dark web or wherever kids these days go for their paranormal drug purchases." Viv plunked her plate across from Bev's and hopped up on the stool. "And speaking of angel dust, where's your source?"

"My source? What are you talking about?"

"Mister 'I hate pop culture and don't know how to use text speak but was secretly watching Buffy from the hallway.'"

Bev stuck her tongue out at her friend. "That is a very, very long name. But if you mean Barachiel, he said he had errands to run. And before you ask, I have no idea what kind of errands. Maybe he needs more leather jackets."

Viv laughed. "To answer your house question, though, it's not done yet. I had to replace the roof, rewire the stuff, fix some plumbing things, and am finally getting to the kitchen. Those appliances might still be running as well as they did in 1967, but I cannot live in a place with a burnt orange and avocado green color scheme. At least I got that carpet out of the kitchen, though. That was so gross." Viv gagged as she spoke.

"That great, huh?"

"The best. At least we didn't find any bodies or anything, though. I was a little worried when we pulled up the kitchen carpet and the stench hit." Viv shook her head, took a drink of coffee, and loaded her fork with potatoes. "No more talk of my kitchen now. When it's done —and this should be the last project, it would've been cheaper to buy a new place—I will have a housewarming and will cook all the things. But I do not bake, so I will have to beg you to make me a cake."

"Anything for you."

*Meow.*

"When did you get a cat?" Viv asked, looking around for the source of the meowing.

"I completely forgot. I don't have anything. No cat food. No litter box. Ugh. I do not want to go to the store this morning." Bev glared back towards the stairs where she assumed the cat noises were coming from.

"You got a cat, didn't tell anyone, and forgot to buy any supplies for said cat? Nothing in that sentence sounds like you." Viv got up and filled a bowl with water, then set it on the ground in an out of the way corner. "How old is it?"

"At least thirty, maybe thirty-five. And I didn't tell anyone because Shelby came home with it last night and refused to let me put it back." Bev opened the internet app on her phone and did a quick search. "The pet store might deliver if they're not too busy and I offer a huge tip."

"Or I can run down to the store as soon as you tell me why Shelby came home with an impossibly elderly cat and your solution was to 'put it back.' I'll wait." Viv took another bite of her breakfast, then waved her fork at Bev.

*Meow.*

This time, it was closer. Just outside the room.

"I think she's shy," Bev said. "Probably her first time with humans in a few decades. As for her origins, I think the pet cemetery didn't get all its residents back after their walkabout last night."

Viv visibly recoiled. "You have a zombie cat in your house? That's disgusting."

"She's not disgusting, and she's not a zombie," Shelby said. She walked into the room with a tiny black cat curled up in her arms. "She's adorable."

"She is cute and doesn't seem to be missing any fur or important body parts. And she doesn't smell any worse than a preteen who is suddenly averse to showering." Bev side eyed her niece and the cat. "And if you're going to keep your undead pet—which is a very big if— you'll be the one responsible for her. You will pay for her supplies, you will scoop the litter box, and I will never, ever smell the existence of a cat in my house."

"What's her name?" Viv asked, curiosity apparently winning out over disgust.

"Xena. It was on her collar." Shelby held the cat out for Viv to inspect.

"Oh my god. It is Xena. You were right—my mother did murder her and bury her in the pet cemetery." Viv held out her hands for the kitten, and Shelby slowly handed her over.

"She's your cat?" Shelby looked devastated and about thirty seconds away from tears.

Viv looked up and handed the cat back. "She *was* my cat thirty years ago. But I'm not the one who raised her from the dead. She's yours now."

"Thank you, Aunt Viv. And Aunt Bev, I promise to take really good care of her. I can sell my clothes to make money for her supplies, but I don't have enough right now." Shelby widened her eyes and cuddled the kitten under her chin while looking at her aunt.

"Don't use that cat's cuteness against me. I still haven't forgotten where you found her." Shelby's eyes widened even more, and she stuck her lower lip out and made it tremble. Bev had no choice but to relent. "I will front you the money for what you'll need to get her set up. Viv, will you take her to the pet store and get her stocked on food and litter and whatever else cats need to thrive? A cat carrier, I suppose, so we can take her to the vet for shots. I'm sure whatever vaccinations she got in the eighties have long since lost their effectiveness."

"Thank you, thank you, thank you!" Shelby danced over to Bev and dropped an enthusiastically loud kiss on her cheek. "I'll get my coat."

"No. You will put your cat on the ground, wash your hands, and have some breakfast. Viv made breakfast potatoes." Bev wrinkled her nose at her niece. "And if any body parts start falling off, I will put her right back in the ground where she belongs."

# CHAPTER TEN

"Aunt Bev! I'm back!" The door slammed behind Shelby as she stomped into the house.

Bev walked into the living room and was greeted by the sight of her twelve-year-old laden with a pink cat carrier adorned with cat skull stickers, a litter box, and a suspicious-looking bag that jangled when Shelby moved and had a long pole with a feather sticking out of one end.

"Did you get food and litter? Those are a little more important than cat toys, I think." Bev put her hands on her hips and shook her head.

"In here." Shelby dropped the cat carrier on the entry rug and grimaced as she flexed her arm. "That was heavy."

"Where's Viv? Couldn't she have helped you in?" Bev picked up the cat carrier and grunted under its weight. "Where do you want to set up the litter box?"

"In the mudroom?" Shelby set down the bag of toys and walked through the kitchen to the mudroom/laundry room. "And I told Aunt Viv I could manage. She wanted to run home and shower and drop off her bags. And probably smooch Sam."

"I thought you were going to renovate that into your sewing

room?" Bev said, following with the bag of litter she'd pulled out of the cat carrier and ignoring the smooching comment. She knew preteens knew all about smooching, and Shelby'd been reporting crushes for the last couple years, but that was not a road she wanted to travel down right now.

Shelby paused and looked around the room. It was spacious, but one end was taken up by the washer, dryer, laundry sink, and folding station. The other side had coat hooks, a shoe rack, and a bench with storage for winter gear. Shelby had planned to take out the bench and replace it with a sewing table and add a cabinet—with the help of one of the friends she'd made in her woodshop class—to store patterns, fabric, and notions.

"It will still work," Shelby decided. "I can move the bench to the other side of the door without compromising the flow of the room, but instead of storage—I'll still move most of those things to the back of the hall closet, I can cut a hole in the side for Xena to go in and out. Then the seat will lift up for easy scooping!"

Bev surveyed the space. "You'll want to measure, but I think that will work. For the short term, we can get her set up in this corner so no one trips over the litter box while we're getting used to having a cat in the place."

"Where is she?" Shelby asked after they got the box set up and filled.

"Snoozing in the chair in front of the fire. On my nice blanket. Of course."

"I'll get her food and water set out, then introduce her to the litter box and food. And then I'll show her the presents." Shelby ran back to the living room and returned with two bowls decorated with tiny paw prints and a bag of food she must've pulled out of the cat carrier. "The carrier can go on top of my storage cabinet Will's going to build for me. That way it'll be accessible but out of the way."

Bev left Shelby in the mudroom to finish setting up her new cat's necessities and poured herself another cup of coffee. She watched Shelby fetch Xena and take her on a tour of her kitty dining room and water closet, then walk back through the kitchen to the living room.

Crinkling paper and baby talk drew Bev into that room against her better judgment.

Shelby was plumping a cat bed in front of the fire and trying to lure Xena off the couch and into the cozy-looking bed. Once the cat had deigned to investigate, Shelby ran outside and returned with a cat tree that was taller than she was. It had three platforms, an alcove for hiding, a climbing rope, and what looked like a hammock.

"How much of my money did you spend?" Bev gasped.

"None. Aunt Viv paid for everything." She looked up and saw the look of disapproval her aunt was sending her way. "What? It's a loan. We drew up papers and everything."

"What else is in that bag of wonders?" Bev asked.

"Catnip, toy mice, a laser pointer, the feather toy, and this!" Shelby produced a wad of cloth with flair worthy of a stage magician's.

"Is that… Is that a witch costume?" Bev asked. "Are you going to put clothes on your cat?"

"It's almost Halloween, and a warrior princess costume seemed too obvious. So, she's a witch cat. Just like us." Shelby's grin was so delighted, Bev didn't have it in herself to throw any negativity on Shelby's happiness parade.

"Fine. Have your Halloween fun with your cat. I'm going to clean up the kitchen, and then we are going to talk about last night."

Shelby's shoulders hunched, and she shrank several inches. "Okay. I'll be here with Xena. Unless you need help in the kitchen?"

"I got it this time, but you should run upstairs and make sure there are no clothes on the floor and your bed is made. We can reconvene in fifteen minutes."

It was closer to a half hour before Bev made it to the couch with another cup of coffee—she'd stayed up way too late watching Buffy last night and was paying the price today—waiting for Shelby to reappear.

"If you don't come back down soon, I'm going to lure your cat in with cat treats and chin scritches!"

"Nooooooo…" Shelby ran down the steps and Bev thought, and not for the first time, that adolescents couldn't go anywhere without sounding like a herd of young elephants was chasing them.

The phone rang just as Shelby was collapsing into the chair in a tangle of limbs that were still too long and awkward for her to know what to do with.

"It's Evie. I'm going to get this to make sure Luc is okay, and then I want an explanation, young lady." Bev didn't wait for a reply and answered the phone. "Everything okay, Evie?"

"Depends on how you define okay. Um. I have a huge favor to ask, and you are not going to like it." Evie sounded out of breath and more irritated than Bev had heard her sound in ages.

"You know I'd do anything for you. Spit it out."

"Can you come to Jer's? He needs our help."

Bev didn't know how to reply, so she just stared at the phone.

Evie's voice broke the long silence. "Bev? Are you there? Did I break you?"

"I think I misunderstood. Did you say you wanted me to come to Jer's? The place where I was last night? The place where your horrible ex-husband lives? And did you also imply that you were already there? What is going on?" Just when you thought the world was out of surprises for the weekend…

BY THE TIME Bev was dressed and she'd asked, cajoled, and threatened Shelby until she agreed to come along—"I should stay home with Xena! It's been a big day for her!"—almost thirty minutes had passed since Evie's phone call. She grabbed her wallet, slipped it into her jacket pocket, and used the keys to unlock the car.

"Aunt Bev? There's someone in the back seat."

Bev's heart raced and every true crime carjacking story flooded her mind. She hadn't realized how much the fear had faded to the background over the last twenty-four hours, but the second it was triggered, everything came flooding back. "Get back in the house and call 911."

"If I'm running away from the danger, why aren't you? We're both closer to the house than the car, and he doesn't look like he's got a gun or anything." Shelby made no move to retreat. "Besides, how am I going to call 911? You won't let me have a phone, and we don't have a landline. No one does. It's the twenty-first century."

"I need to get you a phone. They must still make dumb phones." The door to the car opened, and Bev backed up, feeling for the door-knob behind her. "Shel, get behind me and unlock the door."

Shelby walked around Bev and punched in the code that would unlock the door.

"Hi! Are you headed out to that farm? I thought it would be easier to ride with you than fly. Elle says I'm supposed to keep my wings on the DL." Barachiel waved. "How's your cat, Shelby? I hope she's still alive and in one piece!"

"Elle one hundred percent did not tell you to keep anything on the DL. That is not how she talks." Bev knew that as a retort, it was lacking something, but it was the best her tired, overwhelmed brain could come up with on the fly.

Barachiel folded himself back into the car and slammed the door.

"Why is he sitting in the backseat?" Shelby asked. "That's weird. Adults always take the front."

"Guess it's your lucky day, kid. Front seat for you!"

"So lucky. I get to go to a farm to find out why Evie's ex suddenly needs her help after all these years. Hopefully the cows are still there." Shelby walked to the front passenger door and got in.

Bev shook her head and got behind the wheel. "Are you telling me the cows were on purpose? I assumed it was a loss of control after you tried to find yourself a pet from Dead Cats R Us."

"Whoa. If I tell you it was an accident, can we rewind this conversation three minutes?" Shelby buckled her seatbelt and avoided eye contact.

"Nuh uh. Cat's already out of the bag. So to speak. Tell me about the cows." Bev fixed a gimlet stare on her niece.

Shelby shrugged. "We were there, and I could feel them. I needed something big to practice on, and they were the nearest big animals."

"I don't understand what's happening. Why would Shelby go pet shopping in a cemetery?" Barachiel leaned forward and propped his chin on the back of the passenger seat.

"Put your seatbelt on or we're not going anywhere. You know the rules."

Barachiel grumbled. "I thought that was only for the front seat. If I'd known it was everywhere, I would've sat in the more comfortable seat."

When she heard the click, Bev backed out of the driveway and tried very, very hard not to think about what would happen if another car sped down the quiet residential street while she was pulling out. She slammed on the brakes before she hit the street.

"What's wrong? Are you okay?" Shelby looked around and rolled down her window.

"I'm fine. I don't hear anything. It's been radio silence since I left Chelan. Maybe I'm cured!"

"It's not a disease, and if you don't learn to control it, you'll never be able to live with it. Why do you think I—" Shelby clamped her mouth closed and turned to stare out the window.

"She's right. Maybe they're quiet now, but it's a temporary reprieve. I have a theory if you're interested."

"If it's about pocket dimensions, or the unreality of the void or whatever, I am not interested in your theories," Bev snapped as she turned right onto Main Street. The road would drive through the middle of town, halfway around the lake, and then dump her on an unimproved road that wound down the mountain to Jeremy's farm. Or at least the farmhouse part of it.

"It's about why you don't hear dead people."

Despite herself, Bev snorted. "Fine. Explain." She slowed at a crosswalk to let someone cross the street, then belatedly recognized them as Joanne Mills' deputy, the one who'd insinuated that she punched

Jackson for some kind of weird sexual gratification. "I should've hit him. Or at least scared him."

"What? You're acting real weird, Aunt Bev. I mean, not about the ghosts and zombies and stuff. I mean, you're really…violent. You said you wanted to punch Martin—"

"Martin?" Bev couldn't place the name, but if she was as violent as Shelby was saying, perhaps she'd forgotten one of her many, many victims.

"The kid I got suspended for hitting. Then, you punched your boss. Now you want to run over cops. What's up with you? You're not setting a very good example, especially after telling me a million times that violence is never the answer." Shelby's voice had morphed into a passable imitation of Bev's by the end of her sentence.

"Violence is hardly ever the answer," Bev said. "I maintain that you hitting Martin was just. He was harassing you and no one was doing anything about it. You have the right to defend yourself, especially if you try non-violent methods first."

"Is that why you hit your boss? Self-defense?"

"No. I hit him because he was a jerk, and I lost my temper. I should've walked away and gone with my first plan."

"What was your first plan?" Barachiel asked from the back seat.

"To ask Lily to give him boils on his behind," Bev said.

Shelby dissolved into giggles. "She probably still could, and I know she'd love to as long as you promise not to tell her mom."

Bev pretended to consider it. "I think I'll have to keep that in my back pocket for now. I don't want to hide something like that from my best friend, and I really don't want to explain to her why I asked her child to harm another person." She sped up a little now that she was out of town.

"Can I tell you my theory now?" Barachiel asked. "Or should we come up with more ways to harm your former boss? I remember the sorts of pranks She used to get up to, and I have several ideas."

"Um… Why don't you tell me about your theory and we can do divinely inspired revenge fantasies later."

Barachiel's face appeared between her and Shelby again.

"Barachiel. Seatbelt. Now." Bev held up her index finger on her right hand and poked him in the forehead. Or where she'd assumed his forehead would be. It was hard to gauge that correctly without taking your eyes off the road.

"That was my nose. Why did you touch my nose?" The seatbelt clicked.

"BOOP!" Shelby yelled, then laughed hysterically.

"No more distractions. Tell me why the voices are gone, why the fear is gone."

"Because you broke the void, of course." The window in the backseat rolled down and then back up. "You shouldn't have been able to do that, and when you did, it was like breaking a…" There was a long pause. "Rubber band? I think that's the word. It was like breaking a rubber band. The ends snapped back, they hit the creator of the void, the dark sorcerer, and it pulled the animating force back out of the world. It will take him some time to make his way back, but when he does, I do not think he will be pleased."

"Can you stop calling him a sorcerer?" Shelby asked. "It sounds like we're stuck in bizarro Harry Potter world, but that it's way less fun than it should be."

"What title do you want me to use?"

"The Great Necromancer is what he likes to be called, although I think that's stupid. He says his name is William the Bloody." Shelby pronounced his epithet with a solemnity usually reserved for queens and popes.

"Is he a poet, too?" Bev asked. "Or just a big Buffy fan?" Keeping the questions at the surface kept the anger at bay—kind of. She didn't want it to break through, not at Shelby. There were times to show a kid how angry you were, but not when it was directed at them. At least not in the moment. This was a step back, count to ten, and make Buffy references kind of moment.

"What are you talking about? He's a necromancer, and he offered to train me." Shelby huffed in a way that no other person being accused of consorting with dark magicians could.

"If he's a necromancer, why would he be bloody?" Barachiel asked. "The dead, unless newly introduced to that state, are not very bloody."

"My guess is it has something to do with how he gets the dead to work with him," Bev said. *One. Two. Three. Not working!*

"What? Are you saying that William *kills* people?" Shelby sounded completely aghast at the suggestion.

"If he's a bloody great necromancer, he's doing something that's not on the up-and-up. You knew he wasn't above board, didn't you?" Bev threw that out there and waited for Shelby's response.

"Of course I didn't! If I'd known he wasn't cool, I wouldn't have agreed to hang out so he could teach me how to control what was happening. I swear, Aunt Bev. I would never..." Shelby was almost on the verge of tears, but Bev had one nail to put in that coffin.

"Did you tell your friends? Or did you hide what you were doing and who you were doing it with, even knowing that your best friends have seen a lot and are extremely familiar with moral grey areas?" That was it. If that didn't drive home how big of a mistake she'd made —and that part of her knew she was screwing up—nothing else Bev could say would.

When Shelby didn't respond, Bev glanced over at her as she prepared to take the turn into Jer's driveway. Shelby was curled up as much as she could strapped into the front seat of the car, shoulders shaking as silent tears coursed down her cheeks.

Bev's heart ached with Shelby's. Seeing the silent crying was somehow worse than loud, wracking sobs, but she couldn't put her finger on it.

"Hey Shel, I don't want to say that what you did was okay, but you're not the first person who's messed up big. We all make mistakes, and yours isn't so far gone that it's irreversible. We will fix this, and you will walk away much, much wiser. What did he look like? If he's been walking around town luring impressionable youths into dark magic and zombie raisings, it's probably good to have people keep an eye out for him."

There was a long enough pause that Bev took her eyes off the road to glance over at the passenger seat.

"I don't know," Shelby answered, confusion evident in her voice. "How could I not know? We spent hours together. But when I try to think of what he looks like instead of what he told me, all I see is beige."

"Are you sure? That is extremely weird." Bev couldn't help the doubt that crept into her voice. Shelby'd never had great facial recognition skills, but she usually could remember at least skin and hair color.

"All I do is screw up." Shelby's voice was muffled by tears and the hands she'd buried her face into.

Bev bit back a sigh. This wasn't the first time she'd heard this refrain, and this time it was a lot more justified, but there was a point where continual reassurance of someone's self-worth stopped feeling genuine and helpful. "Shel, you're human. Human and twelve. Part of your job is to screw up regularly now so you can figure out how to do better as you get older and screwups have bigger implications."

"Bigger than hanging out with someone who is a murderer and raises the dead to search for treasure?" She clapped her hand over her mouth. "I wasn't supposed to tell anyone about that part. He said if I told, he'd know, and that I wouldn't like what he'd do next."

The car filled with bright light, and Bev nearly drove off the road. "Turn it off, Barachiel. I can't see where I'm going."

The light disappeared as suddenly as it'd appeared. "Apologies. I was angry. To threaten a child so they will keep a secret is not the mark of a great anything. It is one of the great wrongs a person can do."

"I didn't think you got angry," Shelby said. "Aren't angels supposed to be all peace and light and halos and harps?"

Bev recognized the change of subject and decided to allow it so they could get the last half mile to Jer's safely.

"You need to read more books about angels. We are not fluffy, and most of us do not play the harp. You saw Elle last summer, so you saw her sword. She is not floating on a cloud. And I am older even than Elle. She has walked this world for the better part of ten millennia; that has gentled her. But I rarely graced humans with my presence until recently, and I am not soft. I bring Her blessings and benedictions to this world, all the blessings humans deserve." An overpowering scent of roses filled the car.

"Dude. Do angel farts smell like flowers?" Shelby made a gagging noise and rolled down the window.

Bev almost laughed, which would've broken her twelve-year record of never laughing at her kid's toilet humor. She rolled down the window.

"I looked you up," Bev said. "According to Wikipedia, you're the angel of blessings and lightning, and you bring mirth and shifts in mindsets."

"What did Wikipedia say about angel farts?" Shelby asked. She was nearly unintelligible through her laughter. Kids were a roller coaster of emotions; it was a wonder more of them weren't messed up.

"I neither eat nor drink, therefore I do not have bodily functions. And you are missing the point of my anger." Bev could swear she heard a sliver of amusement in his voice.

"Whatever, angel," Shelby said, twisting around in her seat to stick her tongue out.

"Shelby, manners. Barachiel is older, thus deserving of your respect. You should call him Mister Angel." She parked next to Evie's car and opened the door. "Okay, everyone out. Let's go figure out what Jer's problem is this time." *And if it doesn't come with a hefty dose of groveling, I'm dragging Evie out of here and leaving him to the zombie livestock.* She slipped an arm around Shelby, pulled her close, and led her towards the barn.

# CHAPTER ELEVEN

Bev entered Jer's too-large barn—who knew you could be ostentatious with your farm buildings?—for the second time in two days. For the second time in two decades, actually.

Jeremy Kantek was sitting in his leather recliner with a beer in hand. He was in the same clothes he'd had on the night before, rumpled and dusty farm chic, along with an uncharacteristic seed cap. Bev hadn't seen much of Jer in the almost fifteen years since Evie'd divorced him for cheating on her—with Evie's boss, no less—but she'd never seen him looking this disheveled. At least not since last night.

Evie was perched on his desk on her phone. When Bev got a little further into the room, she saw what was holding Evie's attention. She was super intent on passing level 843 on the match-3 game she'd started playing during late night nursing sessions with Alex. Evie looked up, saw Bev had made her, and grinned before putting her phone back in her pocket.

"Why are we here, Jer? Didn't we help enough last night?" Bev was running low on patience and niceties and had no intention of wasting either on him.

Jer looked up and paled. "You brought that freak?"

Bev looked behind her. Barachiel waved. "Did you call my friend a freak?"

"He has wings. *Wings.* I thought Brandy was lying when she tried to tell me what kind of weird shit you all got up to last summer, just like she lied about the father of her bastard. But that freak has wings." Jer's eyes were wide as they darted back and forth between Barachiel, Bev, and Evie. "I shouldn't have called. Nothing's wrong here. You can go now."

"You didn't seem so eager to get rid of us last night when Barachiel guarded you from the zombie cows with his wings. You might try being a little more grateful and a little less douchey." She turned to Evie. "What does he want, anyway? It must be something big if he called you, and you were willing to come."

Evie shrugged. "He texted me last night, but I didn't see it until this morning, but after what you told me went down, I figured I better answer the phone when he called. It's partly the zombie cows—every time he leaves the barn, they surround him and won't let him go home. I thought you could help with that."

"If it's partly the cows, which... Do I have to get rid of them? They're not actually hurting him, right? Just herding him."

"Quality word play, Bev," Evie congratulated her. "But yeah, you should probably send the cows away."

Bev held her imaginary skirt out and dipped into a curtsey. "Fine. I'll take care of the cows when I head back outside. What's the rest?"

"Make him stop looking at me," Jer interrupted.

Bev turned around. "Barachiel, can you look somewhere else, I guess? Jer is sensitive about people seeing him when he hasn't had a chance to iron his jeans...or shower in re-scent history. Wouldn't mind some of that rosy angel dust now."

"Re-scent? You are on a roll, Bev. I bow in the face of your superior punning. I haven't seen you this humorous in a long time and considering it's in the face of zombie cow dispersal, that's even more impressive." Evie grinned and Bev returned it.

"Turns out hitting the off switch, however temporary, on the whispers of the dead makes everything feel a little less grave." Bev screwed up her face. "Okay. I'm done now. Three was not the charm."

Shelby poked her head in, and when Jer caught sight of her, his face got even whiter.

"You have a freak with wings and a witch? What did I do to deserve this?" He drained the rest of his beer, leaned over, and grabbed another out of the mini fridge next to his chair, and took a healthy gulp from that can.

"Shelby, please explain why he thinks you're a witch." Bev tried to look stern, but no matter how serious the situation, seeing Jer this freaked out warmed a part of her soul she didn't know was cold.

Shelby shuffled her feet and stared fixedly at the out-of-date calendar above the desk. "Maybe he saw me last night when I was here trying to help the Great—I mean William—find the treasure he'd lost. And it's possible he saw me tell the cows not to let him leave the barn." She squirmed under the gazes of Evie and Bev. "He deserved it," she ended defiantly, looking up and glaring at the women before turning her hard gaze on the object of her disaffection.

"Whether or not he deserved it is irrelevant," Bev said. "We don't raise the dead for personal gain."

"It wasn't for my personal gain. It was because he was mean to both of my best friend's moms. No one should be mean to people's *mothers*."

"She's as good as Lily at twisting mistakes into gifts." Evie grinned at Shelby. "Since Jer doesn't appear to be permanently damaged, we can forgive the cow thing. This time. But you do need to tell us why you were here in the first place."

"I think we're all interested in that." Joanne Mills walked into the barn, starched to within an inch of her life and with shoulder pads that must have been directly imported from 1985. "You were reported missing by your... What's Luc Morgenstern's relationship to this child? Oh, right. He isn't. Which means that you, Beverly Hill, left a minor child with an unrelated man who lost her within twenty-four hours. In addition to your assault charges, we're looking at adding some child endangerment charges, too."

Evie rolled her eyes. "Get over yourself, Jo. A sleepover isn't child endangerment. Bev didn't drop her off with the creepy preacher down the road. Shelby was at her best friend's house, a place she's stayed countless times over the last ten years. But if you want to throw a bunch of stuff at Bev to see what sticks, I can get in touch with our family lawyer. She is *really* excited to come do some digging in Eden Valley and has already submitted a request for the phone call Luc made to the station last night when he tried to file a missing person report. I can't wait to hear how that played out."

The sheriff rolled her shoulders back as she tried to regain her verbal footing. "Irregardless—" Bev winced at the word "—I was called here to investigate some vandalism and threats against Mr. Kantek's person, and here you are, admitting this child was here last night without adult supervision. So tell me, little girl, why did you pick Mr. Kantek to terrorize?"

Shelby took a step towards Bev and looked up at her aunt, uncertainty and fear competing for dominance.

"You don't have to answer any of her questions if you don't want to," Bev said. "You're a minor, and I'm your legal guardian. I don't give consent for her to question you, certainly not without your own legal representation." She took Shelby's hand and squeezed it. "Why don't we walk out of here and let the sheriff talk to Jer alone. He can tell her more about his experience last night and why he called her today, what he saw."

Shelby nodded and gripped Bev's hand tight.

"We won't leave the property, Jo. We'll be right outside. I want to see Jer's cows before we leave." Bev looked over the top of Shel's head and widened her eyes at Evie, who returned a slight nod.

Evie walked by and took Shelby's other hand, leading her outside.

"Barachiel, why don't you stay here with Jer and help him answer Jo's questions. After all, you were here for a long-time last night and probably remember things more clearly than Jer."

The angel smiled in delight. "I was here, and I've never been questioned by the police before. This is going to be fun!"

Bev smiled. She didn't know how the interview was going to go, but she almost wished she could stay to watch.

"I'll be outside, Jer. I'm going to check on your cows, okay?" Bev waved at the sheriff, who was sputtering as she lost control of the conversation.

"My cows are dead. That's the problem," Jer said. "They're wandering around out there, mooing at me, and they're dead. That little witch raised them from the dead."

"Okay, Jer. I believe you. I'll just go out there and check for you, okay?" Bev walked out of the room, grinning in complete joy. Everything sucked, and last night had been the scariest of her life, but it was almost worth it for the moment Jer told the cops he'd called them because dead cows were mooing at him. She'd probably feel bad for whatever trauma had happened the night before that had interrupted Jer's calculating assholishness—normally he would've found a slier and more believable way to blame Shelby for his woes—but for now... This was the balm she'd needed. When she gauged she was way out of earshot, she looked around. "Shel, where are the cows?"

"Hiding behind the garage. I think they're waiting for him to try to get to the house so they can ambush him." Shelby pointed towards the large garage that had been converted into a man cave, complete with weight room, tool bench, big screen tv, kegerator, and more leather furniture.

"What's he compensating for, anyway?" Bev muttered.

"His complete lack of personality and enthusiasm for anything that's not him." Evie shrugged. "I wasn't allowed to go into any of the building besides the house. My car wasn't allowed in the garage, not even in winter. Our relationship was fantastic. Sometimes I don't understand how I could've left all this for Luc."

Bev laughed. "It's a mystery for sure."

"Look!" Shelby pointed towards the garage. A long ear that had once been black was slowly emerging, followed by the long face, large nostrils, and large eyes of a black Angus cow. When she spotted the group of people, her head disappeared behind the garage.

"Does she seem too smart for a typical cow? I mean, I'm not a cowgirl, but I feel like I'd know if cows were good at hide and seek. That would be on YouTube for sure." Bev stared at the spot where the cow's face had appeared.

"I lived on this farm for almost ten years, and I don't remember ever hearing the cow's superior intelligence lauded," agreed Evie.

"Sweetie, did you do anything else to them besides raise them from the dead? Now would be a good time to let us know." Bev caught Shelby's gaze and held on.

"Not exactly more, but I was feeling a lot of emotions when I did it. I really don't like that man, even though I've only met him a couple times. And the Great, I mean William, told me the more emotion I could put into the raising, the better the reanimation would work. He didn't say it'd make the cows sneaky, though. I'm sorry." Shelby caught her hands behind her back.

"It's fine. We need to sit down and have a talk about William and everything he told you. But for now, I guess I'll go back there and put out the sparks." Bev pursed her lips. "I wish we could leave a couple to sneak up on him whenever he's least expecting it and just moo."

Evie bit back a laugh. "It's taking all my self-control to not react to your wish. I think if this whole marrying for money thing doesn't work out, I could make a killing as a genie, and I hear lamps are very cozy."

Bev walked slowly to the back of the garage. "Hey girls. I know you are all having fun, and let's face it, that man deserves to be harassed by a herd of undead cows, but it's time to go back to sleep."

There was a loud scuffle and a couple angry moos.

"What the hell am I doing? Two weeks ago, I was a banker. And now I'm sweet-talking zombie cows into letting me return them to the graves from whence they came." Bev rounded the corner and stared into eight pairs of soft, dark eyes framed with long lashes. Well, thirteen eyes on eight cows. They were much less healthy looking than they'd been yesterday. "Right. I'd better take care of this before Shelby tries to talk me into starting a whole undead petting zoo."

Bev closed her eyes and felt for the spark in each animal. Now that she'd found it, it was easy to identify again. Those on their first lives had sparks centered in their brains, but the undead's sparks were in the chest. It made a weird kind of sense if you assumed a pumping heart with no brain activity was the only thing animating these corpses. Kind of. Eden Valley sense, anyway.

"I'm sorry. I really am." Bev reached out and pinched eight sparks in succession, holding them until the un-life left them and they collapsed in a heap of bones covered with the scraps of cowhide that hadn't quite rotted away yet. When she was finished, she was sweating and eight carcasses were on the ground in various states of decay.

Bev walked back out of the driveway. "It's done. I feel bad. I think they were having a great time."

Evie patted her arm. "There will be other undead in your future."

"Did Viv tell you about Shelby's new cat?" Bev asked.

"No. Oh no! Shelby! Are you serious?" Evie looked genuinely horrified, an expression that Bev didn't often see on her nearly unflappable friend.

"She's not undead. And she's nice."

"She doesn't smell bad, and all her body parts are on. And she and Viv spent a small fortune at the pet store this morning, so I guess we're keeping our sweet lil zombie cat." Bev grinned at Shelby.

"Ladies, can you come back in here please?" the deputy whose name Bev couldn't remember, even though she'd spent a lot of time with him this week, called to them.

"Maybe you should've hit him with your car," Shelby said as they walked back to the barn.

"It's not his fault he's the way he is. Not running over him was the best choice, especially since he was in a crosswalk." She put an arm around her niece. "Remember, don't say anything. You'll have to tell us the story without a lawyer later, but for now, keep it zipped."

Shelby mimed zipping her lips, locking them, and throwing away the key. "My ips are heeled."

"Ridiculous child. I love you." Bev glanced at Evie. "Ready to find out how Jer explained it all?"

"Never readier."

Bᴇᴠ ʜᴀᴅ sᴘᴇɴᴛ most of the last twenty minutes suppressing laughter and eye rolls, but at least she hadn't had to excuse herself the way Evie had. Jer's version of events was even more bananas than what had actually happened, and it was obvious Sheriff Mills was confused and very, very disappointed she couldn't pin anything on either Bev or Shelby.

Once the sheriff had sent her deputy out to look for the "zombie cows" Jer insisted were chasing him all over the farm and he'd returned reporting no mobile cows, only a pile of carcasses in various states of disrepair, she was nearly at the end of her patience. Jer's insistence that Barachiel had wrapped him in large snow-white wings to save him from the cows was when she'd pasted an insincere smile on her face before standing to leave.

Barachiel backing up Jer's story didn't appear to have lent it any legitimacy, but it did discredit Jer's insistence that Shelby had been roaming around the property, raising the dead and breaking into his outbuildings.

"The only question I have left is why any of you were here last night. I heard the child admit she was here, and Mr. Invisible Wings over there was clearly here based on his own admission. What about you, Beverly Hill?"

Bev gritted her teeth. No one called her by her full name unless they were trying to get a rise out of her. "Jer texted Evie asking for help. Evie was still on her way back from Chelan, so Luc and I came instead. Barachiel had beaten us here, and since I knew he was looking for Shelby, I hoped that meant she was here. I didn't see her here, though."

"Where was she? You obviously found her."

"She was at the lake." Bev knew she was being short and that it might not be the best way to talk to Jo, but she couldn't help herself.

"So a runaway, after all. Guess I was right." The smugness in her voice made Bev's itchy trigger fist twitch.

"I guess you were. That doesn't negate the fact that you refused to help look for her. She is a child, and you dismissed her disappearance as not worth noting. Is that how you treat every missing child? Because that makes you a horrible human being, and possibly criminally negligent yourself." Evie was vibrating with anger.

"I don't have time to follow up with every runaway in the county. My job is to prevent crime and arrest criminals, not coddle emotional teenagers with anger management issues. Although at least now we know where those anger issues come from." Jo smirked as she looked at Bev.

"I don't understand what you are telling us. Did you say coming here to talk to this man after he reported being harassed by undead cows is more important than ensuring the welfare of a child?" Barachiel was regarding the sheriff the way he'd stared at the television during the opening sequence to Buffy, the way he'd looked when Bev had tried to explain banking and money management. But the scent of roses that was beginning to fill the small office told Bev he was at least as angry as he was confused.

"I think we're done here. I'll be in touch if I have further questions." The sheriff stalked out of the building.

"The cows won't bother you anymore," Bev told Jer. She didn't want him to question his sanity, at least not very much. He'd spent so much of his marriage to Evie gaslighting her that he might deserve just a little back, but Bev knew what it was like to worry about your mental state. "They were here, but I got rid of them. You can go back to your house now, and if it'll make you feel better, we'll walk you over there."

Jer glared at no one in particular. He seemed reluctant to meet anyone's eyes. "I can go by myself."

"Whatever you want. It's up to you. Call me if you see anything walking around that you shouldn't. I'd be happy to show up and lay any of your fears to rest, but I don't think you'll see anything else, do you, Shelby?" Bev fixed her niece with a pointed stare.

"I don't think there will be anything else." Shelby bit her lip and looked at the adults around her. "Can we leave now? I'd like to get the scolding and punishments over."

"Yeah, let's get out of here. The third degree is already overdue." Bev led the way out to her car, trying to figure out how she'd so thoroughly lost control of everything in the last week, and, more importantly, how she was going to get everything back on track.

# CHAPTER TWELVE

Bev sat on the couch next to Evie and looked at her niece, who was curled up on the loveseat next to Lily. Barachiel, as the resident alternate reality expert, was cross-legged in the middle of the floor with Xena on his lap, her legs in the air, purring madly.

"What are we waiting for?" Shelby asked. Fear was making her sound sullen.

"Viv. She's been seeing some weird stuff, some of it about Jer and some about zombies and other undead creatures of the night. If she's here while you talk about what's been going on with you, it might help us figure out where to go from here."

"Why not invite the rest of the town to stare at me while I talk about how badly I screwed up?" Shelby was hunched up against the corner of the loveseat, not making eye contact with anyone.

"Because I don't have room for that many people in my living room, and it's raining outside, so a garden party and blame game is out of the question." Bev took a sip of the peppermint tea she'd made while waiting for Evie to show up with Lily.

The front door swung open. "Hi, sorry I'm late. I had to make a quick stop." Viv walked into the room carrying an enormous box.

"What is that and why is it here?" Bev asked.

Viv propped it against the wall, then spun it around to show the picture on the side of the box. "It's a catio, so Xena can play outside safely."

"Oh my god. I don't even want to know how much money you and Shel spent on pet supplies today. You know this is beyond ridiculous, right?" Bev shook her head.

"I'll be right back. I have one more thing in the car." Viv returned moments later with another huge package. "This one is cat shelves. You can hang them in Shel's bedroom and her sewing room, and Xena can walk on the walls!"

"We'll talk about this later. Now, let's just get down to it. There have been too many delays already, and the anticipation of punishment is starting to be worse than anything I could dream up." Bev smiled at Shelby as reassuringly as she could, but Shel refused to meet her eyes.

Viv grabbed a mineral water from the fridge and dropped into the vacant chair.

Bev dipped her head, trying to catch Shelby's eyes. The pre-teen had momentarily perked up when Viv had brought in the additional cat accessories, but the minute the subject returned to the events of the last twenty-four hours, she hid her face again.

"Why don't you tell us how long you've been talking to William the Bloody Awful Necromancer," Bev suggested. "We can go from there."

Shelby twisted her hands in her lap, glanced at Lily from the corner of her eye, and started talking. "Since right after we helped Kevin. Lily was at Papa Abe's, and I don't remember what Kevin was doing. I was all alone."

"Where was I?" Bev asked, racking her brain for a time when Shelby would've been all alone long enough to have a conversation with a sorcerer.

"Work. I was supposed to be at the library helping to shelve books and reading to the little kids, but story time was canceled and there weren't many books to shelve, so Addie told me I didn't have to stay."

Shelby managed to look defiant and contrite at the same time, a special gift adolescents everywhere possessed.

Bev held back a sigh and took another sip of her tea. "Okay, so you were hanging out at home when some adult showed up and offered to talk to you about magic?"

Shelby's head shot up, and she glared at Bev. "It wasn't like that. I'm not an idiot. I was reading in the park, and he looked normal and nice. He asked me for help finding his wallet, and when I found it, he offered to buy me a milkshake as thanks. I didn't go anywhere with him that wasn't public, and I watched Emily make the milkshake. She gave it directly to me, and I never left it alone."

"I'm sorry. I know you're not an idiot, and I should've known you wouldn't be easily tricked into something you didn't want to do." Bev hated so much that Shelby already knew not to leave drinks unattended in the presence of strange men, but also so happy stuff like that was sticking.

"We sat at a booth, and he told me he was visiting town for a week and asked questions about what he should do in the area, what hikes were good, and why no one was swimming. We just talked. He was super nice." Shelby's shoulders drooped. "Too nice. Why would a grown up want to talk to me that much? I should've known."

"Hey, you are awesome and interesting, and any grown-up would be lucky to talk to you. People like this are really, really good at gaining the trust of people. Don't beat yourself up," Viv said.

"She's right. He sounds like a con artist, and they're experts in getting people to confide in them. What happened after?" Bev asked.

"He asked me if I believed in ghosts. I laughed, because of course I do, and we'd just seen all the dead on the island. But I know what most people believe—or at least say they believe—so I told him I didn't. Then he said he could tell I was lying and told me he believed in ghosts and thought people who wouldn't believe were boring and short-sighted. So I told him about the ghosts I'd seen and heard. He was really interested and asked me how it felt to see them. No one had ever talked to me about it and sounded like they really cared about my answers."

"I care! And we talked about it a lot," Lily protested. "Kevin and I helped you practice raising the dead the same way we helped Kev practice drawing life energy from tourists without killing them, and how you let me…" She trailed off when she realized the attention had shifted from Shelby to herself.

"You're right. I guess I mean he was the first person who asked questions like he understood what was happening to me. And it was nice to talk to an adult who didn't think I was crazy for being able to hear the dead talking." Shelby shot her friend an apologetic look. "Anyway, I told him about the experiments I'd been doing, and he made a couple suggestions to make it easier."

"To make what easier, exactly?" Bev asked.

"Raising the dead." Shelby looked up, and every trace of contrition was gone. "I have so much power and had no idea how to use it. And I thought maybe if I learned how to control it, I could help you. It's already hard enough having to deal with me all the time. I wanted to do something for you for a change to try to make up for everything I've put you through."

"Oh, baby girl. You never have anything to make up to me, and you haven't 'put me through' anything. We're both doing our best. I'm sorry you didn't feel supported." The number of times Bev had failed Shelby in the last year was creating a debt to her niece she'd never be able to repay.

"So, he gave you some tips, you practiced them later and found out they worked, so… He just showed up again?" Viv prompted.

"A couple days later, Lily was still at her grandpa's, Kevin and I were at the pool when I saw him. He waved at me and had a book in his hands. I told Kev I was going to the bathroom and ducked out for a minute. He said he didn't have time to chat, but that our conversation the other day had reminded him of this book he had from when he was young and learning about his powers and that he wanted to lend it to me. He also said I should show it to my friends and parents so everything was on the up and up. I told him I didn't have any parents, and that my friends already knew about the necromancy thing." Shelby shrugged.

"I can't believe you never told us any of this," Lily said. "We're supposed to tell each other everything. We made a pact. I'm mad at you, Shelby."

"You have a parent," Evie said. "You have Bev."

"Bev isn't my mom. She's my aunt. She's pretty great for an aunt, but she's still not my mom. My mom is dead, and I don't even remember her. I just wanted to…"

"Oh no, Shel. Did you?" Bev couldn't even finish the question.

"She hasn't. Not yet." Barachiel set the cat on the ground and stood up. "But that's where everything was leading, wasn't it? Start small—maybe insects and arachnids. Then small animals, individually at first, then in groups. After that would be larger animals—like cows. How could you be so stupid?"

"Barachiel, you cannot talk to Shelby that way. You're here for one purpose only, and making my kid feel bad is not that purpose. Either keep your thoughts to yourself until you're asked for them or get out." Anger was easier than dwelling on the hurt she felt when Shel said she didn't have a mother. It might be true, biologically and legally, but Bev had felt like a mother for most of Shelby's twelve years.

"Fine. I'll be quiet. I was out of line. I believe I am angrier at the sorcerer than at this child, but for some reason, I misdirected it." He sat back down and scooped Xena onto his lap again. "I am sorry, Shelby. I hope you can forgive me."

"You're right. I was an idiot. I just wanted to learn so badly. I thought if I could learn everything, he could teach me, I could talk to her just once." Shelby resumed watching her hands twist in her lap. "After he gave me the book, we started meeting up every afternoon in the park so I could show him what I'd learned and he could tell me how to make it better. When school started, we had to meet less often. Finally, he told me I was ready for the next level, but I had to pass a test. Can I have something to drink? My throat is really dry."

Evie got up and returned a couple minutes later with sparkling waters for the kids, another cup of tea for Bev, and lemonade for her and Viv. Bev looked at her, and she shrugged. "The lemonade is always there when I want it now."

"The lemonade follows you around?" Viv asked. "That is…"

"Handy at picnics," Evie said.

"Can I have some?" Barachiel asked. "I've never had lemonade; it didn't sound pleasant."

"Take mine," Evie said. "I'll get another glass."

Barachiel took a drink, then another. "This is better than Beyoncé led me to believe."

"You are very weird, even for an angel," Lily said.

"What do you know of angels? Elle is your only example," Barachiel said between draws on his beverage.

"And she's weird," Lily retorted.

"I didn't think you consumed pleasures of the flesh," Viv said. "Wouldn't that include music and lemonade?"

Barachiel dropped the glass like it was hot. "I forgot. I was thirsty. I shouldn't be thirsty." He looked down at the broken glass, ice, and liquid on the rug. It disappeared, leaving everything looking pristine.

Bev stared harder at the rug. The area where he'd spilled no longer revealed the effects of being in a high-traffic area. Too bad the rest of the rug was still worn.

"Can I finish?" Shelby asked, setting down her empty water bottle.

"Of course. You have the floor." Bev tucked her feet up under herself and tried to look more compassionate and less judgmental, a task that was easier and easier the more she heard.

"I had just one test left, but it was more like a series of tests. I had to raise bigger and bigger things all in one night, and then he'd teach me how to um…resurrect humans. I was going to do it this weekend, anyway, but it's a lot easier to sneak out of my room than away from a sleepover at Lily's when everyone's in the same room with Sprinkles at the door. Plus, Kevin is a light sleeper and wakes up anytime someone breathes too loud." Shelby stopped, apparently realizing she'd just confessed to knowing the ease with which she could sneak out, and looked at her aunt with a cross between contrition and defiance.

"We'll come back to that some other time. There are bigger issues here." Bev rubbed her temples and tried hard not to think about what sixteen was going to be like.

"Okay, so. We went to the…" Shelby looked at Lily for prompting.

"Go ahead. Kevin and I spilled the beans when you disappeared. They know all about our not-so-secret hideout for evil geniuses with great cosmic powers and very little responsibility." Lily didn't meet her friend's gaze.

"Okay…" Shelby drew out the word, and Bev wasn't sure if she was searching for the next words or hearing Lily's continued unhappiness. "Okay. So. When we split up, instead of searching the rooms, I snuck out and headed to the pet cemetery and called William."

"Like the way Lily calls Papa Abe?" Evie asked. "Is there a ritual we should be aware of?"

"No. Like on the phone." She huffed out a breath, reached into the pocket of her baggy jeans, and pulled out a phone. "I'm already in trouble, might as well get it all out there."

"Where did you get a phone?" Bev didn't think there was anything more that could shock her, not after learning her niece was training with a dark sorcerer to learn how to resurrect her dead mother, but obtaining a cell phone did it.

"It's a prepaid one from a gas station." Shelby looked at the phone, then handed it to Viv, who was holding her hand out for it.

"Did William buy this for you?" Viv asked.

Shelby nodded. "It made it easier for us to contact each other once school started and my schedule got all weird. I'm sorry."

"Honestly, least of the problems right now," Bev said.

"Okay, so I called him, and he showed up, and then I did my test. First, the little bugs that died everywhere, then the small pets. Mice and hamsters and tarantulas and stuff. Just one at a time for a while. Then Xena, and I worked hard on her to make sure she was all the way back and not a zombie. I could feel her in the dirt. She was young and hadn't been sick when she died."

"Why'd you get an undead cat, Shel?" Bev asked. "Why not just ask for a regular humane shelter cat?"

"You told me I couldn't buy a pet until I was living on my own because you didn't want to take care of one. I thought this was a good way to get a cat without paying for one."

Bev wracked her brains. "When did I say that?"

"When I was seven."

"Next time you want to revisit something I told you five years ago, please talk to me first to see if anything's changed before desecrating a grave, okay?" Bev felt a tension headache forming. This kid was a lot of kid. Wonderful, talented, smart, amazing. But a lot.

"Oh. I didn't think of that." Shelby grimaced. "Um. So after I got Xena, I raised everything else in the pet cemetery all at once. They weren't great, though. Not like Xena. Most of them were barely alive and would fall apart in a few hours. But it took so much power, especially after everything else I'd done. Then there was one more thing. I had to raise a group of large animals. It's really hard to find a bunch of big animals all in one place, especially ones that are dead, so we went to a farm."

"And that's why you were at Jer's," Evie said. "Makes sense. He's the only one dumb enough to try to raise cattle in the mountains."

"The cows were an anchor holding a ship in the port," Viv said. Her eyes were unfocused, and she looked a little nauseated. "But he thinks he doesn't need it anymore, so that's why he killed them all. His secret is in the land you can't see." She shook her head and her eyes came back into focus. "Ugh. That was weird and not helpful. Sorry."

"I raised the cows, but I was mad when I did it because I remember how mean he was to Evie, and then to Brandy. And then I was supposed to learn how to do people, but..." she trailed off again.

"But he wanted one more thing?" Evie said gently. "That's often how it works."

"I could've told you that," Lily said scornfully. "We've talked about stuff like that a lot, like how I can't ask for anything in return when I do something with my demon powers, because it's easy to trick people into doing too much when you start small. If you'd just told us what was happening, we could've helped more."

Tears formed in Shelby's eyes, the shine reflecting the soft light of the hall lamp. "It was a little thing. He just wanted me to find something for him. A box of bones. Not even raise something from the dead. Just a box of bones."

"What for? And why couldn't he find them himself if he's so powerful?" Viv asked.

"I don't know." Shelby was on the verge of tears again, and Bev knew she needed a break.

"One more question, sweetheart, and then we're done for today. Did you look at Jer's farm first because you were there for the cows already? Or were you looking there because William thought his box was there?"

Shelby thought it over, tapping her chin with her index while she considered. "I think we went there because he thought Jer had the box, not because of the cows. Actually, it was his idea to go there to find the cows in the first place, but he let me think it was mine all along. I was looking in the dark, trying to find the dark light, the bones without life, and then you came." She shuddered. "He's pissed. I heard him yell when you teleported us or whatever. I don't know. I'm sorry."

"Why don't you go grab another water—or a soda or something— and take Lily and Xena to your room. You need a break, and we want to talk about everything without making you relive it again. If you're down here, we'll be tempted to ask you more questions." Bev stood and stretched. "Anyone need anything from the kitchen?"

"I should probably stay. I was in the mansion, you know, and could probably help." Lily looked around the room with a bright smile she aimed at every adult in turn.

"Nice try, demon child," Evie said. "But no. Upstairs with your friend. She definitely needs you more than we do."

Shelby followed Bev in, grabbed a couple Cokes while staring defiantly at her aunt, then walked back out. Bev leaned against the fridge, resting her forehead against the cool metal, and tried to process everything she'd learned. She heard muffled conversation from the living room that sounded like an argument between Shelby and... Barachiel? She peeked her head out.

"Barachiel, give her the cat," Evie said. "You can always pet her later. Or get your own, although preferably from the pet store."

"Fine," he said stiffly. "I did not enjoy her at all."

Lily followed Shelby upstairs, dragging her feet the whole way and shooting daggers at her mother, who smiled and waggled her fingers at her.

"Fucking fine," Lily mouthed at her mother.

"Well. That's a lot," Evie said. "Are you okay, Bev?"

"I'm more okay than I was last night, but that's not saying much. I don't understand how she got from looking for a box of bones—which I think we can all agree is an inappropriate quest for any grown man, regardless of sorcererousness, to make of a girl—to being trapped in the inter dimensional pocket? What did you call it Barachiel?"

The angel got off the floor and sat gingerly on the loveseat Lily and Shelby had vacated. "I called it a non-reality space because that was the easiest way to explain it to a human. And if you feel better than you did last night, you've missed the entire point of what your child told us. You almost had it. Well, she almost had it." He pointed at Viv. "She is obviously the smartest of the three of you."

"That is not a revelation," Evie said. "Bev and I were solid B students, but Viv is valedictorian of everything she does."

"I don't know what you mean by any of that, but I'm glad you know your intelligence pales in comparison to hers." Barachiel's usually jovial tone had hardened, and Bev had the feeling she was getting a glimpse of the real angel, the one he'd hinted to Shelby existed under his human shell.

"Fine, Evie and I are total idiots. What does that have to do with the situation?" Bev got off the couch and paced in front of the fireplace, trying to put all the pieces together and come up with a solution to the problem she couldn't quite see.

"If he's so all powerful, the 'Great Necromancer,' why does he need a girl to go treasure hunting for him? And why did he think Jer had his box of bones?" Viv asked.

"The answer to the first question is completely obvious. It is hidden from him," Barachiel said, the "duh" implied.

"Duh," Bev said. "That's why he's trying to find it."

"No. It is hidden from him and his senses, but is visible to other necromancers. That suggests it is an object of power that someone more powerful than him didn't want him to find." Barachiel crossed one ankle over a knee and clasped his hands around the other knee. He was a tweed jacket and horn-rimmed glasses away from looking like a pedantic professor giving an even more pedantic lecture.

"I'm going to get some wine. Does anyone else want wine?" Bev marched to the kitchen without waiting for an answer. She unlocked the pantry door and grabbed the first bottle with a screw top she saw. She didn't have the time nor the patience to wrestle with foil and a corkscrew today. She opened the wine, grabbed four glasses by the stems, and returned to the living room.

Evie and Viv took their glasses when Bev handed them out, but Barachiel put his hands behind his back. "I already had lemonade. That is enough vice for one day."

Bev put the full glass on the table next to him. "Suit yourself." She took a long drink of the merlot.

"Did Shelby know where she was? Or did she think the darkness was all mental?" Evie asked.

"It was mental. But the kind of mental that created a pocket dimension that trapped her. It is possible she would've been able to escape had she realized what was going on before too much time had passed, but it's equally possible that she could've been trapped there until such time as the sorcerer decided to release her." Barachiel picked up his wine and took a drink, then grimaced at it and put it back on the table.

"He's gone now, though, right? When we broke Shel out of the alternate reality pocket dimension—and of course the sorcerer is a man, because that was a big damn pocket—it snapped back on him and banished him?" Bev held the bowl of her wine in both hands and tried to remember details about what she'd seen, or not seen, the night before.

"Only for a short time. You are powerful enough to banish him, but do not have the knowledge or training to do so. In some ways, it is good you kept yourself so ignorant. You weren't targeted by the sorcerer. He could've done so much more with you than he did with her. I have no doubt you could've found the box Shelby was unable to locate." He took another sip of wine, grimaced again, and glared at it suspiciously.

"So he'll be back?" Evie asked.

"He'll be back," Viv said. "And as much as it pains me to say, we need to talk to Jer and let him know he's in danger. If William, you know what? That's too formal sounding. If Billy the Creep can't get Shelby to help him find it, he's going to start excreting the bloody part of his self-assumed moniker and start killing people he suspects know something, starting with everyone's least favorite ex, Jeremy Kantek."

"There is not enough wine for this," Bev said. "What do we do? Will he come after her again? How do I protect her?"

"By learning what you need to know," Barachiel said.

"And how am I supposed to do that? Text Mr. the Bloody and ask for a webinar?"

"Your snark is top notch," Evie said. "I get that you're on edge, but you've been on edge recently. Are you okay? I mean, other than the last day or so…"

"Of course she's on edge. She is trying to ignore the voices reaching out to her for help because she's the only person who can hear them and possibly let them find their eternal rest, but she is too selfish to learn what she can and help those who've been woken from their sleep by the bloody evil sorcerer!"

The scent of roses permeated the room, and Bev gagged on the scent.

"Dude!" Shelby yelled down the stairs. "You should see a doctor about that!"

Lily and Shelby laughed uproariously, sending Xena skittering down the stairs and away from the hyenas who couldn't get themselves under control.

"I guess they've made up," Viv said drily, waving her hand in front of her face.

"They'll be okay. Kids are resilient." Evie had her wine glass directly under her nose and was breathing deep.

"None of you are taking this seriously enough. This sorcerer could destroy everything and everyone in this town, could use his power to rip the fabric of reality, and you are...are...making FART jokes." Barachiel stood up, knocked over his wine, and stomped towards the door. His wings unfolded just before he got to the door; he stepped through the closed door and disappeared into the wood.

The three women looked at each other and dissolved into giggles.

"We are no better than the tweens," Viv said.

"We got the angel to say fart," Evie laughed.

"You guys are awful. Terrible influences on the youth of today." Bev grinned at her friends. "We've got this. We're two for two so far, and that's a track record we can get behind. Now I just need to figure out how to stop an evil necromancer, keep my kid safe, and see what I can find out about Jer's box of bones."

# CHAPTER THIRTEEN

Bev sat on the couch, wrapped in an afghan and staring into the flickering fire, a discarded paperback on the armrest. She sipped her cup of herbal tea and tried to convince herself that it was okay to go to sleep. She wasn't afraid—and that's what she was afraid of. It was exhilarating to not constantly hear voices reciting all the ways a person could die, but it'd become such a constant refrain over the last almost two years that the silence echoed and kept her awake.

It was well after midnight. It'd been forty-eight hours since she'd pulled Shelby out of the roomy pocket the necromancer had stashed her in, and they'd spent a blissful twenty-four hours free of zombies and drama. The biggest event of the day had been Xena getting lost in a paper bag.

She knew it was the lull before the storm, and she hoped she'd be enough to stand against it. Shelby had handed over the notebook William had given her, and the two of them spent the day poring over it, looking for clues that would help them keep William from finding the bone box and doing whatever unspecified evil that would doom the town. Barachiel was still off in his angry snit and wasn't answering texts or knocks on the door accompanied by apologies and pleas for help.

"Either this has been the most eventful eighteen months in Eden Valley since the founding, or my history teacher was practicing some real revisionism," Bev said to Xena, who'd abandoned Shelby for Bev's fireplace-warmed lap.

She knew she should go to bed. She had to get up early to take Shelby to school, extract a hundred pinky swears that she wouldn't sneak off at lunch, then meet her friends for brunch and planning.

"We just do so much planning. And it's worked, it's always worked, but I feel like we're never ahead of the game." Bev scratched Xena on the back of her head just behind her ears.

"Mrow," Xena said, before curling into a vibrating ball of purrs.

"I'm not sure your advice is solid, but at least you're a better listener than my previous late-night confidante, peppermint tea. I did get a mug with a face on it to see if it helped, but it's a terrible conversationalist. Between you and me, I am lonely. I want someone besides a cup and a cat to talk to at night. It's not always about the end of the world and zombies and monsters. Sometimes it's just about my crappy boss and my goals and hopes and dreams. Frustration with parenting such a great child who is struggling so hard." Bev sighed. Xena wiggled her head under Bev's hand until she resumed the head scritches.

Bev finished her tea, turned off the fireplace, and made sure all the doors and windows were locked before heading upstairs to bed. She deposited Xena on Shelby's bed and tucked herself in with the book she hadn't read earlier. Her eyes dragged down and sprung back open several times before she gave up and turned off the light.

"Heeeeeellllp me. Hellppp. Vengeance!"

Bev's eyes sprang open. She was covered in sweat and goosebumps. It'd been a blessed three nights without nightmares, but apparently, they were back. She counted backwards in her head until she could control her breathing, then went into the breathing exercise that pulled her back from the edge of a panic attack. When she exhaled, the fog from her breath hung in the air above her.

"What?" she sat up in bed, swung her feet over the edge and into her slippers. She must've turned the heat down too low, or they were having a sudden cold snap or...

Or the room was filling with ghosts. They weren't the faint specters she'd always imagined ghosts to be. No women in white drifting tragically through the halls. No Caspers in formal bed linen. Each ghost was solidly translucent, and every single one bore the decay of the graves where they'd spent the time after their death. The causes of death on some were readily apparent. Blood and gore, still translucent and nearly colorless, marked accident victims. There were children and teenagers, adults in all stages of life. The one thing every one of them had in common was the refrain they repeated in a hoarse whisper.

"Help me. Help. Vengeance."

She thought she'd been prepared for this. She knew the dead had been talking to her. She'd spent hours thinking about what they wanted, how she could help them, and how to ask them for help, but now she didn't know if they were looking for her help or being sent by the sorcerer to seek vengeance on her for some unknown reason and all her good intentions had flown out the window and frozen. Horror curdled in her stomach as a dozen hands reached out towards her.

"Help me. Help. Vengeance." The sound was metal scraping across ice.

Bev tucked her feet back into bed, every fear of a monster under her bed forcing its way to the forefront of her memories. Maybe if it was daylight, or if she hadn't been woken from sleep, or the last three days hadn't happened, she could deal with this. But the dead were advancing, and they wanted something she didn't know how to give them.

"Help me. Help. Vengeance."

Horror curdled her stomach. Her breaths moved faster, puffs of suspended ice leaving her body quicker and quicker.

"Help me. Help. Vengeance."

Bev opened her mouth and screamed, then covered her head with her arms and waited for them to take her. Waited to feel their hands brush against her face, her hair.

"Help me."

The voice was mere inches from her ear, and she almost swore she could smell the musty rot of autumn leaves in a graveyard.

"Help."

Her teeth chattered in fear and with the cold that permeated every cell of her being.

"Vengeance." The sound was next to her skin, but she couldn't feel the breath of the one who spoke.

She drew her knees to her chest and hoped that with her last breath, she'd be able to protect Shelby from the same fate.

A green light flashed in her room bright enough to create dancing orbs on the back of her eyelids. After a minute, she realized the voices were gone, and she was no longer shivering.

She cracked open one eye and looked around. The lights were still off, and whatever had made the green light was dim again. She opened the other eye. There was a figure at the end of her bed, glowing faintly and vibrating with intensity. She shrank back against her headboard, knowing there was nowhere to hide.

"Are you okay? Was I too late?" Barachiel's voice sounded like it was traveling miles through the depths of the sea.

Bev sucked in air and tried to slow her pulse.

"Bev. Beverly. Talk to me. Are you okay?" Barachiel sounded almost panicked, something she'd never heard from him before.

She opened her mouth, intending to reassure him, but instead she burst into tears.

BEV WAS ONCE AGAIN on the couch, wrapped in an afghan and sipping tea—chamomile this time. After a brief flurry of Twitter activity, Barachiel had declared it the best tea to recover from being ghosted if she didn't want a pint of Ben and Jerry's. Bev wasn't entirely sure he knew what being ghosted meant in the vernacular, but she was going to let it go.

Shelby was snuggled up under the blanket with her head in Bev's lap. She'd velcroed herself to Bev's side as soon as they'd come downstairs and refused every suggestion she return to bed. She was mostly asleep now, and the weight of her twelve-year-old body threatened to put Bev's left leg to sleep as well.

Barachiel sat across from her, staring unblinkingly while she sipped her tea.

"Stop looking at me," Bev whispered. "You're giving me the creeps."

"After what happened in your room, I am what gives you the creeps?" He sounded almost indignant.

"Thank you," she said for the thousandth time. "I panicked."

"Of course you did."

Bev braced herself for the inevitable scathing critique.

"Anyone would've done the same. There were at least fifty dead in your room advancing on you with a single purpose in their mind." He looked at the end table next to the loveseat he was on. "Is the wine all gone?"

"That was two nights ago, so yeah. I didn't leave it out. Fruit flies do not need to be getting drunk on my dime." Bev shifted in preparation to move Shelby off her leg so she could get Barachiel wine.

"What are you doing? Do not wake the child." He sat straight up and spread his arms like he was about to run a zone defense maneuver to keep her from going for the wine.

"I was gonna get you some wine. Besides, my leg is falling asleep, so I need to move, anyway. Shel can have the couch." Bev eased as far as she could to the edge of the sofa, supported Shelby's head with one hand, and scooted out from under her. "Pillow," she ordered.

Barachiel snapped to attention and handed her one of the several decorative pillows that were scattered about the room. Bev slipped it under Shelby's head, slowly released her hold, and stood. She froze and stared down at her niece, but when Shelby did nothing more than mutter something about algebra and roll over, Bev breathed a sigh of relief and headed into the kitchen.

"You know, wine at three in the morning is a terrible, terrible idea," she said, grabbing a bottle of port and a corkscrew. She poured the wine into two small glasses and handed one to Barachiel before snagging the blanket from the back of the chair and wrapping it around herself.

He sniffed the wine. "This glass is smaller than the other. Is it because of the hour?"

"No, it's a different kind of wine and needs a smaller glass. Port has more alcohol, and I love it as a nightcap or an after-dinner drink." She raised her glass. "Salud."

Barachiel screwed up his face and gingerly brought the glass to his lips. He took the smallest possible drink, then a larger one. A grin started to spread across his face.

"Do you like it?" Bev asked.

In response, Barachiel drained his glass. "May I have more?"

"Um. Of course, but…"

Barachiel was on his feet and in the kitchen faster than she could follow. He returned with a burgundy glass filled to the brim with port.

"Oh wow, Barachiel. I don't think it's a good idea to drink that much port." Bev was equal parts horrified and curious.

"It's okay. I've been intoxicated by alcohol before. My friend Andy gave me too much Scotch one time to learn my secrets. I can burn it off if I want to." He chugged his port like water on a hot day. "I like this wine."

"Okay. Well. Thank you for saving me. If you'd like to crash in the guest room, you are welcome to. You certainly shouldn't go home in this state." Bev took another drink of her port and watched as Barachiel went to the kitchen and came back with the bottle, pouring the rest into his glass.

"I'll be fine. I don't feel at all like I did when Andras intoxified me. Intoximacated. Intoxined? You know what I mean." He threw back the rest of the port. In less than fifteen minutes, he'd consumed almost an entire bottle.

"Are you going to be okay? Do I need to call an ambulance or something?" Bev let the blanket pool around her feet and stood up to search for her cell phone.

"Nahhh. I'm gonna be okay. Port is warm. You should have port, then you'll be warm again." He grinned at her. His eyelids were starting to droop. If an angel who never drinks consumes a million servings of liquor on a stomach that's been empty for millennia, what happens?

The doorbell rang.

"Don't answer it. Might be the necromancer the great." Barachiel was slurring his words so badly he was almost impossible to understand.

"Would he ring the doorbell?" Bev asked. "It's not like he's a vampire and needs an invitation, right?"

"Maybe he is polite? It's good to ring doorbells unless someone is screaming." His eyes drifted shut, and he let out a gentle snore.

"Some rescue," Bev muttered. "Sure, he saved me from the ghost army, but then he gets drunk and passes out while telling me an evil necromancer might be ringing my doorbell."

She walked to the door and peered through the window, careful not to twitch the curtain. A man stood on the other side with a suitcase and an extremely irritated look on his face. He had a phone out and was thumb typing. Bev tilted her head. He looked almost familiar. Dread pitted in her stomach. Was it the necromancer? Was looking vaguely familiar how he got people to trust him?

The buzz of an incoming text pulled her attention back to the center of the room. A phone had fallen out of Barachiel's pocket and was buzzing on the ground.

Bev only hesitated a second before picking it up and looking at the incoming texts that were saved as 'bartender.' He might have a cell phone and a twitter handle, but he did not have any security on his phone.

*Hey. Angel. I came all this way only to be abandoned in the dark with only a handwritten address and now you won't even answer your texts?*

*Barachiel. Dude. Let me in. The whole place is locked up, and it smells like death.*

*If you don't open this door in one minute, I am hopping back into my car and driving back to Oracle Bay. I don't care what you or Ceri or any of the others say. I can't help anyone if I have to sleep in my car.*

His vague familiarity and mention of his hometown connected the dots for Bev. She dropped Barachiel's phone and pulled open the door. He stared at her, phone in hand mid-text. "Beverly?"

"Hi Russell. Welcome back to Eden Valley."

RUSSELL SAT in the chair Bev had pulled into the living room and regarded the passed out angel on the loveseat. "He's only been here for thirty minutes tops—I don't know how long it would've taken him to get here from where he abandoned me on the highway, but it took me thirty minutes to drive the rest of the way alone. What happened?"

Bev waved the empty bottle of port at him. "This bottle happened. He drank it."

"All of it?"

"All but the one small port glass I poured myself. He finished it off in ten minutes flat, told me he could handle his liquor because some guy named Andras once tried to get him drunk, then passed out well before he could tell me who was at the door. He did mention it might be an evil necromancer who was coming to call in the middle of the night. I hope you're not him."

"I'd like to believe I'm not evil. I helped solve a murder and every-thing last winter." He looked at Barachiel. "Should I wake him up and tell him to sober up? This is embarrassing."

"You're not evil, but you are a necromancer?"

"Yeah. Aren't we all? Hill family curse, I guess. Have you ever met great, great, great Aunt Sybil?" Russell stood and bent over Barachiel, shaking him gently.

"I didn't know we had a curse or an Aunt Sybil, great or not," Bev said.

Russell shook the angel harder. "He is really gone. Usually, you can wake an angel quickly, even when they're drunk."

"A bottle of port. Ten minutes. Tell me more about our family curse."

Russell glanced over at her. "You obviously know. Necromancy. Or mediumship if the power isn't all there. We talk to the dead."

"It's more than just talking, though. That sounds like seance territory. Shelby raised the dead." Bev took a deep breath every time she had to remember the events of the last few days.

"She yours?"

"My niece. Do you remember Holly? Shelby is her kid." Necromancy and family reunions. Neat. She shook herself. She always got a little hysterical when she was exhausted.

"Oh yeah? What's she doing here? Is Holly here? I don't remember her very well. She didn't ping my senses, you know?" He shook Barachiel again, then grimaced. "Can I get a glass of water?"

"Help yourself. Find whatever you need."

Russell returned moments later with a full glass of water. He slowly and deliberately poured it directly onto Barachiel's face.

Bev gasped, and seconds later, the angel sat up, gasping for air and flailing wildly.

"Sober up, Barachiel. We don't have time for this," Russell said.

"Holly died ten years ago. And I think you may have ruined my upholstery." Bev pushed back the pang that always accompanied the memory of her sister's death and fixated on the thing that was more immediately distressing.

"I'm sorry. About Holly, that is. Barachiel will fix the upholstery when he's back to his normal pompously weird self." Russell grinned tightly at her, nerves and awkwardness apparent on his face.

"Why are you here, Russell?" Bev finished her port and watched the angel glare glassily at Russell.

"He brought me. Said you needed help. And clearly you do, although I'm not sure if it's with your ghost problem or your angel problem." Russell sat back in his chair.

"I am not a problem," Barachiel shouted.

Shelby turned over and opened her eyes.

"Sh, baby, it's okay. Let me help you upstairs to your room." Bev helped Shelby stand and led her to the stairs. "Get it together by the time I get back down here, or so help me, your angel ass will be out on the sidewalk."

WHEN BEV RETURNED to the living room, Barachiel was sitting stiffly on the loveseat and there was no sign of the port, water stains on the upholstery, or intoxication.

Russell was on the chair looking a lot more comfortable than Barachiel and drinking a beer. "Hope you don't mind that I helped myself to a glass. It was a long drive, and I am wiped out."

"Of course not. But where did you find the beer?" Bev grabbed the blanket she'd used to cover Shelby and wrapped it around herself before settling back into the couch.

"Brought my own! Or rather, I brought a selection of beer to give to 'that hot demon who knows good beer when she drinks it.' Andy, the owner of the Pour House in Oracle Bay, met her last summer and was impressed with her discerning taste." He tilted his glass and looked at the light shining through the amber liquid.

"It is so very late. Do we need to talk about everything right now? Or can it wait until slightly later in the morning?" Bev asked. Her eyelids felt like sandpaper every time she blinked, and she was having trouble focusing on the conversation.

Russell glanced at Barachiel, who hadn't moved or said anything since Bev had come back downstairs. "Unless the angel thinks we have to get into right now, I think sleep is the better option. It's going to be hard to teach you anything if you're too tired to channel your power."

Barachiel maintained his stony silence.

"Great. I am exhausted, and I'm sure you are, too. The guest room is already made up. It's down that hallway, first door on the right. The bathroom is the next doorway. Help yourself to whatever you need. Breakfast will be served at seven; after that, you're on your own." Bev glanced at Barachiel, but he didn't even acknowledge her presence.

"Barachiel, if you're going to stay, you can have the couch since you don't sleep. There are blankets in the linen closet, and the switch for the fireplace is to the right of the mantle. Remotes are in the door of the table next to you if you want to watch something, just keep the volume low because Russell will be sleeping on the other side of the wall."

Still nothing.

Bev shrugged. "If there's nothing more, I need to know about ghost repellant, then…"

"We've got this," Russell promised. "Go to sleep."

"Okay. See you in the morning." She trudged upstairs, toed off her slippers, and crawled into bed. Maybe it was silly to feel this much more secure with a sulky angel and the cousin she hadn't seen in thirty years downstairs, but she felt safe. She checked the alarm—she had two hours until morning—and closed her eyes.

# CHAPTER FOURTEEN

"Coffee," Russell said as he shambled into the kitchen.

"I know we've had a zombie problem around Eden Valley, but I didn't expect to have one in my kitchen looking for caffeine," Bev said.

"You're hilarious." Russell took a deep breath. "And I'm rude. I would love coffee if you have some, or directions to a coffee shop."

"I just brewed a fresh pot. Do you take cream or sugar?" Bev grabbed one of the big mugs down from the cabinet and filled it with Turkish roast.

"Yes, please. Both if it's real sugar and real cream." Russell rubbed his eyes and perched on one of the stools at the kitchen island.

Bev slid the cup in front of him and grabbed the cream and sugar. "Do you want some food? I can make eggs and toast in a jiffy, or French toast?"

Russell exhaled with a hum of satisfaction. "This coffee is pretty good. Thank you. Eggs and toast sound great. Over easy?"

"Coming right up. If you want juice, it's in the fridge. When you're sufficiently caffeinated, I'd like to talk about what's going on and why you're here." Bev cracked the eggs into a ramekin, then slowly poured them into the hot pan and put the bread in the toaster.

"Yeah. Sure. You are awfully chipper for someone who had their sleep interrupted by an invasion of the dead, then had to watch an angel get drunk before welcoming a virtual stranger into your home before heading off to bed for... How many hours of sleep did you get?" Russell yawned. "I cannot wake up this morning."

"I got about three hours of sleep and two after, so I'm doing alright. Not great, but I'm a morning person and I had an entire pot of coffee before you got up." Bev flipped the eggs, grabbed a plate, then slid the eggs out of the pan onto the plate. The bread popped out of the toaster. Bev added the toast to the plate, grabbed a knife and fork, and handed it over to Russell. "Butter's right next to you. Do you want jam? I have homemade blueberry, raspberry, and strawberry rhubarb. There's also some marmalade, but I didn't make that."

"Strawberry rhubarb, please. That sounds amazing."

Bev cleaned up the kitchen to avoid watching Russell eat and to keep herself from asking the question at the forefront of her mind. It didn't take long to wash the few dishes she'd used that morning, so she puttered around pushing chairs in, wiping a dusting cloth over the already clean surfaces in the dining room, and coaxing Xena out of her hiding place behind the china cabinet.

"You have a cat? I didn't smell it when I came in." Russell did a double take when he saw Xena. "Where'd you get her?"

"She's not quite dead. At least not anymore. Shelby ahhh... obtained her last weekend when she made a stop in the pet cemetery with William the Necromancer."

"Eden Valley has a pet cemetery? Like in the book? I didn't know that was a real thing," Russell said.

"Is it weird? I didn't know pet cemeteries were weird. Maybe I read the book too many times in my formative years." Bev flipped the kitten onto her back and cradled her in her arms while scratching her under her chin. "She's quite a bit more alive than anything else I've seen walking around after being woken from their dirt naps."

"She's in remarkably good shape for an undead," Russell confirmed. "And I'm not asking any more questions about your dead pets. How long was this cat dead?"

"Almost thirty-five years." Bev set the cat back down, and Xena made a beeline for the china cabinet, squeezing into the small gap between the cabinet and the wall.

"Impressive work, especially for a kid. You know this cat isn't going to live long, though, right?" Russell mopped the last of his egg off the plate with this toast, then carried his dishes to the sink and rinsed them off before putting them in the dishwasher.

"Really? I was hoping we'd have a few years at least. Shelby is going to be devastated." She hadn't known how much Shelby wanted a pet—she hadn't brought it up in five years at least—but now that Xena lived with them, she wanted her to stay... And not because the cat was cute beyond words. It was one hundred percent for Shelby's benefit.

"If that's the worst thing that comes out of all this, count yourselves lucky. Now, let's sit down and figure out how I can help you get rid of your necromancer problem." Russell poured himself another cup of coffee from the carafe while Bev made a cup of tea.

"Why don't we sit in the living room. It's the most comfortable, and I have a feeling this isn't going to be a quick discussion." Bev turned on the fireplace and curled up on the couch in her favorite spot. "Should Shelby be here for any of this? I can pull her out of school early."

"How old is she? Not that it matters," he interrupted himself. "She clearly has the power, judging by this cat. Hmmm. Actually, I'd like to talk to you first before we bring Shelby into it."

Bev settled herself in and cupped the hot mug between her hands, inhaling the chai aroma and willing it to melt the tension from her body. "I'm ready."

"Where's your angel?" Russell asked. "I just realized he isn't here."

"I don't know. He was gone when I got up." The question she'd been mulling all morning now didn't feel awkward to ask. "Was he still here when you went to bed? Did he ever say anything?"

"Once you went to bed, he filled me in on what'd happened last night before he came back so you wouldn't have to rehash the whole thing again if you didn't want to. He said he'd keep watch on the house and wake me if there was an encore performance." Russell shrugged. "He'll be back soon, probably just needed to stop at home to polish his halo or whatever morning routine the messengers of god perform."

The disappointment Bev'd felt at not seeing Barachiel that morning was somewhat assuaged by the fact that he'd stayed the night to keep watch over her.

"What do you know about necromancy in general?" Russell asked. "What's your background?"

"I didn't know it was a real thing until about three months ago. I'd spent the previous year thinking I was going crazy and taking Shelby along with me." Bev shuddered. The face of the doctor who'd convinced her that she and Shel were both destined for the nuthouse rose unbidden in her mind. He'd left town soon after Bev had switched doctors in July.

"Why only a year? What did you think before when you could hear the dead talking to you?" Russell leaned forward and propped his elbows on his thighs.

"I didn't think anything. I mean, I didn't hear anything out of the ordinary. It didn't start until April of last year. Is that weird?" Bev wasn't sure why she was so concerned with whether or not her ability to hear the dead talking to her was out of the ordinary.

"It is. Most people I know with supernatural abilities have them manifest when they're children, typically around the time they hit puberty. There are only a couple people whose powers, for lack of a better word, are triggered by a location or an event. What was your trigger?" Russell asked.

Bev chewed on the inside of her lower lip, trying to figure out how much to tell him. She didn't want to leave anything out that might help, but she didn't want to tell Evie's story without permission. "Um, there was an incident with a hell mouth and a car accident. My friend Viv and I were driving and got sucked into a sinkhole that held the door to hell. We didn't go through the door, at least not that day, but we were both branded."

"Branded? Can I see?" Russell set his cup down and stood.

"As long as you don't touch. It's on my left shoulder. Just give me a minute to climb out of my blanket fort and adjust my shirt so I don't flash all of my assets at you." Bev untangled herself and stood, back to Russell, and pulled the back of her light pink sweater up and over her head. "Can you see it okay?"

"Yeah, I can. This is…weird. I've never quite seen anything like this before. Do you mind if I take a picture? That way you can put your shirt down and get cozy again, which will probably be more comfortable for both of us."

"Yeah, go ahead. Just don't Instagram it." Bev shivered. The fireplace might be on, but the heat was off. She hadn't readjusted the thermostat yet to take into account that she wasn't at work all day.

"Done." Russell stepped back, giving Bev space to readjust her clothing.

Bev nestled back into her pile of super-soft heather grey blankets.

"Do you know what this symbol means?" Russell asked, zooming in on the picture with his thumb and forefinger.

"It's the symbol representing the demons of death, rebirth, and treasure. That last one feels like a bit of a stretch but turns out the 'source material' of Germans obsessed with the occult didn't lump related abilities together when passing them out to the demons. Also, they either really admired the demons or really hated liberal arts." Bev arched her back. Every time she thought about the brand, her skin itched and burned.

"I've never seen anything quite like it, but I haven't made a study of demons, to be sure. Is Shelby marked as well?"

"Not that I know of. She's at an age where she's pretty body-shy, which honestly is a refreshing change from when she used to hide around corners and jump out at me in nothing but her skin, wiggle around, then run away laughing hysterically. But I'd like to believe that if she'd found herself in possession of some new body modification, she would've let me know." Bev tilted her head and considered. "She was on the cusp of puberty when I first noticed she was talking about seeing ghosts. But if puberty is stalled, at least for now, then… I don't know."

"Once triggered, it won't disappear, even if puberty is suppressed, just like your gifts won't go away if you have your brand removed and relocate to a sleepy town in Kansas." Russell shoved his phone back in his pocket. "Okay, crash course on necromancy and all things related to the walking, talking dead. As you probably know, necromancy is the art of raising the dead. One might argue, if one was trying to offend a religious majority, that Jesus is both a necromancer and a zombie."

"Should I be taking notes?" Bev grabbed a notebook and pen from the drawer in the end table nearest her.

"There's not going to be a quiz at the end. It's going to be more of a practical exam. Take all the notes you want." He steepled his fingers. "If you're a necromancer, it's likely there are more in the family tree who don't understand what's happening and think they've gone mad. If they do know what's going on, they don't talk about it in case other people think they've gone mad. Your father and my mother are cousins so we can make that family connection."

"Did your mother see dead people?" Bev asked. "I don't think I've ever met her."

"She died when I was ten or so, and she was the reason I lived with you guys that one year. I was passed from relative to relative until I was old enough to emancipate myself and strike out on my own. Her death was what triggered my abilities." He shifted uncomfortably in his chair and looked down at the floor. "She was the first person I heard speak to me. And she was the first person I ever tried to resurrect."

"I must have known that—the part about your mother having died, not the necromancy part—when you came to live with us, but I've forgotten. I'm sorry if I opened old wounds." Bev looked up and grimaced sympathetically at Russell.

"It's okay. I miss her every day, but it's been thirty-five years. What about your dad?" Russell asked.

"If he did, he never mentioned it. I don't know where he is, or even if he's still alive. I haven't seen him in over twenty years. He wasn't with mom and Holly when they died, and he didn't show up for their funerals. He's never met his granddaughter." Bitterness crept into her voice. She tried really hard to give her father the benefit of the doubt, but she was at the point where it'd be better if he was dead rather than continuing to not show up for anything.

"The Woods are a flaky bunch, aren't they? My dad was pretty solid when I was young, but my mom's death devastated him. He knew enough to know he couldn't be an effective parent, but not enough to figure out what to do with me. We reconnected when I was twenty. He was remarried, had a couple kids, and was happy. It was bittersweet for me to see how well he took care of his new family when he couldn't be there for mine, but I think he really did do his best. He died about five years ago." Russell laughed. "Look at us, catching up on the family history with the most depressing news we can come up with. Let's get back to something more cheerful."

"Like necromancy?" Bev asked drily.

"Exactly. Okay. There are two basic ways you can go as a necromancer, although of course there's an entire spectrum between them. You're either on the path of goodness and light or evil and the dark. If you choose the light path, you're typically a medium or something like that. You can communicate with the dead—most of us use a focus so we're not broadcasting to everyone—to get information or, in some cases, tap into their knowledge to predict the future, although it's easier to find out about the past. You can raise ghosts for short periods of time. It's easier soon after they die before their spirits have been away from their bodies for too long. You can help the restless dead move on to the next life. And you help them and the living find closure. I like to believe I'm closer to that end of the spectrum." Russell paused and took a deep breath. Before he could continue with what Bev assumed was the dark side, but without the promised cookies, the doorbell rang.

Bev hopped up, tripped in her tangle of blankets, and righted herself without falling or knocking anything down. She proceeded more sedately to the door, peeked out through the window, then unlocked it and pulled it open. "Barachiel."

"Beverly," he responded stiffly. "May I come in?"

Bev stood back to let him in. He looked exactly the same, if more polished, but his personality had changed so much since just a couple weeks ago when he was buying banana slicers and making her laugh with the sheer ridiculousness of his adjustment to humanity. There was so much the sorcerer needed to answer for. "Only if you promise not to drain an entire bottle of wine."

"That was an aberration. My apologies for my behavior." He strode to the living room and sat on the end of the couch without blankets piled on it.

"I guess if that's where you want to sit, but I am sitting on the other side. Fair warning to keep to your side." Bev picked up the blankets and carefully slid back into her corner of the couch, then arranged the blankets over herself partially as a cozy warming nest, and partially as armor to ensure no part of her touched any part of the angel.

"I was just getting to the darker side of necromancy. Feel free to jump in if you think I've missed anything."

"Of course. I would never allow you to impart incorrect or incomplete knowledge." Barachiel folded his hands in his lap and kept his back ramrod stiff.

"I don't know what's wrong with you. You're not usually this uptight. I've seen you let loose and have fun." Russell paused, but there was no response. "Fine. Let's get on with it. The darker path involves, as I'm sure you've guessed, using the powers for not good. These are the type of people who spend a lot of time raising what we'd call zombies. There are very few reasons to disturb the rest of the long-departed, and on the few occasions I've done it, it's to solve a mystery, close a cold case, something like that. It's usually quick, and there's virtually no shambling or appetite for brains."

"What does one do with a bunch of zombies? Other than raise a few cows and have them moo at a farmer." It wasn't quite funny yet, but it would be soon. Nope, she was wrong. It was funny now.

"That's not the typical zombie apocalypse people make moooovies about, is it?" Russell asked with a grin.

Bev groaned. "Wow. That was... Actually, no words."

"I can't help it. When this is all over, you'll have to come to Oracle Bay, then you'll see that my puns are merely amateur level."

"Isn't levity inappropriate at a time like this?" Barachiel asked. "Why do you insist on making jokes when you should be making plans?"

"If I don't make it funny, I can't get through it. Humor is a time-honored coping mechanism for humans," Bev said. "We know things are scary and dark, but making jokes about it doesn't mean we're dismissing that. It just means we're shining a light on it and laughing to squash the fear down far enough to function. When this is over, come find me. I'll be on the back porch at night after Shelby's asleep, curled in a ball sobbing my eyes out because all the fear I pushed away will rebound and sock me in the chest."

Barachiel turned his attention to Russell. "Is this true? Are you taking this seriously?"

"Of course we are. I'm here, aren't I? But if I laid everything out on the line in one fell swoop, it'd be too much. Bev doesn't have the advantages I did. She's only had this power for a year and a half, and most of that time believed she was mentally ill. I've been practicing, mostly in secret, for the last thirty years. I've met others like me, and I live in a town with more psychics per capita than anywhere else in the world. Even when I was hiding who I was, I knew it was all real. Give her a minute, Barachiel." Russell crossed his arms and glared at the angel.

Bev regarded them. Russell obviously knew Barachiel a hell of a lot better than she did and had no problem telling him where to go. Her stomach growled, and she looked at the clock. It was already two.

"I need lunch. I've been up since six and didn't get much sleep before that. I've hit my limit on caffeine, especially without something more substantial than dry toast seven hours ago." Bev knew she was hitting the edge of sleepy cranky and about to tip into full-on hangry territory.

"We can talk while you are cooking," Barachiel said.

Russell let out a long, low whistle. "You need to go ask twitter what they think of that suggestion. While you're doing that, I'll go grab my shoes and coat. Is there a diner or something nearby? I'm buying."

BEV STIRRED the dregs of her strawberry milkshake and watched Shelby and Russell talk animatedly about their Halloween plans. Milkshake Mondays were a tradition Bev and Shelby had decided to create when Bev found herself suddenly free in the early afternoons, and this was their inaugural time. Bev had imagined it'd be more bonding and less apocalyptic.

"I wonder what'd it be like to get through an entire year without worrying about the end of the world," Bev said. "Didn't we just do this?"

"It's the fault of the demons," Barachiel asserted. He'd declined all offers of beverages, ice cream, pie, and cake, saying he no longer participated in human offerings.

"Kevin isn't the fault of the demons, is he?" Shelby asked. "He was a primordial being. You could just as well say this is the fault of the angels."

Lily and Kevin clattered into the diner and pulled chairs up to the six top where they were sitting.

"Mom and Elle are right behind us," Lily said. "And Alex, of course. But she doesn't need a chair."

"What about Viv and Sam?" Bev asked. "Did you see them?"

"No, but that doesn't mean anything," Kevin said. He was a lot quieter than he'd been before... It seemed trite to say that separating the lake monster from the child had changed him, but he was more serious, less inclined to laugh—at least around adults. Of course, it might also be adolescence taking hold. "They might be smooching in a dark alley or something."

"I never smooch in dark alleys." Viv took one of the empty chairs and scooted close to Bev, who was now trapped between Barachiel and her best friend. "All my alley smooching is done directly under streetlights for all to see."

Lily snorted, and even Kevin cracked a grin.

"I heard there were milkshakes happening. Can I get in on some of that ice cream magic?" Sam slid into the chair next to Shelby, then tipped her head and looked behind Shelby at Russell. "You're new. What's your name?" She clapped a hand over her face and looked across the table at Bev. "He's new, right? I didn't just forget about him like that other guy." She snapped her fingers a couple times.

"Colin," Bev supplied. "The manager of the Silver Dollar where you spend every Friday night trying to con tourists out of their pool money."

"Right. He has such a forgettable face. But this isn't Colin, is it?" Sam peered at Russell as if trying to place him.

"I'm not Colin, and I would like to believe my face isn't completely forgettable. My name is Russell Black. I'm Bev's cousin. You must be Sam. I brought a gift for you." Russell directed his smile at the gorgeous demon whose mahogany skin was set off by a canary yellow tank top under a black leather jacket that looked like it was molded to her skin.

"A present? For me! I like you already. Gimme!" She held out her hands and wiggled her fingers.

"It's at Bev's. It was too big to bring with me, and I didn't know I'd be seeing you."

The light in Sam's eyes glowed yellow and an avaricious expression spread over her face. "I like big presents from strange men. You are already my favorite man in Eden Valley. Please tell me you're going to stay and put the angel out of business."

"He is not staying, and I do not have a business," Barachiel snarled. The faint smell of roses in the rain hit Bev's nose.

Bev leaned towards Barachiel and whispered as quietly as she could without being in touching distance. "Barachiel, I know you're upset—but if you don't want to hear a bunch of middle school fart jokes for the rest of the afternoon, I suggest you get ahold of yourself. No one is interested in stopping to smell the roses right now."

He took a deep breath, released it, and closed his eyes. "Thank you.

I don't know why I am so angry lately. I have never had trouble controlling my anger before."

"Maybe it's the hellmouth, or the disappearing alternate plane island, or the very slow zombie apocalypse. Or maybe it's just extended time in Eden Valley." What had started as a joke had quickly devolved into painful truth. Bev smiled at Barachiel and tried to blink back the tears she knew were brightening her eyes. "Whatever it is, Angel, I feel it too."

Evie and Elle walked through the door, eyed the chaos at the table. Eight chairs, three preteens—including a baby necromancer and a half-demon—an angel, a demon, two necromancers, and a psychic were taking up so much space there wasn't room for a guardian angel, a genie-in-training, and her demon spawn baby.

"Why don't we get our milkshakes to go and head out to the house," Evie suggested. "It'll be easier to talk, less crowded, and about a hundred times less annoying for the servers here."

Bev caught the look of relief on Tami's face as she came to take orders from the newcomers.

Elle clapped her hands to get everyone's attention. "I will pay for everyone's orders, but anyone who has already had their milkshakes needs to get out and make some room."

"That means us," Bev said, looking at Shelby. "Scoot your boot outside. We can walk to the house, drop off your backpack, and drive out to Evie's."

"I'll walk with you. I want to make sure I grab Sam's present!" Russell winked at the demon who rewarded him with a smile hot enough to melt the undergarments off any adult who was prone to such melting.

Bev herded Shelby out the door, Russell close behind them.

"I brought you a present, too," he said to Shel. "I don't know how we're related exactly, just that there are a lot of ordinal cousins in various states of removal.

"Can I call you Uncle?" Shelby asked a little hesitantly.

"That sounds great. I've never been anyone's uncle before. We'll probably need a secret handshake or something." Russell winked conspiratorially at her.

"Ugh. You've been my uncle for like a minute, and you're already being weird." Shelby sounded torn between amusement and embarrassment.

"Pretty sure that's in the job description. Bad puns and weird suggestions. You'll like it. Or at least get used to it."

Bev let them walk on ahead. Shelby was trying to figure out what he'd brought her, and her guesses were getting more and more outrageous.

"They get along well. That's good." Barachiel said.

Bev jumped. "You startled me. I didn't think you were walking out with us."

"It was either leave or have Aurielle force a milkshake on me." He walked stiffly next to her, eyes straight ahead.

"Are you okay? I mean that sincerely. When you first got here, you were a lot more…relaxed, I guess. Maybe you were still staying away from the pleasures of the flesh—except Twitter—but you laughed and had fun. You made jokes, or at least did your best to understand them." Bev looked up at the angel who'd been by her side almost constantly for the last few days. He was close, only a few inches away, but Bev didn't feel like moving.

"I… I don't know. This was supposed to be easy. Stay here. Watch Aurielle to make sure she is still committed to her mission. Don't get involved. Leave." He shook his head slowly. "I don't know where everything started to go wrong, and now it is wrong, and I don't know how to fix it. This wasn't supposed to happen."

"None of this was, but maybe this is the price Eden Valley exacts from us. I thought it was the lake holding us here, but now I think it's something more. Dark things happen here, and I don't understand why." The space between them was hot, and Bev wanted to lean into it. "I don't understand anything that's happening right now. It's all so new."

# CHAPTER FIFTEEN

"We're almost too many people for this porch," Viv said as she set up some folding chairs. Bev followed behind her, laying a porch blanket on each one.

"Do you have room for one more?" Luc asked. He had two more folding chairs. "Sorry they're covered in cobwebs. They were in the crawlspace I didn't even know we had until ten minutes ago."

"I'll take them," Barachiel said, sounding resigned. He grabbed the chairs from Luc and shook them out and set them on the porch. When he let go of them, they were spotless.

"If you and Elle ever run out of your mystery money, you could make a fortune cleaning houses," Viv said. "There's got to be a great business name there, right?"

"I can get the Oracle Bay crew on it immediately, if not sooner," Russell volunteered.

"More important than angel names. Where's my present, necromancer?" Sam demanded as she strode across the porch. She flashed a grin at her big brother, who rolled his eyes at her, then dropped into one of the chairs Barachiel had just cleaned.

Russell grabbed a large box from around the corner and handed it to Sam. She tore off the box tops and looked inside. There was a moment of hesitation, then a smile of pure pleasure erupted. "This is amazing! Look, Viv! It's the demon beer!"

"Andras is not a demon," Barachiel said. He walked as far away from Sam as he could and sat in the Adirondack chair next to Bev.

Sam waved dismissively. "Close enough. He was a literal Grand Marquis under grandfather's reign. Sure, things didn't go so well for him once things got divided up between the Kings and he ended up with Sathanus, but he knows how to brew a little hellfire into his porter." She opened one of the cans and took a long drink. "This is so good. Thank you, necromancer."

"I'd love to take the credit, but it was all Andy's idea. I am merely the messenger." Russell bowed dramatically, eliciting a giggle from the girls who'd just joined them on the porch.

"It's kinda cool always getting to be a part of the grown-up discussions now," Lily said. "We should be invited to brunch next time, too. We bring valuable insights into the conversation."

"We don't want to go to brunch," Shelby said. "I bet they mostly talk about kissing and jobs and other boring stuff."

"Kissing isn't boring," Lily protested. "I bet it's fun. Otherwise, why would so many people do it?"

"Okay," Luc interrupted. "As much as I'd like to see where Lily goes with this… Actually, I am not ready to hear where she goes with this. Sounds like a conversation for later. I will get flashcards or something. Do we have enough chairs?"

Bev counted them out. "Unless there's someone else I don't know about planning to show up, I think so. Russell is the only newcomer to the porch."

"I know it's not even five yet, but the sun is setting, and it feels like happy hour." Evie and Elle passed around glasses. "Besides, I didn't get to try anywhere near the number of wines I'd meant to drink with Charlie."

Luc held out his hand to Russell. "Hello, I'm Evie's fiancé. Welcome to Eden Valley."

"Nice to meet you. Always good to meet the demons next door, right?" Russell reached into the paper bag he had by his chair. "Want a beer?"

"Absolutely. I've had the IPA, but nothing else."

"Uncle Russell," Shelby said, widening her eyes at him in an apparent attempt to look adorable. "Where's my present?"

"I haven't forgotten you!" Russell pulled a gift-wrapped box out of the bag and handed it over.

Shelby tore the paper off a red lacquered box, then carefully lifted the lid. Her jaw dropped. "Oh my god. Is this for real?"

Lily and Kevin crowded around her, blocking Bev's view of what was inside.

"Whoa," Lily said, reaching her hand out and hovering it a couple inches above the box. "This is…"

"Power," Kevin finished.

"It was mine when I was young, and I got it from my uncle when I was a little older than you. It's been in the family for ages." Russell glanced at Bev. "I probably should've asked your aunt first. I've never had a niece, or any child actually, to give gifts to."

"If someone doesn't tell me what it is right now, I'm going to be very cross," Bev said. It couldn't be too bad… Russell didn't seem completely out of touch with the reality of appropriate gifts for kids, but Lily and Kevin absolutely were, and it was their awe that worried Bev.

Shelby lifted something out of the box and held it up for Bev to see. "It's a Ouija board. My very own, and it doesn't feel like the cheap ones from the party stores. Check out this planchette!"

The board was at least an inch thick and fifty percent bigger than the standard game box board. And the planchette was ivory-colored and looked like it had designs carved into it.

"This is bone," Shelby said. "The planchette. It's human bone."

"You gave my kid a human bone toy?" Bev had been wrong. Russell did not know the correct limits on presents for kids.

"It's not a toy, and the bone channels the energy better, so spirits are less likely to overwhelm the medium. It's a lot easier and less terrifying than just running around in the woods raising the dead." Russell leaned back in his chair and looked completely unrepentant.

"May I?" Bev asked.

Shelby walked across the porch and handed her aunt the board and planchette, looking resigned.

"I'm not confiscating it," Bev said. Shelby brightened a little. "I just want to see." The board was heavy, even heavier than it'd looked. It'd been carved from a solid piece of wood, and the numbers and letters were deeply engraved in a heavy, gothic font. The planchette looked ordinary, other than being white. But when she flipped it over, it hummed in her hand. She almost dropped it. "It's vibrating."

"Ooh, got another one of those, Russell? I think I need to pick up some Ouija skills," Viv said.

Bev pursed her lips at Viv and shook her head.

"What? I live with a demon. We're all occult all the time." Viv winked at Bev, then leaned over to whisper something to Sam, whose eyes widened before she gave a throaty chuckle.

"Y'all are the worst," Evie said. "Why is the planchette vibrating, Russell?"

"It recognizes her. The bone came from our great-great-grandmother. When she died at the ripe old age of at least two hundred, records were weird when she was born, as were impossibly long life spans that you hide from the locals, Aunt Sybil, who was even older and is much, much weirder, had this planchette carved from one of her bones. The information is all a bit sketchy. Aunt Sybil likes riddles and being obscure for no reason other than orneriness." Russell grabbed the box and passed it to Bev, who put the board and planchette back in.

Shelby grabbed the box and hugged it to her chest. "Thank you so much, Uncle Russell. This is one of the best gifts ever."

"You are welcome. I'll show you how to use it before I head back home."

"Not to change the subject, but I'm changing the subject," Evie said. "Other than the haunting at Bev's house last night, has anyone heard anything from the dead or William the bloody annoying necromancer?"

"Nothing," Sam said. "I did a flyby of Jer's this morning after Barachiel showed up to tell us what'd happened, and everything looked quiet there. No dead cows or live humans to be seen."

Bev looked at Barachiel. "You went to Sam's house? Voluntarily?"

"They are your friends, and I wanted them to know so they could be on alert. Besides, even though she is an infernal demon, cursed by my lord to spend an eternity swimming in the pits of hell, she is well liked and is well-suited for reconnaissance work." One corner of Barachiel's mouth quirked up, and Bev smiled in return.

"I like this. Jokes about serious business. It's a good look, Mr. Angel." Bev leaned forward, hoping he'd unleash one of his devastatingly peaceful smiles. Oh my god. Was she flirting? She never flirted.

"I thought I'd try it out since you and Russell seemed okay." This time Barachiel's grin was more than just a quirk of the lips, and it reached all the way to his eyes. Bev basked in it, letting the tension melt, if only for a moment.

"You have gorgeous eyes. I don't think I've ever noticed before." She brought her hand up to brush the hair away so she could see his eyes better but stopped before she touched him. "I'm sorry, I shouldn't…"

"It's okay. I know you didn't. And thank you for the compliment. Your eyes are very pretty, although not as beautiful as your nose." Barachiel leaned back, still close enough to be considered friendly, but far enough away that Bev couldn't easily touch him.

"My nose. Okay. That's not a compliment a girl gets every day, but I'm gonna roll with it. Thank you, Barachiel." She wrinkled her nose at him and was rewarded with another smile.

"I don't mind when you call me angel. Just don't tell the others it's okay." He sat back up and raised his hand.

Evie side-eyed him. "Yes, Barachiel? Did you have a question?"

"If it is okay with you, may I have a glass of wine? I promise to not drink the entire bottle." He beamed at her, and for a moment the warmth of it was nearly blinding.

"Of course." Evie poured a glass of wine for Barachiel and handed it to him.

"Careful angel, your halo's slipping," Bev murmured, holding her glass up to clink against his.

"I find I'm not quite so bothered about the idea as I was before I met you." He tapped his glass against hers and took a slow, careful sip. "This is quite nice. The wine and everything. Is this how it always is? Maybe I should come more often."

A crash in the underbrush near the path leading up from the lake grabbed everyone's attention and interrupted Bev and Barachiel's conversation. Luc and Sam were on the edge of the porch, wings splayed, before Bev could stand. Elle and Barachiel flanked the demons, their white wings spread wide.

"Kids, get inside," Bev hissed. "Evie, you too. You've got Alex."

Evie cursed under her breath but herded the kids inside.

"What are we going to do?" Viv asked. "Two necromancers and an unreliable psychic aren't going to be much help."

"We're the last line of defense between whatever's out there and Evie and the kids. It's our job to give them time to get away if necessary." Russell stood and joined Viv and Bev on the porch.

"If whatever it is gets past our first line of defense, I don't think we're going to give it much of a fight," Viv murmured. "I guess I can predict stuff at it until it gets bored with finding out what's going to be on sale at the grocery store next week."

The crashing grew louder. Bev's neck muscles tensed. She had no idea what to do, and if it wasn't for the fact that Evie had been wearing a baby, she would've volunteered to be the one to stay with the kids.

"Relax," Russell said. "Necromancers are great at defense. You remember what that bone felt like, right? And you've touched the sparks of the dead animals. You can use that to find bones and fire them up. You're new, so they won't last long and won't look good—it takes a lot of power and practice to make a cat look as good as Shelby's—but you can have the dead serve as your cannon fodder. If it comes to it, watch me and follow my lead. You'll catch on."

Bev nodded in what she hoped looked like confidence, but was, in fact, incredulity that he thought she had any possibility of raising a zombie army to throw at the enemy.

The light in front of them that had been emanating from Elle and Barachiel went out, and Luc said, "Oh, for fuck's sake. What are you doing here?"

Barachiel came back to the porch. "It's okay. It's not the enemy. Well, not the sorcerer. This might actually be worse." He walked by her and went inside.

Luc's and Sam's wings folded in, and they parted to let the newcomer walk up the stairs.

"Jesus Christ, Jer," Evie said as she walked back onto the porch with Alex strapped to her chest. "I really enjoyed the last twelve years when I barely had to talk to you. Three times in almost as many days is way, way too much."

"They're after me," he whispered, eyes darting from side to side. There were streaks of dirt on his jeans, his flannel shirt was torn in a few places, and his work boots, usually polished and showing no signs of actual work, were scuffed and caked with mud.

"How did you get here? Did you walk?" Evie demanded. She picked up her wine glass, and from the tension in her arm, Bev wasn't sure if Evie was going to drink it or chuck it at her ex-husband.

"I parked downtown; I didn't want them to follow me." His eyes darted from side to side, then he looked back over his shoulder and scanned the tree line near the lake.

"Who? Who's after you? Who are you trying to ditch?" Viv asked in a bored tone that Bev knew had always driven Jer to distraction. He hated being thought boring.

This time, he didn't take the bait. "My parents. And they keep saying, 'Help me. Vengeance.' I don't understand, and they won't stop."

He took two more steps onto the porch, then fainted at Evie's feet.

# CHAPTER SIXTEEN

"I thought he was a pain in the ass when we were getting divorced, but at least he wanted nothing to do with me then," Evie groused, nudging him with her foot. She made up her mind about the wine and took a drink before sitting down and glaring. "Sorry about the baby. Usually, I'd put her down for a late afternoon nap, but I don't want her too far away from me tonight. Besides, she's being really quiet, and we need to take advantage of that while we can."

"That's right. Soon she'll be old enough to talk and the rest of us won't get a word in edgewise," Lily said. She stepped around Jer's prone figure and smiled impishly at her mother. "Finally, I won't be the most annoying one in the family."

"You're not annoying," Evie said, booping her daughter on the nose.

"Ugh. I'll try harder." Lily crossed her eyes and picked up the lemonade she'd abandoned when they'd fled inside.

"Should we check on him? Make sure he's okay?" Russell asked, looking nonplussed.

"The mighty necromancer is ready to raise an army of ghouls to stand against our enemies but is uncertain of what to do in the face of ex-husbands with low blood pressure," Bev said. "But seriously, should we try to wake him up?"

"Probably," Viv said. "If for no other reason than to ask about his parents."

"Since he quoted his parents using the same words as the ghosts who went after Bev last night, I'm going out on a limb and guessing they're dead?" Russell cracked open a beer. "I thought things were weird in Oracle Bay, but it's a whole new level here."

"I think he's waking up." Sam reached out from where she was sitting and nudged him with her foot. "Lily can wake him up the rest of the way if we need him to regain consciousness faster."

"Samiel, you will not use my daughter as your personal defibrillator," Evie said.

"Do it," Viv said at the same time. "We need to know what he knows, and we need it soon."

"It's okay, Mama. Aunt Sam or Daddy could do it, too, but healing is my gift." Lily hopped out of her chair and crouched beside Jer. She put her hands on either side of his forehead and took a deep breath.

"Just a minute, Lily," Viv said. She went forward and wrapped an arm around Lily's chest. "Now."

Lily closed her eyes. It looked like the world's most ineffective head massage until Jer's eyes popped open, and he sat up like a jack-in-the-box. Viv yanked Lily out of the way not a second too late, saving her from a severe head butting.

"Thank you," Lily said, brushing off her knees. "Glad you saw it coming."

"Can anyone keep him from going hysterical again?" Evie asked. "We need the whole story, and he's nothing but a giant pain in the ass."

Barachiel hooked his arm around Jer's shoulders and led him to the porch swing. "He'll answer your questions now, but ask quickly before he remembers who I am."

"When did your parents appear?" Bev asked.

"This morning. They were at the table having breakfast when I got up." He spoke as if hypnotized, which was much better than any other reaction they'd gotten from him in the last couple days. "Bacon and eggs, which was weird, because I don't have any bacon in the freezer. The cows unplugged the chest freezers and everything spoiled."

"How did the cows... You know what? Not the most important question. Did they speak to you other than the words you repeated to us earlier?" Bev wished she had a notebook. It'd be easier to play Miss Marple for Barachiel if she had somewhere to write down all the clues. "Evie, can you get me a notebook and pen? It's for a good cause."

"No problem." Evie winked at Bev, and a moment later a spiral-bound notebook with a shiny Lisa Frank pegasus on the cover appeared in her lap with a black ballpoint pen.

"Thanks for remembering the deepest desire of my nine-year-old heart." Bev opened the notebook and wrote "cows," "no bacon," "help, vengeance." She studied the words for a moment, then turned her attention back to Jeremy. "Back to my question; did they say anything else? Did they recognize you?"

"They talked to each other. It was like every morning from when they were alive. And they saw me and asked why I wasn't out feeding the pigs." Jer's monotone was already wearing on Bev, and they'd just gotten started.

"I'd forgotten about the pigs. They disappeared soon after we were married, didn't they? I don't remember anything else but the few cows you kept for no good reason that I could ever figure out," Evie asked.

"We had two pigs when I was young. No cows, only pigs and chickens. The pigs were named Heathcliff and Rochester. My mother named them. They were so big, like giants. I was scared of the pigs." A tear streaked down Jer's face, and a pang of sympathy ricocheted in Bev's chest.

"So, they were reliving a typical morning from your childhood. Anything else?" Bev wrote down the pigs' names. You never knew when that would be important.

"No. I went out to feed the pigs, then remembered we didn't have them. After my parents died, I had them slaughtered and took their bones as souvenirs. They fed us for well over a year." The grin on Jer's face was a little deranged and erased the pang of sympathy Bev had.

"When did they die?" Russell asked. "Was it recently?"

"No, it was right after high school. They came to the wedding, then died just a few weeks later. Car accident. It was tragic. I genuinely liked them." Evie pulled Alex out of the carrier and stretched her back. "Luc, could you?"

Luc took the baby and sat her on his knee facing him. "You have almost as many car accidents as drownings here." He popped his horns out, then made them disappear again.

Alex laughed and clapped her hands. "Da da da da."

"That is seriously weird, man," Russell said.

"If you have any other questions, now's the time," Barachiel said. "He's fighting my control, and I'd rather let him go than have him break it. We don't need him to faint again."

"Do you know where the treasure is?" Shelby asked.

The look on Jer's face could best be described as crafty. "Treasure? What kind of treasure?"

"A secret box, hidden away so long ago that only the land remembers," Shelby said. "The land and those who are owned by it."

"The land doesn't own me, not anymore. I broke that curse when I sacrificed the cows who were the anchor to the earth and ended my line so that my children wouldn't be forced to carry the same burden I was." The look he shot at Evie was pure venom. "The curse was broken, and the wife my parents forced me to take was driven off. The land has no hold, and the secrets it forced us to keep were moved. There is no treasure, only pain." His voice no longer sounded like Jer. It was hollow and dark and raised goosebumps on Bev's skin.

"I'm letting go," Barachiel warned. He dropped his arm from around Jer's neck and held it away from his body. He shuddered. "I need to change my coat. And maybe my arm."

Barachiel stood and went back to the chair next to Bev where he'd been sitting before. Awareness slowly returned to Jer's face. He glared at no one in particular. "What have you done to me now?"

"Jer, you came here of your own free will. You wanted help—again —and asked us. We have done nothing more than revive you when you fainted and calmed you long enough to give us the answers we needed. If you're going to be mad when we help, stay home and don't ask." Evie straightened her shoulders. A bucket of water appeared over his head and tipped, drenching him completely. "That should cool your temper a bit."

"Nice, Mama," Lily said.

"I know I've made a mistake when the hooligans are impressed," Evie sighed. "I've been wanting to do that for years."

"I'll take him inside and get him dried off and get him something to drink," Sam volunteered. "Do you have any cheap beer in the fridge?"

"We do now," Evie said. "Help yourself."

Sam led Jer inside.

"Is he going to be okay with her?" Bev asked. "She looked kinda pissed."

"He'll be fine. I mean, he might pee himself a little when Sam tells him exactly how she feels about him, but she won't hurt him. Might want to wish him some clean clothes, though, Evie." Viv grinned at her friend.

"Also done. All Chevy branded stuff. He hates Chevy." Evie smiled smugly, but her face fell moments later. "Some revenge that is."

"I'm sorry you had to hear that crap," Bev said. "That was awful."

"It's okay. I knew he was a jerk and that he'd never felt the same way about me as I did about him, but I didn't realize how much he despised me. What do you think he meant about the land and the curse?" Evie smiled in a way that brooked no more comments about Jer's revelation about their marriage.

"Um, I think I know," Shelby volunteered. She worried at her lower lip with her teeth and looked at Bev.

"You have the floor, sweetheart," Bev said. "You know more about the box than anyone else here—at least anyone else who's talking about it."

"The box has bones, like I said before. And it's hidden somewhere. The Gr—I mean, William—believed it was on Jer's property; that's why we were there. And the way he talked, like he knew the land and was trying to break free, makes me feel like we were on the right track?" Shelby flushed under the scrutiny of so many people.

"That's some good connect-the-dots," Russell said. "Does anyone know whose bones are in the box? What's it for?"

Bev shot Barachiel a look, but he refused to meet her eyes. "Anyone who knows isn't talking other than to say that if Billy the Bonehead gets the magic box, life as we know it will be over. Same song, different day."

"I can't tell you," Barachiel said. "It's sacred."

"You mean you won't tell us, even though it's our asses on the line. We can't sprout fluffy wings and zoom off to dance on a rainbow or whatever," Bev retorted.

"He means he actually cannot tell you," Elle interrupted. "Neither can I. We both know of it, and its importance, but we are unable to say more than that. Not out of desire to keep you in the dark, but rather because our words are held back by someone of greater power."

"Oh. Sorry." Bev didn't feel sorry, although she knew she ought to. "You could've just said that in the first place."

"I thought I did. I told you I couldn't tell you. I never said I didn't want to tell you." He crossed his arms and exhaled loudly.

"Fine. It's a magic box full of bones that can destroy the world, and somehow Jer knows where it is. Does that sum up everything we know?" Bev heard the bite in her voice but no longer cared enough to hide it.

"Are the voices back?" Viv asked.

"Yeah, they are," Shelby confirmed. "It's just a murmur, but I can hear them."

Russell closed his eyes for a second, then said, "It's like background noise, you know? If you're in a bar or coffee shop and there are conversations all over, you can tune it out. How many people have died around here? It sounds like too many for such a small town."

"The lake dead are gone, right?" Viv asked.

"If they're not, I'm going to be pretty upset about everything we went through," Evie groused. "No fair having voices floating out of the lake after putting all our lives at risk and doing weird demon magic on a creepy island in the middle of the lake."

"I didn't see an island," Russell said, peering out into the evening dusk settling over the valley.

"It was only here for a couple days," Shelby said. "We're not quite sure where it came from, but something to do with primordial beings and lake monsters and the dead in the lake."

"Why does anyone live here?" Russell asked. "I honestly don't understand, and I live in a weird town also full of psychics and demons and angels."

"They can't leave," Elle said. "That's how the town protects itself. If the humans were to leave, there would be nothing stopping a cosmic fight over this town."

"What does that mean? Why is it so important? And how does the town keep people here?" Russell's focus on the lake didn't waver, and he sounded nervous for the first time since he'd arrived.

"You'll be fine," Bev said. It helped to know she wasn't the only one who could hear the dead. "You aren't from Eden Valley, so it doesn't recognize you as something to hold on to. If you stayed a while, you'd be part of the town."

"And you're all okay with this? Why not try to leave?" Russell sounded more bewildered than worried now, and he turned his focus back to the people on the porch.

"Bev and I both tried," Viv said. "I stayed away for years, but I'm back now. The only people I know who've managed to leave are old people—well, older than us people—who are retiring, but even then, they are drawn back to die here."

"Yeah, our cemeteries are exceptionally large for such a small town," Evie chimed in. "Lots and lots of dead to raise."

Kevin inched forward on his chair. "The spirits of the dead that were in the lake are gone. But their bodies are still there. I...the lake monster...kept the people he took because he fed on the life essence, and when it was too drained to be enough to sustain the monster, he took another. But they still had their spirits. They were trapped with their bodies, and that's what was released."

"Oh. So a lot more bodies are in play," Bev said. "That's awesome."

Barachiel leaned towards her until their arms were almost touching. A layer of heat washed over Bev, coating her and dimming the sound of the voices until she could ignore them as well as Shelby and Russell.

"Does it help?" he whispered quietly enough that only she could hear.

"Yes. How? Please don't say pocket dimensions."

Barachiel cracked a grin. "The only pockets I have are in my jeans. And my coat. But that's it."

"Thank you. I know that being this close to someone for any length of time is difficult for you." Bev didn't add that it was usually difficult for her, too; at least when it wasn't Shelby or someone in her intimate circle of friends. Strangers were difficult, and men were…not an option. But for the moment, it was okay and the chill of the grave and the cold of loneliness were both kept at bay with the angel's presence.

# CHAPTER SEVENTEEN

"They're getting closer," Shelby said, scarfing down the last of her dinner.

Bev scooted away from Barachiel, and the weight of the dead hit her. "It's not just ghosts, things are moving."

"How close?" Luc asked. He looked at the playpen next to where he was sitting, and Bev could almost read his thoughts. Alex wasn't even a year old yet, and already this was her second potential apocalypse.

"I don't know," Shelby's voice was tight with frustration. "Close enough to feel that they're coming this way, but not close enough to make out individuals. There are a lot, though."

"One of you should go and take the kids," Bev said. "It's foolish to stay here, Evie."

Evie looked between Bev and Alex, indecision on her face. "You're right. I won't be able to help, and this is one fight the kids can't win for us. Lily, why don't you call your grandfather?"

"Will you take Kevin?" Elle asked. "I cannot take him to heaven, nor can I go with you into hell, but I would have him be safe."

Kevin and Lily started yelling, speaking over each other so loudly that it was almost impossible to determine what the crux of their arguments were. "We have helped. A lot." Lily crossed her arms and glared at her mother. "You couldn't have helped Kevin without me and Shelby."

"They're not going to make Shelby leave," Kevin said. "Just us." His lower lip jutted out.

"It's my mess. I have to clean it up," Shelby said. "But you guys should go be safe."

Lily's lip trembled. "We're supposed to be together. Always."

"I'm sorry; I screwed up everything. But you have to leave. Please." Shelby held out her arms, and Lily and Kevin went in for the group hug.

Bev heard Shelby whisper something to her friends but couldn't make it out.

"Fucking fine," Lily muttered. She closed her eyes, said something in a language Bev didn't know, and glared at the floor.

The doorbell rang.

"I'll get it," Kevin said. He jogged to the door and opened it wide.

Abaddon—Abe to his friends and family—walked in. Today, he was dressed casually and without his usual sartorial flare. Khakis, a mint green Lacoste polo, and…

"Were you golfing?" Evie asked.

"We all need hobbies, and golf is a great place to meet new people. If it'd been anyone else who called me, I would've stayed to finish my round. But, for you, Liliana, I told the rest of the guys I had to go perform an emergency transplant." He bowed to Lily, and when he stood up, he was wearing a bright yellow suit and a black shirt with a matching yellow tie that almost glowed against his dark skin.

"You were pretending to be a transplant surgeon?" Bev asked, wrinkling her nose against the stench of sulphur that accompanied Abe's rapid costume change.

"No, I told them I was a lawyer," Abe said, completely deadpan. "But you didn't call me here to criticize my career choices. What do you need, granddaughter?"

"Can we come visit for the next couple days?" Evie asked. She picked Alex up and grabbed the diaper bag that was always in the hall closet. Luc folded up the playpen and slipped it into the carrying case.

"We who? All of you?" Abe looked at the group gathered in his son and almost daughter-in-law's home.

"No, just me, Alex, Lily, and Kevin," Evie said. "Things are getting a little weird here, and it'd be nice to have somewhere safe to hang out until it blows over."

"What kind of weird? I love weird, and you never invite me." Abe pouted as his eyes darted from person to person. They paused first on Bev. "Beverly. Looks like you finally figured out how to use the gift I gave you."

"You didn't give me anything," Bev said. "You only woke it up."

"You say potato, I say necromancer." He winked and continued his survey of the room. "There are new people here. Another necromancer—"

Russell nodded in acknowledgement.

Abe's gaze fell on Jer, who was sitting in the recliner looking like he was debating between fleeing or crying. "You're human. Nothing special at all. But there's something about you. You've touched an object of power. Where is it? I can help you better than anyone here. Tell me what it is, and we'll go get it together."

"Nope!" Evie said. "As much as I'd love to send you on a quest with my ex, not this time. You can exchange numbers and hang out later. But now, please take us home with you. For your granddaughters. Help me keep them safe."

Abe grunted. "Okay. But I'll be back to talk to your friend later. Good luck with the zombies. They'll be here within the hour."

There was an explosion of sulphurous yellow smoke; when it cleared, Abe, Evie, and the children were gone. A moment later, there was another puff of smoke and Shelby reappeared.

"Now would be a great time for you to get angry," Bev said to Barachiel. "Roses are much better than this stench." She waved her hand in front of her face, trying to clear the smoke.

Barachiel shot her an apologetic look. "I am having trouble feeling angry at the moment. I am relieved the children will be… I'm not sure safe is the correct word, but at least out of immediate danger. I am worried about you. And your friends. But I am not angry."

"Russell, how do we defend against the zombies?" Bev asked, leaning back in towards Barachiel in an effort to clear her mind long enough to figure out what to do.

"Ideally, we'll be able to put out their sparks, as you called them, as they approach. The necromancer might not know I'm here, but he knows you have enough power to break Shelby out of where he'd trapped her, and he trained Shelby, so if she can raise an entire pet cemetery, she can put them right back where they came from." Russell tapped his index finger against his chin as he stared out the window towards the lake.

"It's a trap," Viv said. She was pinching the bridge of her nose while Sam rubbed her temples. "Ugh. Too many too-small visions that aren't giving us nearly enough information. It's a trap. The zombies are a diversion, but for what, I don't know. Everything keeps coming back to Jer."

"There's a first time for everything," Bev said. "Must be nice to finally be wanted."

"If he is the key, there must be something he hasn't told us," Barachiel said.

Bev leaned away from the angel again, and the voices of the dead returned.

*Help me. Help. Vengeance.*

She shuddered and tried to concentrate. "Shel, you said the necromancer was certain the box was on Jer's property, but you didn't feel it on the farm."

Shelby nodded. "It wasn't there. Or if it was, I couldn't find it."

"Jer said he moved it. That the secrets they were forced to keep were moved." It was hard to think over the sounds of the dead chanting louder and louder as they moved closer.

*Help me. Help. Vengeance.*

"Would he be able to throw it away? Or take it somewhere else?" Luc asked. "It's hard to know the limits if we don't know what it is."

"No. He should not be able to dispose of it. Even if he believes the curse was broken and he was no longer tied to it, the box wouldn't leave Eden Valley." Elle grimaced. "It may not be where it was first hidden, but it wouldn't have let go of its guardian so easily."

"Jer, do you own any other land, anything we don't know about?" Bev asked before leaning back towards Barachiel for another respite against the voices echoing in her head.

Jer glared at her but didn't answer.

"Is there a way to find out? Maybe the Jeff Bezos knows?" Barachiel suggested.

"Why would he know? And how would you suggest we get that information from him?" Russell asked.

"According to Twitter, there is nothing safe from Jeff Bezos. He is in our homes and watches everything we do. Like a lesser god," Barachiel clarified.

Viv grinned. "He probably does know, but he is more of an information gatherer, and not a sharer. Property records should be publicly available. Luc, is your laptop available?"

Luc snagged the laptop from the other room and handed it to Viv. She pulled up the county's website and found a map of every plat in the county, along with its appraised value, property tax, and owner of record.

"Will it have to be within official city limits, or is anything in the area fair game?" Viv asked, clicking on the lots one by one.

"The farm isn't in Eden Valley proper," Bev said.

"Eden isn't city limits," Barachiel said. "Lines drawn on a map are artificial boundaries and do not contain anything other than rules."

"That'll take a little longer, then," Viv said. "I don't know how to do this faster, though. It'd be so much easier if he'd just tell us."

"I can make him," Sam volunteered. "He wouldn't like it, but he'd tell me, anyway."

"If I don't find it in the next ten minutes, feel free to extract the information out of him any way you think will be the most effective." Viv grinned at her girlfriend. "I bet you learned some really cool things in hell, what with all those damned souls to play with."

"I'm no expert and could always use the practice." Sam glanced at Jer, who looked like he was trying to turtle his way out of view.

"Still no?" Viv asked. She waited for an answer, but Jer stayed silent. "Fine. Ten minutes, and then I'm going to let my girlfriend have her way with you."

"Who owns the haunted mansion?" Shelby asked. "William wouldn't come there, and I always felt safer there."

"Ooh, good idea. Let me check." Viv clicked a couple times, then grinned. "Nice job, Shelby. You're right. Looks like Jer bought that piece of land right after his parents died. They must have left a tidy sum for him."

"I had to hide the money from my personal gold-digger, didn't I?" Jer muttered under his breath, almost, but not quite, too quietly to hear.

"That's why you got cows," Shelby said before looking back at Viv. "Do you think it's there?"

"That seems likely," Bev answered. "We have our what and possibly our where. What I don't know is what this diversion is diverting us from."

"They're here," Shelby said, her attention snapping towards the window overlooking the lake.

"Let's go," Russell said to Bev. "We can take care of the zombies as they approach. Someone should stay here and guard Jer in case he's the target. Shelby, you stick with us. The necromancer might want you back."

"I'll stay with the mortal," Sam said. "We're getting to be such close friends."

Luc looked at Elle. "Wanna do some recon? We can fly over the mansion and see if there's any activity there. We might not be the only ones who thought to look at Jer's other property holdings."

"That's a good idea." She walked outside, followed closely by Luc. There was a flash of light, and they were gone.

"So, they're just winging it then?" Russell asked.

Shelby laughed.

"Just the kid? No one else got it?"

Bev shook her head. "I love a good pun, but that was not one."

"Tough crowd. I'm going to make a pit stop and then head outside.

Let's put this thing to rest." He waited for a moment, then huffed out a breath and walked towards the hall bathroom.

Barachiel met Bev's gaze. "I will stand by you and protect Shelby. I swear it on my immortal soul."

"Thank you." Bev reached out her hand, and he took it. For a moment, they were joined, and it felt right.

"All right, troops, once more into the breach!" Viv said. "Bev, can you come here for a moment? Barachiel will stay with Shelby while we get all set up, won't you?"

"Of course." He let go of Bev's hand and moved to Shelby's side.

"Anything you want to tell me?" Viv asked Bev as they stood side by side halfway between the house and the lake, buffeted by raindrops the wind was flinging in their faces like a thousand tiny daggers.

"About what?" She was glad it was dark enough Viv couldn't see the blush rising into her cheeks.

"You were holding hands. With a boy." The look Viv gave her penetrated the darkness and the curtain of rain threatening to come between them.

"We weren't holding hands, we were..." Bev trailed off.

"Do go on. What were you doing? And what have you been doing all evening? There has barely been any space between you since he got Jer to talk. You never get that close to anyone."

Bev shivered and rubbed her hands over her arms in an effort to warm up. "When he's close, the dead aren't so loud. It's self-preservation."

"So you're using him?" Viv asked.

"Of course. What else would it be?" Bev tried for light and airy and was pretty sure she'd nailed it.

"You don't have to be alone. Just because you don't want the kind of relationship Sam and I have doesn't mean there isn't anyone for you. Plenty of people aren't into the naked parts of love."

Maybe she hadn't nailed it after all. "It's not that. He's an angel, and he's leaving in the summer. I don't think there's such a thing as an 'occasional cuddle' fling, especially with someone who considers Buffy a sin of the flesh." Darkness clawed at the edges of her awareness, and she swung her head towards the woods to the west of the house. "It's almost time."

"Fine, but don't leave happiness on the table because you're afraid of all the ways it might not work. You deserve to be content." Viv wrapped an arm around Bev. "I love you so much, and all I want is for you to be happy. Whatever that looks like for you, you know I have your back."

"Thanks, Viv. You know you're the best, right?" They turned and walked slowly back to the porch where Russell, Shelby, and Barachiel waited for them.

The window to the kitchen was open, and Sam was waving frantically from the other side. "Is it okay if I tie him up? I'll keep an eye on him, but this way I don't have to sit on him to make sure he doesn't run away."

"Tying up people is probably wrong," Bev said.

"Unless it's for their own good. Or for fun," Viv countered.

Bev shot a look at Shelby, but the tween hadn't seemed to notice the innuendo.

"Go ahead, Sam. If it'll make you happy, you should go for it," Viv said.

Bev reached back and grabbed a thick handful of her hair and squeezed the water out.

"That looks uncomfortable. Why were you in the rain? Couldn't you and Viv have talked on the porch?" Barachiel reached out and took her hand.

"Girl talk, Barachiel," Viv said, looking down at their linked hands and smirking.

Bev shivered and felt warmth return to her extremities. "My clothes are dry. And my hair. Wow. That is a handy talent." She smiled up at Barachiel. "Thanks, angel."

The smile he directed back at her warmed her even more. "My pleasure."

"Sam, think you could do me a solid and get me dry?" Viv asked.

Sam snorted. "Not a chance, babe. Not now, not ever."

"I love you, but you are the absolute worst sometimes." Viv shook her head, flinging droplets of water from the ends of her jet-black hair.

"That's why you love me," Sam corrected.

"It's time," Shelby said. "You'll see them in a moment."

Bev scanned the trees at the edge of the yard. "I see them."

Viv backed up to the house, giving the necromancers—and Barachiel—room to work.

*Help meeeeeeee...* The words were spoken in a unison by dozens of different voices.

*Vengeance.*

"That is eerie AF," Russell said. "I wish I knew what vengeance they're seeking."

"Is it really time to figure out their motivation?" Viv asked. "But since you mentioned it, I'll see if I can get a bead on it." She pulled one of the chairs against the wall below the window where Sam was standing.

"I'm scared. I wasn't before, but now I am," Shelby said in a small voice. "What if we die?"

"We're not going to die. I will not give that stupid necromancer the satisfaction of driving my body around." Bev smiled encouragingly at her niece. "Stay behind Russell and me and close to Barachiel. A gentle squeeze on her hand reminded her they were still connected. She tightened her fingers in response, then let go. She was going to need all her zombie-senses to tingle to get through this.

"With my immortal soul," the angel promised in her ear. "Fear not."

"I bet that's what you say to all the mortals," Bev teased. She wasn't ready to step away from him yet.

"I've never said that to a human before. Is that a joke?" He frowned, one hand hovering above her shoulder.

Bev raised her hand and almost, but not quite, touched his cheek. "I'll explain later. Thank you." She dropped her hand and stepped forward to take her place beside Russell. Shelby moved up between them, Barachiel behind her.

"Ready?" Bev asked no-one in particular.

"Ready," Shelby said firmly.

If Shelby could sound that confident, Bev owed it to her—to everyone—to take this necromancer out with the powers she'd only just started to embrace. She squared her shoulders, took one last look at Shelby, and closed her eyes.

The sparks of the dead winked on in front of her. First two or three, then a dozen more, until there were hundreds walking towards them. "It's so many," she breathed. "How are there so many?"

"Don't let the numbers scare you," Russell said. "They're pinpricks of weak light. You can do this."

A spark went out, and Bev knew it was Russell taking the first swing. She concentrated, found a spark, and flicked it off. It disappeared, but there was another in its place.

*Help.*

*Help me.*

*Vengeance...*

# CHAPTER EIGHTEEN

"There are so many," Bev said. She'd given up on standing twenty minutes ago and pulled up a chair for her anti-zombie work. It felt weird and oddly lazy, but it was easier to find the sparks she needed to put out when she wasn't concentrating on remaining upright.

"For every one we take out, it feels like two more take their places." Russell gasped between gulps of air. "Something is raising them as fast as we're felling them. We're barely keeping them from overwhelming us, but I don't know how much longer we can keep this up."

Shelby was the only one who didn't look like she was on the verge of collapse. In fact, she looked better and more rested than when they'd started. She was doing her share—more than her share, if Bev was honest—and appeared ready to go for a jog and climb Mt. Rainier after.

"How are you still standing?" Bev said. Sweat was running down her face. Who knew fighting an army of zombies with your mind was so exhausting?

"I don't know. But every time I put out a spark, I feel stronger." Shelby grinned. She was almost glowing with good health.

"Shelby, how are you putting out the sparks?" Russell asked. He leaned back and turned his attention to Shelby.

"What do you mean? I put them out. Just like you and Aunt Bev." Shelby wrinkled her nose at him. Unlike Russell, she was able to divide her attention between zombie fighting and conversation.

"Describe the process to me." Russell took the glass of water Viv held out for him and gulped it down, waiting for Shelby to respond.

"Um. I find the spark in their chest, grab it, and pull it into me until it goes out. How are you doing it?"

"I find the spark, then mentally blow it out, like a metaphysical candle," Russell replied. "Bev?"

"I pinch the spark, like putting out a candle with my fingers." She growled in exhausted frustration. "They just keep coming and coming. How is this possible?"

"Shelby, who taught you to lay the undead to rest like that?" Russell asked. He wiped his forehead on his sleeve. "I am not a fan of fighting zombie hordes in the rain."

"I've only had one teacher, so who do you think?" Shelby snarked.

"Is something wrong?" Bev asked.

"Take a break, Bev, get some water. I'm back at it." Russell closed his eyes and his face immediately tensed until his jaw muscles looked like they might flex through his cheeks.

Bev opened her eyes and took a breath. "We're not doing anything but stemming the tide, but we're going to be overwhelmed soon. There are only three of us, and hundreds of them."

"Something needs to change soon," Russell agreed. "But first, Shelby—you need to stop what you're doing. Every time you pull the spark forward into yourself to extinguish it, you're taking the rest of the life force and assimilating into yourself. You're... I don't know quite how to explain it. You're fueling your body with the power of death, of the grave."

"Well isn't that a good thing? That way I'm tapping into my own energy and can keep going for ages. I almost have enough energy to take out whole rows at a time." Shelby waved her fingers in what was probably supposed to be a mystical gesture, but looked more like she had something sticky on her hand.

"It is not good. If you pull too much grave energy from the ghouls in front of us, you will soon have more of their energy than your own."

"Yeah, and? It'll fade out of me, and soon it'll just be me again. And in the meantime, I'm kicking butt and you guys are passing out."

"That might work if it's just a few here and there, or if you used your own energy to raise them. But this is hundreds of them, hundreds of sparks you're pulling into yourself that were created by someone else. Think it through." Russell opened his eyes. "We have to try something else. Where are Luc and Elle? I would've thought they'd be back by now."

"Unless that was where the trap was set," Bev said. "But it couldn't be. Viv would've seen that, right?"

"The only thing I'm getting other than some super short-term stuff is Jer's stupid giant face. It's on top of everything obscuring my view." Viv kicked the wall next to the door and muttered, "some help I turned out to be."

"I can go check on Luc and Elle," Sam said. "In and out without being seen."

"And if you get snatched, too? How's it going to help us if seventy-five percent of our winged team members are out of the picture?" Viv turned and glared at Sam.

"Oh my god," Shelby said. "Their energy will outweigh mine and whoever created the sparks will be able to control me, too. What do I do? How do I stop it?"

Bev glared at Russell. "You could've just explained it to both of us instead of freaking her out and now me, too."

"I'm tired," Russell snapped. "The ghouls are less than a hundred yards away, and I don't know what to do."

Bev took a deep breath and tried to think through the problem. "Our plan was to decimate the zombie hordes, spring the trap, take out the necromancer, and secure the magic box. So far, we have accomplished none of those things unless Luc and Elle were successful and went to Disneyland to celebrate without letting anyone know."

"I think if they'd taken out the necromancer, the undead he'd created would return to the earth," Barachiel said.

Bev bit her tongue before she could snap at him. When she had control of her temper, she said, "I think you're right. My point was meant to be 'our plans have failed.' Elle and Luc are missing. The zombie horde is undying, and if the trap was sprung, we were all caught up, anyway."

"We need a new plan. Obviously," Shelby said. "If I put out the sparks the way you guys do, will I be using my own energy or the other energy? I don't know what to do."

Russell considered. "It's probably best not to risk it. I'm worried about the balance already. I should've asked sooner—that's my fault and I'm sorry."

Shelby crawled into Bev's lap, all hard angles and elbows, and settled in with her arms around her aunt's neck. "Are we going to die?"

Bev opened her mouth, not sure what was going to come out—a comforting lie unlikely to be believed or the probable truth.

Barachiel beat her to it. "You are not going to die. None of us will die. We are the good guys, and the good guys are supposed to win."

"Did you read that on Twitter?" Bev asked.

"No, I learned that from all of you. And from my friend Andras. And Russell and his friends. Sometimes winning doesn't look like what we expect, but it's still winning." The fierceness in his voice reverberated through Bev's entire being. Her spine straightened and a modicum of confidence returned.

"He's right. We just need a new plan. We know this is the diversion, and I think since Elle and Luc haven't returned or called, we figured out where the main focus is. So all we need to figure out is how to get from here to there through an army of undead who need help and are seeking vengeance." Bev clapped her hands and smiled.

"I love you like a sister, Bev, but when you're chipper like this, it scares me a little." Viv grinned. "Of course, it also makes me want to kick some ass. Your confidence is contagious."

*Help me.*

*Help.*

*Vengeance.*

The chants hadn't faded, but they were starting to exist on that subliminal level that became background noise.

"Has anyone tried to talk to them?" Bev asked.

"About what?" Russell asked. "How they fell about their new undeath? Best evening wear for an autumn zombie uprising?"

"To ask them what they want. Are they asking us for help? Are they seeking vengeance on us? The dead have been saying that for weeks, even before the undead masses marched against us. What do they want?" Bev hugged Shelby, then pushed her gently off her lap. "Help me up?" She extended her hand to her niece, but it wasn't Shelby who grabbed it and hauled her to her feet. She stumbled forward a couple steps when she was upright, and Barachiel grabbed her shoulders to steady her.

"I would like to hug you, if you wouldn't mind," Barachiel said. "I've never really hugged someone before, but I understand it can be pleasant and comforting."

Bev opened her arms and took two more steps forward.

Barachiel's arms encircled her, and she wound her arms around his neck. They pressed into each other, and Bev closed her eyes with the sheer pleasure of being held. A soft flutter drew her attention, and she opened her eyes. They were hidden by the expanse of his wings. "They cannot hear us as long as my wings surround us. I have a plan, but you will not like it."

"Why are you telling me, and why like this?" Bev loosened her hold slightly. She wanted so badly to touch his wings, but the first time she'd asked, he said no, and after Viv shared some more rather salient details of how Sam felt about having her wings touched and what kind of activities resulted from said touching, Bev knew better. That was not a path she ever wanted to walk down, but especially not here and not now.

"The plan will need your approval, your blessing, because Shelby is the key to making it work and it would put her in great danger. I cannot share the plan unless you agree to leave the choice to her. If you say no, the others will think we are sharing a long and uncharacteristic hug, nothing more." His wings vibrated, creating a breeze that swirled around her body.

Bev closed her eyes and let the breeze wash over her. It was almost as good as an angel smile at blowing her worries away. "Tell me then. I don't want to agree to anything that would be Shelby in danger, but I won't reject it out of hand, at least not until you've told me the details."

BEV LOOKED out over the lawn. "At least they're not speedy ghouls. I'm glad the dead shamble as slowly as they do."

"Can't go fast if your circulatory system is the only one online, and it's faulty. Not to mention the danger of dropping a limb." Russell leaned against the porch railing next to her. "This is not how I thought I'd go out. After the last couple years in Oracle Bay, I thought it'd be poison or a trickster god. No one warned me it'd be the zombie apocalypse."

"Do you often get warnings like that?" Bev asked. She was trying very hard not to think about what Shelby and Barachiel were talking about inside.

"All the time. Too often, actually. When you live in a town full of psychics, someone's always up in your future business. When this is all over and we are triumphant, your friend Viv needs to come for a visit. Her girlfriend can hang out with Andy and drink all his beer, and Viv can meet a bunch of other people who see the future, although in very different ways than she does." Russell flashed her a weary grin. "And I will make everyone cocktails and give you a tour to see how many puns you can withstand before begging for mercy."

The screen door opened and was caught by the wind, which slammed it against the side of the house. Bev jumped. Her nerves were wound too tight, even with the tension tamer she'd gotten when sheltered in Barachiel's wings.

Shelby walked out a lot more slowly than she'd walked in.

"Well? What do you think?" Bev asked.

"I don't want to do it. I'm so scared." Shelby's voice was thick with tears.

"You don't have to do anything you don't want to. We will find another way." Bev stood and pulled Shelby in for a hug.

"I have to, though. I made this mess, and I have to fix it." She rubbed her face with the back of one hand.

"Sure, if you'd messed up the kitchen, you'd be expected to clean up after yourself. But even then, I'd help if you asked. This is several magnitudes more than a messed-up kitchen, and you weren't the only one who messed up. We can find another way." Bev forced as much confidence into her voice as she could find. Barachiel's plan was a good one—much more likely to succeed than any of the several plans she'd thought up and dismissed. But it all hinged on the acting abilities and strength of a twelve-year-old girl.

"It's a good plan," Shelby said. "But it's scary, and I'll have to go alone."

"Not alone," Barachiel said. "I'll be with you. An angel in your pocket. Pockets in pockets." He smiled down at Shelby and Bev's fear melted away, just a little. Barachiel spread his wings wide and fluttered them around Shelby, and Bev relaxed a little more.

"Can you get me out if something goes wrong?" Shelby asked, sounding less scared than she had a moment before.

Barachiel looked at Bev. She nodded. The truth was important now. "I don't know," the angel admitted. "I couldn't have without Bev's help the first time, but I didn't know you as well then, and I wasn't as able to…feel the walls of reality. I cannot promise that I can."

Sam and Viv walked onto the porch. "I'm coming with," Sam said, staring at Barachiel.

He opened his mouth as if to protest, then closed it again. "If Shelby agrees, that's probably a good idea."

Shelby nodded. "Sam is a good choice. And then I'll have an angel and a demon, one for each pocket."

Viv looked at Sam and an entire conversation passed wordlessly between them.

"You walked into hell to save Evie's kid. Let me do this for Bev's. Your family is mine, now." Sam snapped out her wings and the red-veined black feathers spread the length of the porch.

Viv took three steps forward and pulled Sam close. Their kiss was so blisteringly hot that Bev had to look away.

She dropped a hand in front of Shelby's eyes. "Don't look. Smooches will corrupt you."

Shelby pushed Bev's hand out of the way. "I've seen kissing before, and I know what sex is. I'm twelve and a half."

"Gasp!" Bev fluttered the back of her wrist to her forehead and closed her eyes dramatically.

"Mom, you're being silly," Shelby said.

Bev's eyes snapped open, and she looked at her niece. She didn't want to say anything. Didn't want to draw attention to Shelby's slip of the tongue.

Shelby blushed. "Sorry. I know you're not my mom. Sometimes I just wish you were."

"I love you, Shelby. So much. And I'm here for you in whatever role you want. I couldn't ask for a better kid. You be safe in there and kick some ass." Bev pulled Shelby close and blinked furiously, trying not to cry. This was so irresponsible, letting her kid walk off with a couple supernatural creatures to find a necromancer and take him out. The lawn in front of them was full of the undead. The house was surrounded. They were waiting.

"Go. Be safe. I love you."

Sam and Barachiel walked up to Shelby and stood on either side. "Close your eyes, Shelby, and use the sparks you took in to find the source of the magic. Grab it, hold on, and then let that life energy find its way home. We've got you." Barachiel put a hand on Shelby's shoulder.

Shelby looked at Bev. "I love you, too." She closed her eyes and disappeared.

# CHAPTER NINETEEN

Bev ignored the encroaching horde that was almost to the porch and stared at the spot where Shelby had disappeared until Russell grabbed her by the shoulder and shook her a little. Bev shrank away from him, then relaxed. Russell was a known quantity.

"Best to ask before touching," Viv said. "At least until you're granted standing permission."

"Of course, I am so sorry. That was rude. We only met again yesterday, or very early this morning, actually, although it feels like much longer." Russell took a step back and looked at Viv. "Thanks for the reminder and… Where is the farmer?"

"He's all trussed up like a Christmas pig," Viv said. "And Sam helped me hack into the baby monitor feed so we can keep an eye on him." She brought up an app and showed Russell and Bev. Jeremy was bound hand and foot and handcuffed to Lily's bed with the monitor camera pointed right at him.

"Um. Maybe don't tell Evie and Luc that's where you kept him," Bev suggested.

"Where'd you get the handcuffs?" Russell asked.

Viv winked at him.

"Why are the good ones always taken?" he sighed. "Just once, I'd like to meet a single psychic who carries her own handcuffs."

"Call me," Viv mouthed with her thumb and pinky held up to her ear. She intercepted the side eyes Bev was throwing her way. "What? Your cousin is very cute, and Sam is very understanding."

"Cool. But maybe arrange your assignation after we save the world. Ready for our part?"

"Whatever. Go forth, Bev. Speak to the dead and find out what they want so we can all go home." Viv waved her forward.

Bev walked to the steps that led down to the yard and took a deep breath. This wasn't as terrifying as letting Shelby enter the place she was deliberately not calling "the void" in her mind, but walking into a horde of undead was right up there in the top two scariest things she'd ever done.

She glanced back at Russell, and he nodded encouragingly and came to stand at her side.

"You've got this, and I've got your back. On three?"

"On three," she agreed. "One. Two."

They stepped down and walked forward into the teeming mass. Bev hoped Russell was doing his part and projecting an aura of calm through the horde. He'd said they were more like an insect collective mind than humans, or even herd animals. A collective that all drew their power from one source but were interconnected. The calm would travel through them but would fade before it got back to the source. And that's where Bev came in.

"Hi." As a greeting to a plague of zombies, it was woefully inadequate, but she hadn't had time to write a speech. "My name is Beverly Hill, and I want to help you."

*Help me.*

*Help.*

*Vengeance.*

A cold wind that carried the odor of old dirt and forest floor swirled around her, fanning her hair around her face and running goosebumps down her spine.

"Tell me how I can help. Tell me what vengeance you seek." Bev put every bit of command she'd learned from Russell that afternoon, every bit of power that coursed through her into her words.

*Vengeance.* The word reverberated in her mind, bringing with it a cascade of fear, hatred, and pain.

"I will help you find your vengeance if it is within my power to do so, but you must tell me where to look. Is there one among you who can speak?" Bev was shivering hard enough to knock her teeth together. If she didn't draw the attention of the necromancer soon, it would compromise Shelby.

The horde parted before her, and she spent a moment enjoying her Moses cosplay before a lone figure appeared in the boulevard of rotting corpses. It walked towards her, and she tensed, prepared for the wave of emotion she knew would wash over her when she spoke with her sister for the first time in ten years.

"Holly…" she trailed off and regarded the figure in front of her. "You're not Holly."

"No, but I can see if there's someone named Holly available if you'd rather?" The mousy man—boy, really, he looked so young—shuffled his feet in front of her. "I was the closest person who can talk to you. Do you want someone else?"

Bev peered closely at him. "You look familiar. Do I know you?"

The boy took another step forward and examined her. "You're Miss Hill! We know each other. You hired me for my first job at the bank right after I finished high school. Remember me? Joe Jones?"

"Of course, I remember! How are you… Never mind. I wondered why you didn't come back after your first week, but I guess this is why?" She gestured at him. He was wearing a suit that was a couple sizes too big and that even before it'd started rotting would've looked cheap and terrible, and when he turned around to look at the ghouls behind him to flash an enthusiastic thumbs up, she saw the side of his head was caved in.

"Oh, no… This happened a couple years later. I just really hated that job, so I decided not to go back. I took off to hitchhike across the country instead. Find myself, you know?"

"That sounds dangerous," Bev said. Someone she'd lost control of the situation. "Is that how you…"

"Nope! That was an amazing trip. I ended up at Burning Man, and that's when it hit me." He winked at her with his good eye.

"When what hit you? Did you find yourself there?"

"No, I was hit in the head with a huge rock that had gone off course from the homemade trebuchet contest some guys were having. Died on the spot. They flew my body back here and my mom buried me in the cemetery next to my dad."

"Oh. Well. Um. What I actually was hoping to find out is what kind of help y'all need and what sort of vengeance you're looking to take?" Bev steered the conversation back on course again and put the steel into her voice that she knew would get him to stop reminiscing and give her the answers she needed. At least, she hoped so.

"Right. Most of us aren't very happy about being woken up and forced to run around, sometimes without our bodies, which is easier, and now this, which is flat-out uncomfortable. We're supposed to be chasing you, but you feel different from the other guy we had to keep an eye on. You can hear us. And so, speaking for the group, we'd really like your help getting back to sleep. This zombie business is not as much fun as the movies made it look." Joe Jones, who Bev only remembered because of his ridiculous name and job ghosting, beamed at her, an expression not quite as happy as it could be when the skin on one side of his face detached from his skull and flapped free. "Oops! How embarrassing." He lifted the skin back up and smoothed it on like a hopeful window cling.

"Okay, you want to rest, but then how come every time I try to send any of you back, your numbers don't diminish?" Bev demanded.

"I don't know. A few of us went down and stayed down. But most of us fell over, then popped right back up again. It's a real roller-coaster of a week." Joe took a step back, and a shadow crossed his face. He froze—and with him, every other ghoul within eyesight—then they quivered in unison and all stared right at Bev.

Bev tried not to freak out. Freaking out would help no one. But this was so far from the weirdest thing that had happened. "Joe, are you still with me? Joe?"

He shook his head and his face flap broke free again. This time, he didn't bother trying to fix it. "Yeah. I'm here."

"What was that?" Bev put steel in her voice to keep it strong and steady. The first rule of necromancy was "never let a zombie see you sweat." Probably.

"Messages from on high." The cheerful boyishness disappeared from Joe's face and was replaced by the hatred and anger she'd felt before. "We are to kill you and your friends and subdue the girl until he arrives for her. I'm sorry, Miss Hill…"

"I understand. Just one more question. What vengeance do you seek?" She crossed her fingers that they'd guessed correctly, and Joe wasn't about to request she take down Bank of America.

"Vengeance against the man who made us. Vengeance against Jacques." His face contorted into a rictus. "You should run now."

"You can't have Shelby," Bev screamed. "She's safe inside, hiding in the bathroom!" She turned and ran, Russell on her heels. Viv had the door open for them and slammed it closed and locked it behind them.

"If a horde of zombies destroys Evie's house, we are going to be in big trouble," Viv said.

"I know, but it'll be okay. I promise. Now lock me in the bathroom and get out the back!" Bev pulled her hair back into a low ponytail, grabbed an oversized sweatshirt from Shelby's stash she kept in Lily's room, and tucked Xena into the front pouch of her hoodie. She looked nothing like Shelby, but hopefully it was close enough to convince the zombies. She curled up in a fetal position, careful not to squish Xena, and tucked her head down and waited.

Light flared around her, and she slowly uncurled herself and looked around. It was too bright, but somehow it looked familiar. It felt almost the way it had when she'd crossed into the non-space with Barachiel, but instead of relaxing, she felt like throwing up. "Where…"

"You're not my apprentice," a voice boomed at her from all sides. "But maybe you'll do."

It was like living in a bass drum; the voice echoed around her. She glanced up and squinted against the light. Speakers. The room was wired for surround sound.

"William the Bloody Annoying necromancer, I assume. Nice setup you've got in here. What's this, like fifty-sixty dollars of AV equipment. Your parents must give you a pretty great allowance." Bev scanned the room, looking for an exit.

"You think you can bait me? It won't work. Greater minds than yours have tried to anger me and failed. But tell me, where is your niece? The poor girl who is so neglected by her aunt that she seeks out the company of strangers to confide in. Do you have her stashed away somewhere I can't see? Or did she run away again? It's not easy to keep track of a willful child, especially when you're too wrapped up in your life and your job to hear the cries for help." The voice was naggingly familiar, but she couldn't quite place it.

"You can't bait me, either. I may lack many things—a villa in the Italian countryside, a hot tub in my back yard, the training I should've had to deal with losers like you—but I do not lack in confidence. I am a great mom, and I have a great kid. I find that it's often the people so willing to find fault with other's parenting who had the worst experiences as a child. Did your parents not love you enough? Is that why you turned to the dark arts?" There it was. The vaguest outline of a door. She had to assume he had eyes on her, but the cameras were more difficult to spot than the speakers.

Bev pulled Xena out of her pocket and set her on the ground. "Find your spark," she whispered, then stood and stretched expansively, hopefully keeping the attention on her. She watched Xena run to the wall opposite the door Bev could see. After a moment of sniffing the ground, the cat walked through the wall and disappeared. Bev walked towards the visible doorway to see what William would say.

"I'll find her, you know," he said conversationally. "She took the light of so many of my creations that I'll be able to track her for days, maybe later if she was unwise and took too much. I didn't tell her there were limits, and you didn't know enough to help her, either. Too bad that other necromancer didn't show up a few months earlier. He doesn't have as much raw power as your niece, but his training is exquisite. Unfortunately, you fall behind in both. Destined to be middle of the road forever, eh, Beverly?"

"Jackson? Jackson Allen? What the actual? Oh, wow, I never would've guessed it was you. You are so...beige. I worked with you every day for almost three months, and I have no idea what you look like. I guess I could check the impression your face made on my fist if I really need to know."

"My camouflage was impeccable, was it not? You never suspected a thing. Every afternoon when I left early, something I would've punished any of my employees for, I was spending it with your niece. Luring her in with promises of knowledge and power. Training her enough for her to fulfill what I needed her for, but not enough for her to realize how much she didn't know. That's how you get them, you know. A taste here and there with nothing asked in return. Then a bit more until they're hooked. Now there's a price for more." He laughed too long and too loud... "I gave a talk to the elementary students about the dangers of drugs. Little did everyone know that power over life and death is the greatest drug of all."

Bev edged around the room, trailing her fingers across the walls. She had to keep him talking so he wouldn't notice what she was doing. With any luck, he was focused on her and not paying attention to anyone traipsing across his pocket dimension to get to the other side. "Where are my friends? What did you do with them?"

"You mean the angel and the demon who went looking for the box? They're gone. Poof!" He laughed again, and the edge of insanity that seeped through set Bev's teeth on edge.

"How did Shelby not know who you were? She must have seen you at the bank a few dozen times. Did she never put two and two together?" There it was. A seam in the wall. She didn't pause. A few seconds later, her fingers crossed another seam. It felt like a door, even if it didn't look like a door.

"Do you think I am a villain in a Bond movie who will give up all my secrets then say, 'And now, Beverly Hill, you *will* die.'"

"I'm sure you're much too clever to fall for that. Besides, I'm sure it's probably dollar store costumes, a wig, and a dramatic cloak or something—a cheap Halloween charlatan who can only fool children."

"I fooled you, didn't I?" he sneered.

Bev stopped walking and headed back the other way, her hand a little higher this time. "How was I to know my boring, incompetent boss was an evil necromancer? Although I should've known something wasn't right when you got the promotion over me. You were neither qualified nor competent."

"Shows how little you know. That wasn't the first time we'd met, but I needed a way back in once you'd refused to see me in my previous guise."

"Your previous guise?" Bingo, there was the doorknob. She stopped walking and looked up towards where she assumed there must be cameras. "Oh. Doctor Allen. Same last name and everything. Let me guess, your William persona is a William Allen as well?"

"Clever girl. I'm inordinately fond of that surname, although it might be time to change it again." He lapsed into silence.

Bev reached behind her, concentrated on the doorknob being real and solid and functional, and turned it slowly and silently. One more question occurred to her. "Why? Why do you want the magic box, and why do you want Shelby?"

"You haven't guessed?" His laughter reverberated throughout the room. "Shelby is a tool—an effective one, but a tool. And box is my salvation. It will shatter the bindings that have been placed on Eden and reinstate paradise on earth."

"So you're what, just a weirdo evangelical with a revelations fixation…oh my god. Do you by any chance happen to know Guenevere Kane?" Bev couldn't believe she'd forgotten her suspicion that the great necromancer was the dark magician who'd given Viv's mom the knowledge and power to banish demons and lure people into the lake, keeping them in a deathlike suspended animation. Power of life and death…

"You are a clever one, although only compared to the rest of your compatriots. I've been here for as long as there's been people to corrupt. And I am not, as you say, a 'weirdo evangelical.' I don't want anything to do with gods or devils. I want the paradise that existed before their endless wars settled on this plane and ruined it for me."

"Are you saying you're older than god?" Bev forgot about leaving. He was evil but fascinating; no wonder Shelby was ensnared. He knew so much about time, history, and Eden Valley. She shook her head. "Actually, you know what? I don't care how old you are and where you came from. All I need to know is that you are evil, and you're trying to destroy the world. Your motivations really aren't important." She pushed the handle, concentrated on William/Neil/Doctor Allen, and stepped through.

Pocket worlds were weird. She was in the dark again, but there were lights on the floor showing her a path—like in a movie theater or airplane. But whether it was a true path or a diversion wasn't immediately clear.

Miaow. Something furry head butted her ankle.

"Hey Xena—do you know where we're going?"

The black cat trotted off into the darkness, leaving a trail of sparks behind her. Bev followed the trail and hoped that they'd been right and that the cat would take her back to the necromancer who'd created her. Xena stopped and the sparks that were emanating from her dimmed. Bev put her hands in front of her and felt for the wall she knew was there. Once her hands touched a solid surface, she slid them around until she found first the seam of the door, then the doorknob.

"This is it, cat. Back in the pouch." She picked up Xena and tried to ignore the faint sickly sweet smell that was emanating from her kid's cat.

Cat safety seen to, she grabbed the doorknob and pushed the door open. A figure in a long gown studded with glowing stars and wearing an indigo pointed hat and carrying a staff with a black rock—like the one Gwen had used to focus the magic that allowed her to banish demons—stood in the center of an impossibly large room that looked like a sports arena.

"Do you like it?" He twirled, and the wizard's robes swirled up around his knees. "I wanted you to recognize me."

Bev grinned and set the cat down. "I'd recognize your foul stench anywhere." She took a deep breath, bounced up on her toes, and sprinted towards him.

"What are you doing?" he gasped.

She tackled him to the ground, and they slid along the floor. Bev screwed her eyes closed, hooked an arm around his neck, and felt for the spirits of the dead who wanted their vengeance. She pulled towards them, anchoring herself to them—made easier because they were tied to the sorcerer in her arms. There was a rush of wind, then cold air and rain cascaded over her.

She let go of the wizard, rolled away from him, and pushed back out of the way and towards Jer's barn. Bev watched in fascinated horror as the zombie horde melted out of the woods and closed in on him.

"No! You are mine!" he screamed at the approaching undead.

"They might be yours, but the pigs are mine," Russell said. He walked out of the barn flanked by two enormous pigs.

# CHAPTER TWENTY

**B**ev and Russell stood with their backs to the barn and watched as Jackson tried to bend the will of the zombies enough to retake control and send them after Bev, Russell, and the pigs. He was having little luck.

"Heathcliff and Rochester?" Bev asked, raising her voice to be heard over the wind.

"The Brontë sisters' douchiest heroes," Russell replied. "It felt appropriate, and they were about the only thing he hadn't raised from the dead around here."

"It's a good thing he'd gotten too cocky to remember even the Great Jackson Allen has limits. And at least we had you to ask the right questions to figure it out," Bev commented.

"There was no way he was in complete control if the dead were able to reach out and ask for help. And since he was so distracted else-where—angels and demons needing capturing near the mansion and a child walking through his pocket dimension without invitation—he lost control enough that they could be redirected, if not laid to rest."

"Nice work on getting them here." Bev watched as the first row of ghouls collapsed and turned to dust in a foul-smelling whump.

"It was easy once you and Shelby both disappeared from this

plane. A suggestion to Joe and the other more...aware...ghouls that you and the necromancer were heading back here and the absence of any argument from him was all it took to get them to change direction. The hardest part was getting them to go quickly enough to make a difference." Russell lifted his hand off the back of the pig on his left side. The pig's head was even with Russell's shoulder and was missing one shoulder.

"If animals are slaughtered for meat, how can they even be raised as zombies?" Bev regarded the animal—she didn't know if it was Heathcliff or Rochester—with clinical curiosity.

"Considering a career as an animated taxidermist?"

"Ew. No. I just don't understand the mechanics of it." Bev wrinkled her nose. She knew what was coming next, what had to come next, but she was wavering in her commitment to commit a murder.

"They are attached to the idea of their bodies. The more intelligent the animal, the easier it is to raise them. Pigs are smart, and their bones were here in a chest in the garage. I don't want to know why, but it came in handy." He dropped his hand to his side, and the pig took half a step forward.

"Wait." Bev stepped in front of piggy number one. The flame of hatred for this man burned bright, and that scared her. She didn't want to be someone driven by vengeance. She didn't want to be a mindless zombie. "There has to be another way. He's human. Doesn't he deserve a chance?"

"I think he's used up all his chances," Russell said. "But it's not my town, and it wasn't my kid he screwed with. However, he's probably even less human than the zombies he sent to kill us and reclaim your kid."

"He could turn himself in..." Bev's voice trailed off as she thought about it. "I guess he could turn himself into another jerk intent on ruining my life and destroying the world. It's just murder is kinda against my personal moral code."

"Is he human?" Russell asked.

"I don't know. Does it matter? Barachiel isn't human, and I

wouldn't try to kill him." Bev crossed her arms. She wasn't sure why this was a sticking point for her.

"But you have no problem sending the zombies back into the ground," Russell pointed out.

Bev locked her gaze on Allen the Awful. The area around him was no longer packed shoulder to shoulder with the dead he'd raised, and their voices no longer called out to Bev.

"We need to do it now, or we won't get the chance. He's doing what he taught Shelby to do. He's taking the sparks back into himself." Russell took his hand off the other pig and they stepped forward in unison. "Please, get out of the way. Think of Shelby. Your friends. That angel you're sweet on."

Bev stepped out of the way. "Are Shel and the others through?"

Russell nodded. "She texted a couple minutes before you showed up. She's through and fine. You ready to give her the signal?"

"Luc and Elle?" She was stalling.

"I don't know, but we can't wait any longer. Look at him." Russell shouted over the wind as it whipped into a frenzy.

Bev looked. The necromancer was growing. He was almost a foot taller than he'd been a few minutes ago.

"What is he doing?" she screamed.

"Preparing himself to take us all out, probably. I don't know, but I don't want to find out. Send the signal." The pigs took another step forward.

Bev pulled her cell phone out of her pocket and typed one word and hit send. *Vengeance.* "Do it."

The pigs charged.

Bev wanted to look away, but she was the one who'd signed this man's death warrant, and it felt like she had to watch, had to see it carried out.

Pig one, who Bev deemed Rochester, took the necromancer out at the knees, tumbling him over into the mud and Heathcliff trampled his body. The necromancer screamed, and it raised the hairs on the back of Bev's neck and curdled her blood.

She couldn't bear it. She screwed her eyes closed against the rain and wind and searched for the sparks of the pigs to blink them off.

The rain stopped and the icy wind that'd been whipping her hair into her face died down. Bev opened her eyes and saw nothing but whiteness.

"Am I dead? Did he kill me after all?" she asked.

"Turn around," Barachiel said.

She did as instructed and came face to face with his chest. His wings were spread wide and encompassed them, blocking the weather and outside sound.

"What are you doing here? Where's Shelby?"

"Shelby's fine. She is in the care of Sam, Luc, and Elle—and nothing will get through those three while they still stand." He reached up a hand and tucked a strand of hair behind her ear. "She's safe. I promise."

"What are you doing here?" Bev moved a half step closer until she could feel the warmth of him on the front of her body. She was shaking, but didn't know if it was fear, cold, or relief—or a combination of all three.

"When I got your text and knew you were here, that you'd made it through, I couldn't be anywhere else. You needed me to tell you this is the right decision." He dropped his hand and skimmed it along her side until it settled at her waist.

"I am committing a murder," Bev said. "Maybe not by my hand but by my will." She took another step closer.

"It's not a murder, it is justice. He has been judged and found wanting. I have that authority—and it is much higher than the authority granted to your small-town sheriff." His wings pulled inward and brushed against her back. "I cannot give you what the demons give their partners. You will never have the kind of relationship Evie and Luc have."

"I have never wanted that. I want love and companionship. Someone to talk to at the end of the day. Someone to hug and curl up with in front of the fire. A partner but without all the implications that come with that."

"You can hug me. I will shield you to the end, and I will watch this sorcerer meet his end so you don't have to." His other arm slid around her body and tugged her closer.

Bev gave in and twined her arms around his neck and stepped into what he was offering.

*Miaow!*

The angry snarl came from inside Bev's sweatshirt. She jumped back and bumped into Barachiel's wings.

"What was that?" he asked.

Bev scooped Xena out of the pocket. She was no longer the lanky, sleek kitten who'd curled up with Shelby at night. This cat was emaciated and rotting, barely holding onto what little life it had left.

"She's going to be so upset," Bev said. "I'll get her another one, but it won't be the same."

Barachiel reached out and touched Xena's head with one glowing finger. The light left him and surrounded the cat. Her skin became less scabrous and repaired itself in the places it'd sloughed off.

"Did you resurrect the cat?" Bev asked.

He shrugged. "Minor miracle. I am allowed."

"Thank you." She set the cat down and stepped into his arms for the hug. There was nothing in the way now.

"It is finished. The necromancer is gone," Barachiel said. He dropped his wings and once again, the fall weather buffeted her face.

Bev turned around. There was nothing left. The ghouls had died with their master, and the zombie pigs were no more.

"We saved the day!" Russell said.

"There's one more thing to do," Barachiel said. "We have to secure the bone box. The sorcerer may be gone, but others will take his place. It must be hidden again, new guardians found for it. Whatever happens, it must never be opened."

"To the mansion?" Bev asked.

"I will be your chariot." The angel bowed.

"What about me? Where's my chariot?" Russell asked.

Bev laughed. "We can take your car most of the way, then hike it in the rest of the way. The old driveway's so grown over we'd never get a car close enough."

"I do not like cars," Barachiel said.

"You can ride on top! There are tie down bars to hold onto," Russell suggested.

The angel scooped up the kitten and tucked it into the pocket of his leather jacket. "Don't be ridiculous. If we are taking your car, I can sit inside. Unless you will allow me to drive."

Russell opened the driver's door and got in, locking it behind him.

"Do you even know how to drive?" Bev asked.

Barachiel opened the front passenger door and ushered her in. "I do not, but if I'm staying, I should learn, and what better time than the present?"

Russell turned around and drove down the long driveway. "Dude, just about every other time is better than the present."

"You're staying then?" Bev asked as evenly as possible.

"I thought it was decided." He leaned forward from the backseat and propped his chin on the seat next to her head.

"It's nice to hear it though." Hope blossomed. She finally had a chance to find the one thing missing from her life, the kind of companionship she hadn't been certain existed for her. Someone she could call home.

# CHAPTER TWENTY-ONE

Bev walked up the overgrown driveway towards the house that had been abandoned since before she was a child. It'd been an occasional playhouse for her, Evie, and Viv when weather drove them away from the witch's clearing, but she hadn't thought of it in years.

"I wonder when Jer moved the box here?" Bev said as she climbed over a fallen tree blocking the driveway.

"Why would it matter?" Russell asked, grunting as he followed her up the driveway.

Barachiel spread his wings and rose over the obstacles, then beaned himself with a tree branch. "I'm okay!" he called.

Bev and Russell exchanged a glance and snickered.

Bev looked around, then shone her cellphone light at the ground in front of her, trying to avoid more obstacles and remain upright. Barachiel was, as always, a cautionary tale. "I used to play here, but I'd forgotten about it until we found out the kids had been here. If it was meant to protect itself from everyone but the guardians, maybe that's how it does it. It doesn't really matter now, but I was curious."

"What will you do with the box? Is it protected here?" Russell asked.

"Too many people know where it is now," Barachiel replied. "It will have to be moved. Aurielle will secret it away again and choose another otherwise ordinary family to serve as its protectors."

"Does this happen a lot? Supernatural beings choosing humans to guard stuff? Doesn't seem very efficient," Bev huffed.

"It does happen often. Humans are usually so ordinary that they escape notice, but they have their own kind of magic that is tied to the earth and is difficult to detect, even if one of us knows what we're looking for. The problem with a town like Eden Valley is that after a while, even the most ordinary families become something more." He held out a hand and helped Bev climb over a larger tree.

"That's how the town works, isn't it? The object resided with one family, but the failsafe is the rest of the town. We are kept here because we are the guardians." Bev scanned the ground, looking for obstacles and thinking it through. "But if we're the guardians, are we guarding only the box? And is something guarding us?"

Lights appeared in front of them, bobbing up and down like flashlights.

"Only a few more feet," Barachiel said. "Once we get over this last tree, we will see the others."

Bev sped up. It'd been less than two hours since Shelby had disappeared in front of her, but it felt like longer, and she was desperate to see her again.

Shelby sat on the front steps of the huge wrap-around porch with a large box balanced precariously on her lap. Her hands were on the ornately carved wood. She was flanked by Luc and Sam on one side and Elle on the other.

Barachiel rushed forward. "You can't open it. Aurielle, you must stop her!"

The other angel spread her silver wings wide and looked at Barachiel. "I have so advised her, but as you know, I cannot interfere, nor can I explain my reasons. The limits placed on us are unfortunate."

"Shelby, what are you doing? Opening this box can lead to the end of all things." Barachiel knelt beside her and moved his hands as if to hold the lid down, but they froze before they could reach the box.

"All things end, and endings are just the beginnings of something new," Shelby said, her voice sounding more like an ancient evil sorcerer than a twelve-year-old girl. "Childhood must end for adulthood to start. Night must end for the day to be born."

Something about her voice was eerie enough to make Bev shiver. She walked forward and stepped between Barachiel and Shelby.

"Shel, don't open the box. Please. If Elle and Barachiel say it would destroy this town, this world, I believe them." Bev put her arm around Shelby and leaned in. "Give the box to Elle and let's go home."

Shelby looked at the demons next to her. "And you? Do you also want me to hand it over to the angels?"

Sam shrugged. "It's all the same to me. I'm not going to push you one way or another. If you'd asked me a couple years ago, I would be cheering you on, but I've come to trust the angel."

"I advise against it," Luc said. "Like Sam, I want it to be opened for curiosity's sake and to go counter to the wishes of our traditional adversaries, but Evie trusts Elle, and I trust Evie."

Shelby's fingers twitched as they hovered above the box. Bev held her breath, then reached out to take the box from Shelby to hand it off to Elle.

When her hands touched the box, she heard Barachiel sigh in relief.

"I cannot touch it, so you will have to take it to the place I instruct," Elle said. "I will tell you alone who to give it to, and they will be the only ones to know where it is to be kept. Hopefully it will spend the next few millennia hidden."

Bev moved to a crouched position to lift the box, which was much heavier than she'd anticipated, but the moment her weight shifted enough to make her lose contact with the box for just an instant, Shelby pulled it back down and pushed off the lid.

"Yessssss…" a voice hissed from the edge of the driveway. A dark shaped flowed into the being in front of Shelby. "Now give it to me, child. You have fulfilled the command I gave you, and for that I will release you."

"We killed you," Bev said. She jumped to her feet and stood between Shelby and the necromancer who refused to die.

"You killed my body, but it'll take more power than you'll ever possess to kill me completely." He had no face, and thus no smirk, but Bev swore she saw it, nonetheless.

"Jesus Christ," Russell spat. "What will it take for you to stay dead."

"Wrong branch of the family tree. I am much older than my dear, departed cousin." He flowed through Bev, and she fell to her knees, vomiting as the oily darkness of his essence ran through her.

"The box."

Bev turned just in time to see the necromancer's hands solidify enough to touch the ornately carved box.

Shelby looked up, reached into the box, and grabbed what looked like a broken femur, sharp and jagged on one end. "It isn't yours." She ripped the bone across her forearm and let her blood drip into the box.

"Noooo! What have you done?" the necromancer wailed.

"What have you done?" Elle whispered.

The bones rose out of the box and took shape until a full skeleton floated in the air. Then the bones snapped together, and flesh and sinew swirled around, covering the skeleton. Feet hit the ground, and a being rose to his full height, towering over everyone who was staring at him. He was naked and beautiful. Black skin glowed under the weak light of the flashlights wielded by Sam and Luc, and long, black curls cascaded down his back. Wings sprang forth from his shoulders and the feathers shimmered with all the colors of the rainbow.

He stretched up, raising his hands to the sky, then arched his back before relaxing his stance and opening his eyes. His irises were so light grey they were almost white. He radiated beauty and etherealness in a way that eclipsed even the angels Bev had seen. His eyes lit on Elle, and he smiled.

Bev ached at that smile and wished it was directed at her.

"Aurielle, my light. It has been too long since I have been permitted to gaze upon your beauty." His voice sounded like music, like water dancing over rocks in a stream, like birdsong.

Tears sprang to Bev's eyes. He was too perfect. This is why he had to stay locked away; she couldn't look away. He didn't impart peace the way Barachiel did. He inspired worship. She dropped to her knees.

Elle looked at him. "You are not supposed to be here. I was meant to keep you locked away and safe, so that your bones could guard…"

The figure spread his wings wide, blocking the darkness behind him. "Come away with me, Aurielle, like you meant to do. The world has moved on, but we don't have to. I will find us a paradise where we can live together as husband and wife."

"I can't. I have to protect what you would not, what you gave away with no thought to the future." Elle's voice was choked with tears, but Bev still couldn't look away.

"I looked to the future, and all I saw was you. You tricked me into leaving you to better serve your god, but I never stopped loving you." The sorrow in his voice created an ache in Bev's chest. It was the sorrow of centuries, of millennia. He reached out a hand, and from the corner of her eye, Bev saw Elle's hand stretch out to meet him.

"Brother." The black form flowed between them. "It is I who found you, who caused this child to lift your tomb from its resting place, who taught her how to resurrect you. I created her to serve you."

The man's eyes flicked down to Shelby and compassion bloomed in them. He reached out and placed a hand on her head. The deep gash on her arm shrank and disappeared. "The link is broken now. You will not be able to use her again. You must leave now, my brother, son of my father."

"Brother!"

A flash of light and a belch of sulphur interrupted the necromancer's pleas.

"As much as I hate to break up this family reunion, I'm afraid I must. I wondered where you'd gotten off to! Your mother is simply aching to see you." Abaddon wrapped his arm around the ethereal being and grabbed the box. "Oh, Shelby darling, I am leaving you a present as a thank you for finding my brother. You're welcome." Papa Abe, King of Hell, disappeared. The world swam in front of Bev's eyes and darkness took hold.

BEV BLINKED her way to consciousness and was met with a raging headache and Shelby's face hovering much too close. "Aaaaaah!" Bev screamed.

"Sorry," Shelby said, backing away. "I was trying to see if you were awake yet."

Bev pushed herself to a seated position and held her head as a wave of dizziness hit her. "Where am I?"

"You are in the gift Papa Abe left for me for being a stupid Pandora." Shelby hung her head and looked at Bev through a curtain of hair. "Just one more screw-up on my list."

"We're not in a creepy demon pocket dimension, are we?" Bev looked around. She was in a bright cheery room on a huge fourposter bed. Sunlight streamed through the window, illuminating the gauzy white curtains and reflecting off the light-yellow walls.

"No. We're in the mansion. It's been restored to its former glory." Shelby rolled her eyes. "Turns out Sam is a huge architecture freak and has a lot of decorating ideas."

Bev swung her legs over the side of the bed, and with that motion came an overwhelming pressure on her bladder. "I don't suppose part of the restoration included working plumbing?"

Shelby pointed at a small door Bev had assumed was a closet.

When she came back out with an empty bladder and a freshly scrubbed face, her stomach growled. "How long was I out?"

"Just the night. It's right after sunrise. Luc took off right away to find out what his father is doing and to fetch Evie and the kids. Sam headed back to the house to see Viv, and Russell leaves his best wishes and an invitation to visit him any time and drove back to our house where he intends on getting four hours of sleep before going home."

Shelby slipped an arm around her aunt's waist. "We all just woke up a little bit ago, too."

"And Barachiel?" Even though he'd said he was staying, fear still clenched her chest.

Shelby didn't answer right away, and the fear intensified.

"Shel? Where's Barachiel?"

"He and Elle were both gone when I woke up, as was the empty box. There was a note for me from Abe making sure I knew he'd done this and not some 'holier-than-thou' angel. Of course, since Jer owns the land, I'm not sure how much good it's going to do me." Shelby led Bev down the hall to a wide, open staircase that went down to the first floor.

Bev's stomach growled again. It'd been a while since she'd eaten. She had to stop doing this to herself.

"I texted Viv when you were in the bathroom. She'll be here in a few minutes to pick us up. But in the meantime, I have snacks." Shelby rummaged through her backpack and pulled out a soggy looking sandwich and a granola bar.

"I'll take the granola bar. I think that sandwich has seen better days." Bev opened the granola bar and scarfed it down. "Don't suppose you have anything to drink in there?" Her tongue stuck to the roof of her mouth, glued there with the force of chewy peanut butter snacks and dehydration.

"Sorry. I drank it all last night. But I can get you a glass from the kitchen."

Bev followed Shelby into the kitchen, and her jaw dropped. "This is…" She spun around, taking in the spacious counters, gas stovetops—more than one—immaculate, light tiles, gleaming stainless appliances, and the largest refrigerator she'd ever seen. "Wow."

"It's completely stocked," Shelby said. "No food, but everything else you'd need." She handed Bev a glass of water. "There's one more thing I want you to see."

They walked through the adjacent dining room that boasted a table that could seat about twenty and into a solarium. The interior wall had a row of tall cabinets, and along one side was a sewing desk with three different sewing machines on it. The other side of the room was a cat paradise—the cat condo Viv and Shelby had picked out along with plush-looking cat bed, several toys, a food and water station, and a litter box in the corner.

"It's self-scooping," Shelby said in awe. "Like magic."

"If it's a gift from Abe, it might be magic. I hate that it's from him, and that all this belongs to Jer."

A tiny black face peered out from the hammock attachment on the cat condo.

"He fixed Xena, too!" Shelby exclaimed. "She's 100% cat now with zero zombie additives!"

"That wasn't Abe. Barachiel did that for you." A tear slipped down Bev's face, and she dashed it away before Shelby could see.

"That's even better. I hate feeling this nice about Papa Abe and want to split up the gratitude a little."

The sound of a car coming up the driveway grabbed Bev's attention. "How did anyone get a car up here?"

"All part of the demon magic, I guess. The driveway and parking area and lawn are all cleaned up, and it has a new paint job." Shelby scooped up her cat and deposited her in the cat carrier by the door. "No more travel by pocket for you!"

Bev looked around the room as Shelby bounded out of the house, yelling for Viv to look at everything. It was pristine and perfect, and plans Bev shouldn't be making were already brewing. And her heart was breaking.

She walked out into the main living space. It was beautifully furnished—the king of hell did have excellent taste.

"Are you coming?" Viv called. "Evie's making breakfast, and I'm starving."

"On my way!" Bev took one last look around. She'd be back.

# CHAPTER TWENTY-TWO

The kitchen was filled with conversation and the noise of a table being set.

"Just in time!" Evie handed Bev a large plate stacked high with pancakes. Viv grabbed the platter of breakfast sausages, and Shelby took a handful of flatware.

"I am so hungry," Bev said, filling her plate with pancakes and sausage and drenching everything with syrup. "I need to get back into the habit of regular meals."

Sam handed Shelby and Bev large glasses of orange juice. "What'd you think of father's gift?"

"It was beautiful," Bev admitted. She took a drink of the orange juice and sputtered.

Sam grinned and winked. "Maybe it's Tuesday morning, but I figured we all deserved a mimosa after that."

Shelby grabbed her glass and took a sip. "Where's my mimosa?"

"Your aunt would murder me in my sleep," Sam said. "Hit me up next time she's out of town, and we'll do a grownup brunch."

"Well, there goes any possibility of me leaving town if Sam's around," Bev said.

"No fair," Shelby pouted.

"You'll get over it, I promise."

The pounding of a young elephant galloping across the porch rattled the plates. The screen door burst open, and Sprinkles skidded to a stop near the dining room table. She looked around, then one of her heads homed in on the cat carrier near Shelby's feet. Her hackles rose and a low growl formed in her throat. Shelby edged forward to grab the handles and move Xena out of harm's way. A paw worked its way through the zippered close and swiped Sprinkles in the center of her center nose.

The three-headed hellhound whimpered, whipped around, and ran back the way she'd come, nearly knocking over a breathless Lily.

"Sprinkles! What happened?" Lily called after her.

Kevin slipped around Lily and grabbed her hand, tugging her forward. "Forget Sprinkles for a minute. You know she'll be fine."

Lily turned around and spotted Shelby. The girls tripped over their feet and tumbled into each other's arms. Kevin wormed his way into the hug.

"I told you it'd be okay," Shelby said. "Easy peasy. No more zombies. No more ghosts. Someone got rid of all the bones from the dead zombies."

Sam raised her hand. "You're welcome."

Shelby grinned at Sam, then turned her attention back to her best friends. "And best of all, Xena is a real cat now!"

"No more Jer?" Lily asked.

Bev and Viv exchanged horrified glances with Sam. "Um…" Viv slid out of her chair and tiptoed to the hallway that led to the stairs.

"What are you doing, Genevieve Kane?" Evie asked, stepping out in front of her and blocking her way into the hallway.

"Bathroom?" Viv asked.

"It's right behind you," Evie pointed out.

"Mama! Look!" Lily grabbed the baby monitor from the end table in the living room and brought it to her mom.

"There's that stupid thing," Sam muttered. "That would've been much easier."

Evie looked at the monitor screen, then at Viv. "Why is there a man tied up in my daughter's bed?"

"It's Jer," Viv said, still trying to slide by Evie.

"I can see it's Jer. And I can see he's trussed up like a Thanksgiving turkey. And I can also see that he is HANDCUFFED to my daughter's bed. I just want to know why."

"We had to keep him here somehow," Sam said. "And he's boring. So we tied him up. Your headboard didn't work with Viv's cuffs, so we had to use Lily's. Alex's crib would've been better, but he didn't fit."

Evie closed her eyes and stepped back into the kitchen. "You're both lucky I love you. Go get that man out of my house, and then someone needs to change her sheets."

"Do you want me to do Alex's sheets, too?" Sam asked.

"Yes. Clean it all."

The doorbell rang.

"I'll get it. It's probably my mother," Kevin said.

Bev followed him to the front door, stomach twisting in excitement to see *her* angel again.

Kevin opened the door. Elle was there. Alone.

Bev's shoulders drooped, and she turned to go back to her breakfast.

"Beverly, I have something for you," Elle said. She reached over her shoulder and pulled her sword out of the hidden scabbard.

"I'm not sure I want what you're offering," Bev said. "Unless you're knighting me? That'd be cool." Jokes in the face of pain and fear—time-honored coping mechanism.

"No. Of course not." She ran her hand along the blade and peeled a single, glowing white feather off. "Barachiel asked me to give this to you."

"Where is he? When will he be back?" Bev knew she sounded desperate, but she didn't care.

"He has some business to take care of, but he will be back. He said to keep the feather, and you will know when he is on his way home." Elle opened her arms, and Kevin stepped in for a hug.

Bev ran a finger along the rachis and smiled. She picked the feather up and brushed her thumb over the downy wisps.

It was the twin of the one she'd found in the pet cemetery, but somehow different. Lighter. Like a gift.

Bev slipped the feather into her purse. It was a promise. A pledge. And enough to keep her hope strong.

# EPILOGUE
## THREEISH MONTHS LATER: DECEMBER

Bev stood in the middle of the living room of the mansion Abe had gifted her and looked around. She wasn't going to question how he'd wrested the property away from Jer. Luc had looked the paperwork over and declared it perfectly legal, and that was enough for her. Between that gift and having all charges against her dropped when it turned out Jackson Allen had disappeared, leaving a trail of evidence connecting him to various unsolved murders in the area, everything was perfect. She walked outside and flicked her dusting cloth over the sign hanging at the end of the drive, knocking the snow off and setting it swinging in the wind.

### B&B's

Her first guests would arrive tomorrow, just in time for a long winter holiday. She had the menu planned, transportation to nearby ski resorts available, wine from Charlie ready to decant, and a selection of desserts ready for tomorrow night's happy hour.

She also had something for Shelby. If that child ever came home. It was winter, and the days were short. She, Lily, and Kevin spent almost every daylight hour outside, and often came home wet from the snow with cold faces, red noses, and the last vestiges of childhood joy on their faces, but Shelby had promised to come home early for dinner that night.

Bev grabbed the large envelope that had arrived earlier and propped it up on the mantle next to Barachiel's feather. He'd been gone for three months. Three months without a word. Every time she'd resigned herself to never seeing him again, his feather caught her eye. He'd made a promise, and he was an angel. He kept his promises.

She reached out to brush the wispy end with her finger as she did every time she saw it. She froze with her hand hovering above. It wasn't white anymore. The brilliant, almost blinding white had changed into silvery grey shimmer.

He was right. She'd know when he was coming home.

"Mom! I'm home. What's so important that you're depriving me of quality daylight and fresh snow?" Shelby kicked off her shoes and slid into the living room on her stocking feet. "What's that?" She pointed at the feather.

"It's Barachiel's. He'll be home soon. But I have something even better." She grabbed the envelope and handed it over.

Shelby ripped the top off the envelope and yanked out the document. "What is this?" Her brow wrinkled, and she peered at the official document. Light dawned in her eyes and tears traced down her cheeks.

"It's officially official," Bev said.

"It's my birth certificate. It says I'm a girl and that my name is Shelby Wood Hill." Shelby thrust the birth certificate back at Bev and burst into tears.

"I thought you'd be happy?" Bev said slowly.

"I am so happy!" Shelby wailed. "I'm a girl, and I have your name. You're my really real mom, and I'm a really real girl!"

"You've always been a really real girl," Bev said. "And you've always been my kid. And you'll legally be my kid when the adoption is finalized."

Shelby sniffled and wiped her nose on her arm. Bev winced.

"Since this is an auspicious day, I deserve pizza and ice cream. To celebrate. And you should have wine!" Shelby beamed at her.

"You know the way to my heart," Bev teased

"And you know the way to mine."

Bev spun around. Barachiel stood in front of the fireplace. He was wearing a graphic tee-shirt depicting an angel hula-hooping with their halo, dark designer jeans, and a leather jacket. His wings were spread out behind him. They matched the silver grey of the one he'd left behind.

"Your wings? What happened?" Bev asked.

"I am no longer an angel of heaven. Instead, I have taken the grey, much like my friend Uriel. And kind of like Andras. I serve Her in a different capacity now. It was a long negotiation, but one that I believe will work best for me. And for you."

Bev felt like her grin would split her face. "I'm so happy you're back."

"How could I stay away?" He strode towards her, arms open, and pulled her into a hug.

"Where are we?" he asked, looking around. "This isn't your house. I would've remembered if it was this big. I think."

Bev grabbed his hand, led him outside, and pointed at the sign.

"B&B's? Isn't it supposed to be B&B?" he asked.

Shelby rolled her eyes. "It's Bev and Barachiel's. Mom thinks she's soooo clever. I'm glad you're back, B-Man, but you're interrupting my celebration. Buy me an ice cream, and I'll forgive you."

"B-Man? I do not like that."

"Buy me an ice cream, and I'll stop." Shelby stuck her tongue out and ran back to the house.

"She is growing up, but also not," Barachiel observed.

Bev grabbed his hand and rested her head on his shoulder.

"I missed you so much." The light-hearted tone he usually used was gone, replaced with a hoarse scratch. "I love you, Beverly Hill."

Bev squeezed his hand and looked into his eyes. "I love you too, angel."

GUARDIAN OF EDEN, the fourth and final Eden Valley novel, will be released on February 24, 2022 (which is, not incidentally, the author's birthday). Preorder Guardian of Eden now and keep reading for a sneak peek!

# GUARDIAN OF EDEN
## CHAPTER ONE

**February**

*Six Months Later*

Aurielle Jones paced back in forth in the small house she'd called home since moving to Eden Valley twelve years ago with a baby and her faux husband in tow. Living in town was vastly different than her previous situation, and even with more than a decade behind her, she wasn't quite used to it. It'd been much less anxiety-provoking when her sole responsibility was protecting the town without worrying about the town's people.

She checked her watch. It was after five. A full hour past when Kevin was supposed to arrive home after school. She grabbed her phone and hovered a finger over the button that would open the group chat Evie had created to keep her and Bev—the mothers of Kevin's best friends—up-to-date on the children's schedules. Elle knew Kevin hadn't planned on going home with either of his friends today. The calendar—also Evie's creation—clearly stated that Lily, Evie's half-demon child, was scheduled to spend the week of Spring Break at her grandfather's and Shelby, Bev's adopted daughter and unpredictably powerful necromancer was flying to Oracle Bay to visit her uncle Russell. Kevin was the only one who didn't have plans for the week off school. Not that he hadn't tried to convince Elle otherwise, but she'd held firm.

She looked at her watch again. Five fifteen. She started typing, finger flying over the tiny screen of her phone.

She hit send, and the door slammed open.

*Never mind. He's here.*

There was a clatter of footsteps on the stairs and a second door slammed on the second floor. More often, Kevin retreated to his room when he was home, refusing to spend quality time with her. It wasn't fair nor was it right. She had sacrificed herself for him. Become mortal for him. Hid his sins for eleven years and broken the first veil of secrecy she'd shrouded herself with in order to separate him from the primordial lake monster he'd been. He owed her love and affection and respect. And punctuality. And an occasional hug—something he'd never been free with, but that she'd seen his friends offer to their mothers.

Aurielle set her shoulders and headed upstairs. Raucous music poured out of his room, nearly vibrating the walls. She knocked. There was no answer. She knocked a second time, but when there was no response, she opened the door. Then closed it again and went back downstairs, scarlet heat staining her dusky face. Some things that were seen could never be unseen, and it occurred to her that she may need to do some research on what it meant to parent an adolescent child who'd recently plummeted over the cliff towards adulthood.

Her phone beeped with an incoming message.

*Are we still on for this evening?* Bev asked.

*Yes. Please bring wine and advice on almost teenage boys.* This time Elle entered the words without bothering to use her fingers. It was faster just thinking the words at the phone, but she usually tried to make an effort to appear human, even when there was no one around to appreciate her efforts.

Viv's reply appeared almost immediately. *I don't even want to think about teenage boys, but I will bring a sympathetic ear and a crate of gym socks.*

Three dots appeared under Evie's name, then disappeared and reappeared again. Elle stared at them in consternation. She knew it meant Evie was typing a response, but why did they blink on and off? And what did it mean when no response ever came? And why was Viv bringing gym socks? Did boys have particular feet issues she'd not been made aware of?

Twenty minutes later, Kevin thundered down the stairs with his laundry hamper balanced under his arm. Elle raised her eyebrows. She might not know much about parenting almost-teens, but according to popular culture, they never did their own laundry without prompting.

"Would you like dinner?" she asked Kevin's back as he walked back through the living area towards the stairs. He still hadn't made eye contact with her.

"I kind of need it to survive now," was the biting retort.

Elle took a deep breath and counted to ten. She'd been under the impression that counting and breathing were the tools humans used to develop patience and calm. So far, it hadn't worked reliably. "That is why I asked. Would you like pizza? I know pizza is a particular favorite of children in the United States."

"I'm not a child. And I'll get my own food." He grabbed the backpack he'd dumped on the floor under the hooks in the entry that had been designed to store such items up and out of the way and opened the door. Or tried. He turned around and glared. "Let me out."

"No. You are a twelve-year-old boy and it is getting dark. Your friends are out of town, so I know you aren't planning on hanging out with them this evening. I know we haven't been close, but I think it would be nice to have dinner together. You can tell me about your day and how school is going. All those things that parents and children talk about with each other." Elle beamed at him, hoping her willingness to engage with him was apparent and that it caused him to reciprocate.

"You can't keep me at home. I'll just wait until you go to sleep and leave then." He crossed his arms and glared at her. He was too young to look that angry.

"I don't sleep, and you don't have anywhere to be for ten days. We have a lot of quality time we can spend together. I haven't been the best mother—"

Kevin snorted.

Elle raised her voice. "—but I am trying to step into that role since you became human and needed more care than simple food and clothing. I didn't have parents, nor did I know any parents until I moved here. I am doing my best, but it would be appreciated if you would also make some effort. We can have pizza and soda and watch a movie. Or we can talk! Do you have any crushes at school?"

"It's pretty obvious you know nothing about parenting. You've made that abundantly clear over the last two weeks." He continued glaring, and Elle's eyeballs ached in sympathy.

"If I have done something wrong, I would appreciate it if you would tell me what it was so I can ensure I never make that mistake again." Elle thought back over the last couple weeks, her mind sifting through every conversation with Kevin—there hadn't been many— and couldn't recall any promises broken or disagreements about anything except his spring break plans.

"If you don't know, why should I tell you?" His stance didn't change at all, but his face relaxed infinitesimally.

"So I will know what it is? That is a very silly question. Is this about your Spring Break plans? I know it is difficult to be left behind. You have seldom been separated from your friends, but they are both going on educational trips to better learn how to channel their inherent powers. You no longer have any, so you don't need a similar experience." Parenting was difficult, and there were times she rued the day she'd agreed to take on this assignment. Not that she had much choice. Assignments were often phrased as requests but were seldom treated as requests in practice. She shook her head. She was thinking too much. As usual. Elle took another breath, counted to twenty, and pasted a smile on her face.

"It's not that." Kevin made a grunting noise that was completely inarticulate but perfectly conveyed disgust, frustration, and eye-rolling.

"Please have dinner with me. We can talk about what I've done wrong and how you would prefer I interact with you. I have board games we could play?" Her phone beeped, but Elle ignored it.

"You know what? I'm not hungry after all." He stomped up the stairs and, for the third time in less than an hour, slammed a door hard enough to rattle the house.

Elle sagged into a chair and picked up her phone. She should've paid more attention to other parents when Kevin was younger, before he needed things like boundaries or affection. Maybe if she'd gotten into practice then, parenting now would be easier. She looked at the phone screen. She had a new text from Evie—the result of all the on-and-off dots.

*I know nothing about raising almost teen boys, but I will bring the vast wealth of experience I have raising an almost teen girl and being one myself, many, many years ago. I will also bring a bottle of sémillon.* There was a small picture of a glass of wine next to a smiling face with tears spurting from its eyes. Elle knew what they represented, but it still intrigued her that humans considered pictographs a primitive form of communication, but used images to convey complete ideas in phone communications.

*Maybe we will need two bottles. And a magic spell for one person in this house to sleep through the next few years.* Elle ended her text with the image of a skull and crossbones and hit send, then thought through the potential interpretations for the skull. *I don't want anyone to die. The icon is inadequate.*

Three thumbs up pictures quickly responded, and Elle breathed a sigh of relief that her icons had not been misinterpreted. She blew a strong breath out, bouncing her dark curls off her face, and looked around. Her usually immaculate house needed a quick once-over before she was ready to welcome her friends. She seldom hosted—Evie's large porch just out of town, overlooking the lake was the usual gathering place—but Elle hadn't wanted to leave Kevin alone, and since his friends were out of town, it seemed a kindness to not force him to hang out at Lily's house without her. The baby was very cute—and an unholy terror on two legs—but she was an inadequate companion for a twelve-year-old.

Elle put a frozen pizza in the oven and set the timer. Even if Kevin didn't want to eat food, she knew if she left it on a plate outside his door, it would disappear as soon as she was out of sight. Perhaps a lock on his door would be a good addition as well. She wrote a note to him to leave with the pizza and bottled water and willed the lock into existence. One more minor miracle, and the house was spotless again.

She shrugged, and her silvery white wings stretched out from her shoulder blades and brushed against the walls of her expansive home. It felt good to let this part of herself out, to have *friends* who knew who she was, even if she still kept most of herself hidden.

For their protection. Definitely not for her own. There was no other reason to keep them in the dark. It was for their own good.

One hundred percent.

Elle sighed and after one last stretch, folded her wings back in, tucking them into the hidden spot between this reality and the next where they nestled against the sword that was almost as much a part of her as her wings.

It was enough. It had to be enough.

Preorder Guardian of Eden and read it on February 24, 2022!

# NOT IN THE CARDS
## ORACLE BAY BOOK 1

Not in the Cards is the first book in the Oracle Bay series—a paranormal romance series set on the Washington (state) coast. It's a separate series but in-world with the folks of Eden Valley (and you might even find the connecting character!).

**W**elcome to Oracle Bay, the town where the local psychics were already expecting you!

Oracle Bay has always attracted the preternaturally clairvoyant. When anyone with seers' blood in their veins steps foot in this quaint coastal town, their powers awaken. They receive a visit from the Psychics Union, and shenanigans ensue.

Sandy Franklin is on the run from her old life and her almost-ex-husband. Lured to Oracle Bay by a too-cheap-to-be-believable apartment with attached tarot reader shop, she has found new friends and a job she didn't know was possible. Hiding from her past while building a new future.

When Vincent, the handsome stranger who owns most of Main Street, announces he's selling Oracle Bay to stave off personal problems, Sandy and the other resident psychics devise a plan to save the town using their divination skills and a little old-fashioned sleuthing.

The one thing Sandy couldn't predict was how hard she'd fall for the one man who could crush Oracle Bay and her hopes for a new life without blinking an eye... Will Sandy get a second chance at true love with the man whose past might be even more dangerous than her own?

TAKE A TRIP TO ORACLE BAY. Come for the scenic Pacific Northwest, stay for the paranormal romance in these (mostly) standalone novels.

Once Sandy has you hooked, check out the rest of the psychics in Oracle Bay.

## ABOUT THE AUTHOR

Amy Cissell is a USA Today Bestselling Author of urban fantasy and paranormal romance novels. She lives in Portland, OR with her husband, her haunted house-obsessed daughter, their three cats, and the murder of crows she's conspiring to turn into her vengeful army.

When she's not working or writing, she's sleeping because that's all she has time to do! There are few things Amy loves more than a well-timed pun, a good book, a glass of wine, and time at the Oregon Coast.

Although she reads anything and everything, her first love is fantasy. Eleven-year-old Amy discovered fantasy when she 'borrowed' her father's copy of The Hobbit and an enduring love affair (mostly with dragons) was born.


facebook.com/acissellwrites

twitter.com/acissellwrites

instagram.com/acissellwrites

bookbub.com/authors/amy-cissell

goodreads.com/acissellwrites

# ALSO BY AMY CISSELL

**Paranormal Women's Fiction**

***Eden Valley***

Raising a Demon (June 2021)

Devil and the Deep, Blue Lake (September 2021)

Valley of Angels (November 2021)

Guardian of Eden (February 2022)

***Eden Valley World Novellas***

Match Made in Hell (June 2021)

Hell's Bells (December 2021)

Fall From Grace (January 2022)

Devil May Care (February 2022)

**Paranormal Romance**

***Oracle Bay***

Not in the Cards (October 2018)

First Hand Knowledge (November 2018)

Belle of the Ball (December 2019)

Hell and High Water (2022)

Tempest in a Teapot (2022)

Bad to the Bones (2022)

***Oracle Bay World Novellas***

Wing and a Prayer (January 2019)

**Contemporary/Urban Fantasy**

*The Eleanor Morgan Novels*

*(complete series)*

The Cardinal Gate (February 2017)

The Waning Moon (June 2017)

The Ruby Blade (October 2017)

The Broken World (March 2018)

The Lost Child (June 2019)

The Iron River (May 2020)

The Dark Throne (February 2021)

*The Eleanor Morgan World Novellas*

The Throneless King (March 2020)

www.ingramcontent.com/pod-product-compliance
Lightning Source LLC
Chambersburg PA
CBHW071252190726
48292CB00007B/2510